The

FIRST BOOK

of

CALAMITY LEEK

The

FIRST

BOOK

of

CALAMITY

LEEK

Paula Lichtarowicz

FLATIRON
BOOKS

THE FIRST BOOK OF CALAMITY LEEK. Copyright © 2013, 2016 by Paula Lichtarowicz. All rights reserved. Printed in the United States of America. For information, address Flatiron Books, 175 Fifth Avenue, New York, N.Y. 10010.

www.flatironbooks.com

Designed by Steven Seighman

The Library of Congress Cataloging-in-Publication Data is available upon request.

ISBN 978-1-250-08793-5 (trade paperback)
ISBN 978-1-250-08791-1 (e-book)

Our books may be purchased in bulk for promotional, educational, or business use. Please contact your local bookseller or the Macmillan Corporate and Premium Sales Department at 1-800-221-7945, extension 5442, or by e-mail at MacmillanSpecialMarkets@macmillan.com.

Originally published in Great Britain by Hutchinson

First U.S. Edition: April 2016

10 9 8 7 6 5 4 3 2 1

For my parents, and for Lydia

The

FIRST BOOK

of

CALAMITY LEEK

THE STARTING OF THINGS

It was plain-cooked perfect, the night Truly did it. There was a good stack of cloud cover above the Wall, and the first apples of autumn for supper. The Pontefracts were off in Nursery Cottage like usual, and we thirteen other sisters were cleansed and moisturized and shut up safe, with only seams to finish on cushions. I don't even remember much bothering from the pigs next door.

The light bulb went off like usual. The High Hut went dead above us. And along the row, thirteen bodies nestled down for beauty sleep. Safe as corpses, just like usual. Until we were woken in the night by a scream. Which was most unusual.

It went something like this—

"AAAAAAAAAAAEEEEEEEEEEEEEEEIIIIIIIIIIIIIIIIIIIIIIIIIIIIIIIIIIIIIIIIIIIIIIIIIIIIIIIIIIIIIIIIIIIIIIIIIIIIIIIII."

"Oh?" A body sat up along from me, puffing out steam

in the dark. Annie St. Albans, that was, scratching her bushy head. "Did I just hear something?"

But before I could answer, a crash landed far off.

"Truly?" Annie flashed green eyes up and down our row. "Truly Polperro?"

I sat up and patted about next to me. "There ain't nothing between us, Annie."

"Oh, Truly," Annie said.

"Her fur's gone," I said.

"Oh, Truly, you didn't, did you?" Annie said.

And Annie was answered by a far-off moan, "UUUUU UUUUUUUUUU."

Annie's green eyes turned black. And my own heart flipped over.

"I'm coming," Annie said. "Oh, Truly, I'm coming."

And while the rest of us were still shaking yawns from our throats, Annie was jumping up and buttoning up.

"No, Annie," I said, low and warning. "Don't, Annie."

She ran down the row and pulled a torch from the trunk. She snatched her headscarf from her hook, and went yanking at the door.

"Better not, Annie." I got up quick. "Out of Bounds at night and all."

But Annie didn't hear me, being busy staring into the night. "Oh, Truly, did you really do it?" Annie was shaking like a bag full of lice. "Please say you didn't."

And away, long and lonely as a sad cow's fart, it came again—"UUUUUUUUUUUUUUUUUUUUUUUUUUUUU UUUUUUUU."

And Annie ran off into the yard.

Well.

Well, keeping safe under the eaves, I watched her go, chasing her torch puddle and leaping her feet over sleeping hens. Racing through the gate and into the Glamis Castles, without even checking the sky lid for safety once.

Oh Annie.

I looked quick about. The Garden was blanketed black, thank goodness, all over the yard and the roses, right up to our Wall of Safekeeping. The High Hut sat snug and protecting as a shell on a snail on top of us, and thankful, there weren't a bark to be heard. But when I checked the night above the Wall, well, my heart stopped jumping and all my breath died in me too. Because it was then I saw it—swollen and stinking and gobbling holes in the clouds—a full-grown Demonmoon.

I spun back inside. Except before I could slam the door and keep us rest in safe, every one of my ten sisters was racing down the row.

"Stop, sisters!" I said.

My sisters were buttoning furs and flinging on headscarves.

"This is foolsome, and deadly dangerous, sisters!" I said.

"Come back to bed, sisters," I said.

But, weren't no matter what I said, my sisters went turning on torches and bumping past me to go flapping their feet after Annie.

Well.

Well, I had to have a quick spit then. Nothing left in our dorm but empty straw.

Empty straw and a *PAM PAM PAM*ing noise starting up.

3

PAM PAM PAM—which weren't none other than our lunatic sister, Maria Liphook, banging her head in her Hole below us, after joining the commotion.

Which was all I needed now, it really was.

PAM PAM PAM went Maria, so the pigs thought to start up next door, bashing their snouts about like they were keeping time—and wanting the High Hut waking too.

So, there really wasn't nothing for it now—I knotted my headscarf, and poked my head out low and careful into the yard. Past the gate, the rose crop acre spread peaceful and pale as a mighty cloud, and still nothing to be heard shifting in the High Hut. So then I did it, I did. I took out a torch and I raced round for the Hole door. And far off in the sleeping roses, somewhere beneath that stinking Demonmoon, Truly let out her moan.

"Come on, Maria," I whispered, sliding back the bolts and cracking open the best smile I could find. "Quiet as you can now. Hope your belly's set steady for what we're going to see."

We ran east, me and Maria, down the path between the rose rows, me gripping her big potato hand, Maria whirling her big potato feet. Our heads tucked in, our breath puffing ice clouds, the soil slipping cool and wormy beneath our running heels.

Out of the Glamis Castles and into the Silver Anniversaries we ran, the blooms shut up tight and white as shrouded mice, oozing out their perfect perfume against his Demon stink up there. Halfway along, I stopped and turned up an ear for sisterly commotion. But there was nothing to hear but that sorry UUUing.

4

Squeezing elbows between protecting thorns, we kept on down the rows, hunting Truly. Truly, who had been so busy at supper, pinch-measuring the holes in the sky lid and giggling into Annie's ear, that her soup turned cold. Truly and Annie, who wouldn't do nothing but giggle, "Tell you later," when I went and asked them why.

Out of the Silver Anniversaries, into the nosy Icebergs, the roseheads waking to nod and nudge behind us. I popped up for a breath and a look. Eleven yellow lights were grubbing about beneath the Eastern Wall. "They're only in the blessed Boules, Maria!"

We raced east into the Boules de Neige. And there, in the plumpest and palest, most Heaven-scented crops in all the Garden, in the black shadow of our Wall of Safekeeping, we found a circle of gorming faces, a fallen ladder, and flung on a bush like slapdash laundry—our sister, Truly Polperro.

"Oh, Truly," I said, and I dropped my hold on Maria and shoved in to get a proper look. Truly wasn't wearing her headscarf, nor her fur. Her dangled arms were milkskin in the torchlight. Her throat was pale as the sorry petals she'd crushed and killed. And her face was flopped back in broke-up thorns. Yes, Truly's face was exposed bare bone white beneath that Demonmoon.

Bare bone sick, that's how I felt at that.

"Mind out," Annie said, shoving me back, and throwing her own fur over Truly.

"Oh, Annie," I whispered, "she went and did it, didn't she?" And words came tumbling out of me all unstoppable, like they do sometimes, "She went up that ladder bare-faced and unprotected, didn't she? Oh, Annie, look at her face. She wasn't—she didn't—oh, Annie—what if she—"

But Annie wasn't saying nothing for shaking. And none of my other sisters were saying nothing. And Truly wasn't saying nothing either. Oh no. Dangled on that sorry bleeding bush, Truly wasn't bothered with nothing but moaning. "UUU," she moaned. "UUU."

And I am sorry to say it, but a punch landed on my ear then.

It was my sister, Nancy Nunhead, doing that. And you might as well know it here, Nancy was not the most well-mannered sister we ever had. Most probably on account of being too close a friend of pigs.

"Devil's pubes," Nancy said, her pig eyes shrunk to pus spots in the torchlight. "Like that's a clever idea." She pointed her torch where a shadow lump of Maria Liphook was off, bouncing potatoey through the Boule rows, crashing into perfect roseheads, and howling all senseless at their protecting thorns. "Like bringing the lunatic was about the cleverest idea there is."

"Shut up, Nancy," I said, and I thought about a spit at her. But we already had a sackful of trouble to shift tonight, and we didn't need no more. "Stay close, Maria," I called out. "Stay close."

Nancy snorted, "Like the mashhead can understand you."

So then I did, I did shoot Nancy some spit.

So Nancy flung me a fist.

So Annie forgot to be all shaky and turned and stamped her foot. "Devil take a dump on the two of you, will you both just SHUT UP!"

But Truly was the one that did.

And right then was when it started. Yes, the ruination started right then, with Truly Polperro shutting up when she shouldn't, just after she'd gone climbing where she shouldn't, exposed like she shouldn't. So, really, ain't like it should have been a surprise that Truly would get ruined, was it?

But, see, the real surprise was, it wasn't just Truly who got ruined, but us all.

Yes, down in the Boules, all our Garden's ruination was about to start right then. And there weren't one thing a body could do to stop it. Not one thing at all.

INJUNS

Now, Truly Polperro didn't die right there and then. No. Just after her UUUs turned off, just when we were all shivering in our furs and shifting on our heels, and trying not to listen to our eldest, prettiest but most chicken-brained sister, Sandra, wailing out what was sneaking up on all our tongues—"Is that Truly done for? Is a demonmale going to jump over the Wall to take her down to Bowels?"—well, just then, Annie shone her torch on Truly's mouth and said, "Her lips are moving."

Course, we all gasped.

And course, Annie St. Albans was straight up then. Before anyone could stop her, Annie was throwing back her curls and sticking her ear to Truly's lips. So it weren't like anyone else heard what Truly said. And that needs remembering. On account of the ruin that happened after, it really does.

"Yes, Truly," Annie said. She stepped back and frowned, "Are you sure, Truly?"

"What is it, Annie?" I asked, stepping up quick. "Do you need me, Annie? Shall I ask her a question from the Appendix, shall I?"

But Annie was too busy bent over Truly's lips to hear from me.

Annie frowned and nodded, and frowned and nodded some more. And then halfway to a nod, she stopped and stared down at Truly's mouth.

"What is it, Annie?" I said.

Annie swallowed down a long old breath before she found some words. "No injuns, you say? But I don't understand you, Truly, I don't understand."

And all the air flew out of my throat and black fear flew in.

"Definitely no injuns?" Annie said. "None at all?"

And all my sisters cried out, and I did too, "Injuns? What's she saying about the injuns, Annie?"

And Annie went, "Tell me again, Truly. Tell me more about the injuns."

But Truly didn't.

No, I am sorry to say, her lips fell loose, and no matter how many times Annie went at her with, "Truly, it's Annie. Your Annie. You can talk to me." And no matter how Annie waggled her torch, or jiggled Truly's arms, it seemed that Truly Polperro, having spoken such terrible things, wasn't for bothering with talking to no one, no more.

Up on the Wall rim, an owl screeched watchful at the Demonmoon.

"We should take her down right now," someone said.

This was Dorothy Macclesfield, course, come grasshopping up to the bush. "Dear, unfortunate Dorothy" was what our Aunty liked to call her, seeing as she had grown twitchy and twiggy and disappointing. "Abandon hope all who enter here," was what Aunty liked to say. Which was going to be sad for Dorothy when she went to War, but we never minded because she had a brain busy with good ideas. It was so busy it never stopped rattling. And right now, Dorothy's head was near rattling itself off her neck.

She lifted up Truly's wrist and watched it flop down on broken branches. "You know how in the Showreel, Marius gets stuck on the barricades and Aunty runs up and helps him onto a stretcher?" Dorothy said. "Well, we should make a stretcher from two fur coats and lay Truly on it like that, watching out for her neck." Dorothy looked out across the roses to the black clot of yard. "We should do it right now. We've been Out of Bounds far too long as it is."

Clever Dorothy, like I said.

"Eldest sisters, take up a corner of Truly with me, nice and gentle."

Except before even one of us had grabbed a leg, the Silver Anniversaries let off a scream. It went on loud and forever, like a pig being gutted chin to tail.

And all my bones turned to jellymeat. And two smacks stung my ears at once.

"Devil's pubes, Flap-ears, I said she'd be trouble. Didn't I say don't bring Maria the mashhead? Didn't I say that?"

"Not now, Nancy," Dorothy whispered. "Maybe Maria's just having herself a shout at the thorns, maybe it's just that."

But it wasn't. Because the scream started running toward us. And then we heard something coming after. Yapping.

Chasing after Maria Liphook's scream came yap-yap-yapping, that meant only one thing on this terrible night.

"We're done for," Sandra wailed.

"Sure are," Nancy said.

We sure were, because chasing after screaming Maria Liphook, and that nasty yapping, came something else then— the only sound ever known to hatch instant maggots in a body's stomach—

I feel pretty, oh so pretty—

Sandra gave a sob. Annie ran to cover Truly's face with fur. Nancy flung me a third thump. And all our youngest sisters started to wail.

"Quiet down!" Dorothy hissed. "Turn off your torches, we'll have to run." She spun about, and faced nothing but the Wall of Safekeeping.

And though I wanted to spit at Nancy, and shout it wasn't my fault that Maria Liphook had been woken by a herd of sisters with their brains in their chicken feet, Dorothy was right, there weren't no time at all, because over the crops that song was swelling—

I feel charming, oh so charming, it's alarming how charming I feel—

There weren't time to do nothing but set my feet racing after my sisters into the only hiding place around—the mangy-petalled, good-for-nothing-but-prickling dog roses straggling up the bottom of our cold stone Wall.

Weren't two seconds later that our softbrained sister skidded into the Boules, that fleabag dog snapping at her ankles. Maria stopped and stared at Truly, like she'd never seen her in her whole sorry life before. Maria stood and stared like she was a sign saying "This way to Out of Bounds, nieces." Which was all we needed, it really was.

I poked my head out of prickles. "Maria, over here! Maria Liphook! The dog roses! Come on!"

I ran out and kicked the dog off Maria, and pulled her in with us. I slid down against the Wall and jammed a hand over her lunatic mouth. Thirteen fur lumps and twenty-six jelly eyeballs, shrunk down under weeds, plugging up ears and swallowing breath, as that song kept coming our way.

Soon enough we could hear the sound of thrashing in between words—

See the pretty girl in that mirror there? Thrash thrash.

I shrunk myself into my fur, quieter than a slug in buds. Or a worm. Better to be a worm, sneaking down to soil safety. Breathe all quiet under soil, worms do.

Such a pretty face, such a pretty dress, such a pretty smile—

All sudden it stopped. It had arrived, that song, in the Boules de Neige, and we had nowhere to go.

I scrunched my eyes blind and tried to keep the shake out of my bones. I pressed Maria's mouth shut and groped my free hand out for a sister's warmth. It was Nancy's fatty paw I found next to me, worst luck. But never mind, I took it.

Up high on the Wall, the owl screeched. I could hear nothing else in my ears but my own smashing heart.

Course, that dog came snarling on up to the dog roses then, snarling and sniffing and snapping for toes. And for a few seconds there weren't nothing happening in the Garden but that owl screeching, that dog sniffing, and the sound of a bottle unscrewing. So I began to hope it was just a Constitutional being taken, and some medicine would be drunk and then the singing would turn around for the yard, and we could be back in our dorm faster than my sister Mary Bootle could say Supercalifragilisticexpialidocious. And I was turning to mouth this at Nancy, when a voice said, "How very curious, the Boules de Neige appear to have grown a lump."

And all my hopes of getting back safe died off.

A white light smashed into the dog roses and wobbled over us. "Toto! Toto-tots, get away from those dratted weeds, and come here at once!" the voice said.

Now, I don't mind saying right here, the voice, course, was our dear Aunty's own one, and like *Ophelia Swindon Volume III: The Glory Years* says it much better than me—

Never was a larynx more loved. As powerful as the Phantom's, as pitch-perfect as Poppins, its eviction from the theaters of the West Midlands left a vacuum as vast as a black hole, a situation as vacant as a womb, and a memory more mourned than a dodo on the dinner plates of the Indian Ocean.

"How very curious, I was saying, there appears to be something cancerous clogging up this Boule bush. See, Princess, bits of bone and fur and hair. Dear oh dear, how messy it looks. And do you know what, Princess, this is very sad news, because cancers are bad news. Cancers spread, see, and soon enough they are gobbling up every inch of an otherwise healthy organ. Before long, they are on the rampage, ruining years of TLC, not to mention best-laid plans for the future." The medicine bottle sloshed. "So, what on earth are we to do with this one?"

Someone moaned. Someone else somewhere else was eating down tears.

Aunty's voice turned butter-soft, "After all, it can't be

13

allowed to spread. It certainly can't be allowed to do that. What's that, Princess, do we have a choice? A lady always has a choice, sweetie. However, in this case, I fear our options are somewhat limited."

Nancy pumped my hand. I forced an eye to look out where she was looking. Our dear Aunty was jabbing about the Boules with the correcting stick, her lantern held high and her shadow thrown protecting as a wall over the bush where Truly dangled.

Aunty slammed the correcting stick into the bush and sighed. "I suppose we'll have to chop it out. Either that or mash it to a pulp. What do you reckon, Toto-tots?"

A hot tear fell on my left cheek and ran away quick.

"What's that?" The shadow skull of Aunty's head turned down at the fleabag dog itching its bottom in rose roots. "Chopping would probably work best, you say? Chopping it into teensy pieces and hoovering them out would work best of all? Oh, but damn and drat, I haven't a knife on me. What's that? Oh no, Princess, I don't think your stumpy old gnashers are strong enough to tear it up. But I won't say it wasn't a charming thought, and terribly heroic of you to offer." Aunty shook her head. "I guess we're just left with plan B. We'll have to mash it to a pulp."

"Come along, Mr. Stick," Aunty said. The correcting stick rose to striking position, in two-handed steadiness above Truly. I shut up my crying eyes. It didn't do to think of my sister right now, it really didn't.

"Are we ready, Mr. Stick?" Aunty said. "I do hope you're feeling energetic—"

And someone shouted, "Stop!"

Someone in the dog roses. "Please stop!"

Well.

Well, Annie St. Albans, that was. None other. Jumping up out of the weeds, like a statue to her very own stupidity. And Devil take me if Annie didn't go running on up to Mr. Stick, like it weren't the nastiest bruiser ever made. Annie went running on up, shouting, "Please don't strike, Aunty! It's me, Annie St. Albans. And it ain't a cancer in there, it's Truly Polperro."

Well, Aunty lifted her lantern high at that. And the light crawled up her silver furs, and over her chins, and past the scoop of her melted cheek and into the socket of her empty eye, and set its skin to twitching. "You're Annie St. Albans, you say? And you say there's something Polperroey curled up in there? Dear oh dear, I wasn't aware we had started growing children in this part of the Garden."

Aunty set Mr. Stick to turfing off fur from Truly. "Well, Toto, this is even more curious than I thought. It appears my niece was spot on, there is indeed a little girl snuggled up inside. It seems it was a good job Annie St. Albans just happened to be passing, otherwise Truly Polperro might have become Truly Mushy Peas by now. What's that, Toto? Annie needs correcting for being Out of Bounds? Oh, pup, I think perhaps you're right. Sadly, I think perhaps she does. After all, she's clearly come all this way alone, while her good little sisters are tucked up safe as corpses, getting their beauty sleep in the dorm. Aren't they, Annie?"

Well, Annie really had gone and dived herself down a well now. And she was stuck deeper than a drowning mouse. And now she was about to pull us all down there too. Because it weren't but the worst thing you could do, to tell Aunty an untruth, because she would crack them open like a louse on a hair when she found them. And she always found them, never mind she only had the one eye for the hunting.

"Aren't they, Annie?"

"No, they're not, Aunty." Would you believe it, this was Dorothy. Grasshopping out of the dog roses before I could grab her fur to tug her back in. Clever Dorothy, being not so clever about it now. "We all came. We heard Truly scream, and we came because we were worried for her."

Aunty's empty socket twitched at Dorothy, and from her living eye it seemed she wiped a tear. Except, of course, she didn't, because Aunty had no tears left, after crying them all away when she suffered her Splashback.

"Such solidarity in the sisterhood," Aunty said. "How sweet."

I shut my eyes again, but it was too late. The lantern swung onto the dog roses.

"Choppity-chop, up you pop, every darling one of you, before Toto takes it upon herself to dive in there and tear you all to pieces. Splendid. Now then, my precious little pension plans, who'd like first go with Mr. Stick?"

After we'd received our correction, Annie and Nancy pushed a barrowful of Truly Polperro back to the yard. Me and Dorothy opened a fresh bale and forked it out in the skinny room built on the other side of our dorm. It was a room made whitebricked and cozy enough for one, with its own door and bolt. The mending room, it was named by Aunty, being a place for mending hearts and minds, and possibly broken-up bodies like Truly's, if she was lucky—it was possible that might happen too.

Annie and Nancy laid Truly out and tucked her fur coat over her. Annie fetched rabbit scraps from our trunk to keep her feet warm. Dorothy went for the *Reader's Digest Home Medicine Manual* from the schoolroom, which Aunty took off her.

Aunty looked down where Truly lay deadmeat or dreaming in straw. She had a drink of medicine and said, "That'll do fussing, nieces, off you pop."

And we were sent out into the yard and bolted inside our dorm until we didn't know when.

JANE JONES

G ood afternoon, dear," a voice says, coming into this room I have been trapped up in. It is a white room with no shade nowhere, and without one single wormhole for the air to fly away free. Also, my left leg has been potted up like a sick rose, which they say is for mending me, but is to stop me running, I know it. "I hope I'm not disturbing you."

Well, I keep on with my pencil, like to say, "I'll thank you to let me be, otherwise I ain't never going to get the truth of everything set down before I leave tonight, what with all these interruptions, am I?"

But the voice keeps on at me. "I don't think we've been introduced. I'm a nurse here, my name's Jane Jones, and you must be—"

A hand touches mine, so I have to look up. And my hand drops the pencil.

A female is standing over me, and she is charred like she's

taken ten turns on the Devil's spit. Charred like her hair should be shrivelled to wisps. Like all her flesh should be dripping off her bones.

But it isn't.

Her hand is charred all over, but not one bit of a finger is dripping off. Her face is charred from top to chin, but it hasn't even started to melt. Her lips are plump, her eyes are swivelling in their sockets, and her nose is all in one piece.

Well.

"Is that a diary you've started there?" she says, holding out my pencil, never mind my hand is shaking too fast to take it. "Goodness, but you're a neat writer."

Well, it's some minor miracle how she can even speak, it really is.

I grab for my pencil. Not one scrap of her skin has come off on it. I rip a page from this writing book and I write quick—

YOU ARE DEAD. WHY ARE YOU TALKING, DEAD WOMAN?

"What's that, sweetheart?" she says. "Oh," she says.

I write more—

HOW DID YOU GET OFF YOUR ROASTING SPIT AND COME BACK UP?

"Oh," she says. "Oh my." And her shoes step back quick from the bed.

So I give her a good look over, and try to think logical, like Dorothy would. She is wearing trousers and a smock and a cap. She is only exposing her arms and face and neck. Then I realize it. And if I was speaking, I would have a good old laugh at her.

But I'm not. So I write and tell her I know she ain't really dead, she has just creosoted her exposed parts for protection,

19

like Truly Polperro tried once in the summer, when she got bored of wearing her headscarf.

Except this Jane Jones ain't for answering. She is unpacking a wash box.

Well, I ain't letting her touch me and not say an answer.

I bang my pencil on the bedpost for her attention, and I write—

SHOW ME A PIECE OF YOUR UNCREOSOTED SKIN.

And she reads them words and she stares at me awhile. And when she's finished with staring, she says, "All right, sweetheart, shall we stop playing games?"

IT WON'T STOP THEM COOKING UP YOUR INSIDES.

"What won't?"

CREOSOTE WON'T STOP THEM COOKING UP YOUR INSIDES.

IT WON'T STOP YOUR SKIN FROM CRACKING UP NEITHER.

Her eyes see this and they get small with thinking. And then she starts trying out a smile. Like all this might be something funny to her. Like I might be something funny. Which I am not.

"May I?" she says, and she comes and sits her bottom on my bed, right by my potted leg, even though I didn't ask her to. There is a smell of Gloriana tea roses about her.

"Listen, sweetheart, I'll tell you what my big sister told me when I was your age. 'Black don't crack,' that's what my sister said. That is unless you smoke sixty a day, and sit in the sun drinking rum from morning to night." This Jane Jones smiles teeth that are white as Icebergs. "Black skin doesn't crack, sweetheart, that's just the luck of the draw."

She pats my leg and stands up. "Now, are we done with the silliness? Because I can see five grubby toes peeking out the end of this cast." She is still smiling, and I have to say, it is uncracking.

And I check all over again, but there ain't one rip on her face. Not even the skinniest little seam is coming undone under her eyes.

Well.

Well, I think about what it says in the Appendix. And in my head I go back to the Garden and I pull it careful off the schoolroom shelf, just like I did every morning to read out a lesson over our porridge, and every night to read another over our stitching. And never mind it is lost now, in my head I can still open its black casing. I turn the pages through the metal hoops to O and find O *for Outside*, but, course, there ain't never been nothing set down nowhere about uncracked females living Outside. And in my head, I go and check on *F for Facts about Females* and also *U for Ugliness, Ungainliness, Unfeminine Conduct, also all Unsavory Urges*—but there was no word on uncracked skin set down there neither.

Dorothy Macclesfield might think up the logical answer. But I ain't heard Dorothy's voice once through these walls, even though they said my sisters were all here. All of them still leftover, that is.

And I hope Dorothy is still leftover. And I think of shouting out to check. Shouting out to say, "Dorothy, get ready for going tonight, because I'm off to War and you can come too if you fancy. And by the way, Dorothy, I have a question for you."

But then I don't.

Either this Jane Jones is a deadmeat wanderer from Bowels, gotten so cooked up her brain's dripped out of her nostrils, dripping her sense out too. Or she has coated herself with creosote, and she ain't telling me the truth about her uncrackable skin.

Or she is.

Well.

Well, I watch her close. She uncovers my unpotted leg and sets to wiping between my toes. The wetness doesn't make her hands go streaky, like Truly's did after Aunty put her under the standpipe for an hour. And all sudden I'm thinking what Aunty said once, "My eye, but there's more to you than meets the eye." All sudden, I'm thinking about me and Annie in the barn, weeks after Truly fell down into the Boules de Neige, and what was said then between us, that couldn't ever be unsaid. And my heart starts battering in its box. I write quick—

ARE YOU PROTECTED WITH BLACK DON'T CRACK SKIN
BECAUSE YOU ARE A WEAPON LIKE ME?

And before I know it, I write—

TELL ME THE TRUTH, JANE JONES.
HOW MANY DEMONMALES HAVE YOU KILLED?

Jane Jones doesn't look at my words until she has done wiping me all over. Then she looks at them words a long old while. Then she looks at me awhile. "I'm afraid we'll have to wait until tomorrow to carry on with our chat, sweetheart."

TELL ME NOW.

Because I have to leave tonight, Jane Jones. I have to start the War. It can't wait.

Jane Jones packs up her box, "Tomorrow should be a quieter day for me. We'll have plenty of time to chat then. I'll be sure to come armed with some answers, now that I know what kind of a grilling to expect."

And she gives me a wink.

Well, I saw it good and proper, that wink. Like Aunty says it was "a quickie but a goodie." And then I know it. She didn't just come to wipe me over. Course she didn't. She came to show me this special skin protection of hers. This Jane Jones has purpose. Just like us. She came to show me that. And just to be sure, she winks her eye again.

And now she is going at the door.

Words rush up my throat. Whole ones that don't melt to nothing on the way.

"Wait," I shout out. "Don't you want to know my name?" Because happen she will need to know my name. "My name is Calamity Leek."

And this Jane Jones lifts her wash box in a wave at me. "Well, it was very interesting meeting you, Calamity Leek. I look forward to catching up tomorrow."

And she shuts the door behind her, leaving her Glorianas flavoring my air.

OUR DORM

"W as it the lid then, Clam?" a voice whispered in my ear.
Little Millie Gatwick, that was, two years and
four months my junior, come crawling up the row to me.
Gretel rat sat on Millie's head, pink rat fingers knitting up
Millie's yellow hair. "Only I was thinking, maybe Truly
climbed up to the sky lid, and it was what she saw when she
opened it that made her fall down dumb."

Now, you're probably wondering why Millie was asking
me. I mean I ain't the most-Spitting-Imaged sister. Nor am I
so clever in sums as Dorothy. But the truth is, I do have about
the best knowledge of the Appendix that a head could ask
for. And like our dear Aunty says it best of all, "If my Appendix doesn't answer the big questions in life, nieces, nothing else will!"

And I expect you're wanting to know why I have the best
knowledge of the Appendix, but like Aunty also says it,

"Well, niece, that's a story probably best kept between me and you, and you and me, don't you think?"

Only I will tell you this, I had one problem right now—there weren't no answer set down nowhere from *A for Aunty Swindon* (see also *E for Eternal Love*) to *Z for Zebra stripes (which are to be avoided during all plump periods in life)* that I could think of for climbing after the sky lid. I sighed and unwrapped my ears from their cloth strips, and sat up in my straw. Wasn't like I'd been sleeping anyway, was it? Not with my Mr. Stick-worked shoulders. Not with Truly tramping about my head. Truly and terrible injuns tramping unnecessary everywhere.

"Well, Clam, was it the lid?"

"All right, Millie Gatwick, wait on, will you."

I looked about. Looked like it was day at last. The Sun was shoving Himself sneaky through cracks in the planks, and sizzling holes in our straw. Down the row, most of my sisters were still curled in sleep. Next door the pigs were farting for their breakfast. In the mending room, well, it was really best not thought about what was in there. And down in her Hole, Maria was starting up her howling.

"Well, Clam?" Millie's eyeballs boggled close. Millie Gatwick, I don't mind saying, had uncommon wobbly eyes. "My dear frogspawn friend" was what Aunty most liked to call her. And one day it was most probably true, like Aunty said, that them eyes would plop right out of Millie's face.

"Well, Millie—" I said. Except then my head filled up with thinking about Truly.

"Yes, Clam?"

"Well, Millie—"

Well, first I thought on reminding her what the Appendix says straight off, on the page stuck inside the casing, *"Remember! Some truths are for Mother and Aunty to know and for nieces to never find out!*, and happen lid-opening may be one of these, Millie."* Then I thought on trying the easy explanation, "Well, you ain't actually old enough to be told." Then I thought about saying the sad but likely one, "Actually, Millie, Truly was mighty foolish to go climbing, and it is a sad but likely truth that she got too close to His moonstain without her headscarf on. Happen that's why her words burned up."

But then I didn't say none of these. "Well, Millie," I said loud and clear, looking past Truly's cold straw space to the fur lump along from me, "Annie St. Albans knows exactly what Truly said she saw up there. Annie knows, and Annie ain't said yet, has she?"

Annie's bushy head popped out of her fur, and two green eyes flashed at me. "Will everyone hush up a second, I think I heard something." She jumped up and raced up the other way, past Dorothy and Sandra, to the wall next to the mending room. She tapped on a plank. "Truly Polperro, it's me, Annie. Truly, can you hear me?"

"It's only wind you can hear," Dorothy said. "That or something knocking."

"But what would be knocking?" Annie said.

I lay down, listening to the thumping noises that had started up, far off outside.

"Why is something knocking out there?" Annie whispered. "What could possibly be knocking?"

Well, there weren't nothing set down nowhere in the Appendix about outside knocking, so I flung some straw over my head, and curled up tight. And I shut my eyes and ears, and I shut out Annie's why and what-ing, and that non-stop knocking, and poor deadmeat Truly, and the whole sorry day.

The dorm door stayed bolted up all day. The knocking kept on. Now and then a bored pig snorted next door. At some point I dreamed. It was my demonmale, tormenting me like they are sent to do to us. Which Aunty said, when I told her, was a "sadness," but what wouldn't kill us should make us stronger for War. *D for Demonmales* explains more. Only I should say Adelaide Worthing was rescued youngest, and she don't have no demonmales in her dreams, none at all. Which is a blessed relief for her, it really is. And I'll just say here, the worst, if you're interested, was Nancy's. He was a fat one in her dream, always bubbling pans and sharpening knives. Mine weren't so bad as that, but he did have hair all over his face. Most times mine was laughing at me and grabbing for me, so I had to wake up fighting him off. This dream just gone, I was trapped up in a chair he was pushing through trees. He bent over to rub his demonbeard on me. I grabbed his ears. They were red with cold. He was laughing, and I was laughing.

I woke cold and full of his nasty laughing.

The dorm was black and breathing quiet. I turned away from Truly's straw and shuffled myself along to Nancy's warm bottom, so as her snores might carry me back to a safe and empty sleep.

Course, Nancy felt me shunt her. And her teeth were something curdled when she turned and smiled at me and whispered, "I've been laid here thinking, Clam. I've been laid thinking ain't it funny how the loonhead was all quiet in her Hole, eh, until a certain Calamity Sneak dragged her out. A Calamity Sneak who knows Maria ain't ever known for staying close and quiet in crops. Who knows she always runs back for the yard in the end. Eh, sister Sneak, what do you reckon to that?"

Well, what I reckoned was Nancy hadn't got over Jean Valjean. "Nancy, I can't keep saying sorry for Jean, he was a sick piglet," I whispered. "Like I wanted Truly to turn deadmeat, and us all to get corrected and bolted in, like I really wanted that. And like I said to everyone, 'Don't go Out of Bounds,' but that hasn't been remembered by no one, has it, sister?"

Nancy grunted, but she didn't throw me a fist.

So I didn't spit her.

"I think my stomach has eaten itself up," a voice said from down the bottom end of the row. Possible it was little Adelaide doing it. To say true, in the dark it weren't ever easy to tell which squeak came from Adelaide, Cinderella or Fantine.

"Well, I tell you, my skin is certain cracking up," Sandra said. She jumped up, and went running down the row to peer at her face in the water bucket by the door. "Either that or I am sprouting blackheads. And I never sprout blackheads."

Course, this from Sandra set all my sisters to stirring, never mind that outside was night again. All except for Annie, who was sat up by the mending room wall, and didn't look to have ever slept. Annie, who had her whole body glued to the planks between her and Truly, who wasn't doing nothing but shaking her head like it was trapped full of worry bees, and she didn't want to let them out.

"Has anyone seen Gretel?" Millie called out from the middle of the row. "Only she's gone and gone off. Don't nobody go squashing her, will you?"

"Has anyone seen my red shoe?" Sandra said, poking about under the bucket. "They're the ones Aunty gave me to practice walking for War, because I'm going first, because I'm eldest. Only I can't go if I can't find my shoe, and I can't find my shoe being stuck in here with so many blackheads." Sandra Saffron Walden—pretty as a snowdrop and about as senseful as one too.

"Once a stomach has eaten itself, will it start on eating up everything else inside a body?" little Adelaide called up from the bottom end.

"No," clever Dorothy said. "Least I think not. Least it's not written in the *Digests*. Happen we should take our minds off our tummies and Truly and everything. Shall I shout out some sums?"

"We could sing," Mary Bootle said. Mary, who didn't have a better dream in her life than one with a bagful of babies. "How about 'Hushabye Mountain' or 'Stay awake, don't rest your head'? In fact, I've got a truly scrumptious lullaby all ready I could sing, couldn't I?"

No one said nothing.

"It's truly scrumptious, truly truly scrumptious."

"Will you quit saying about Truly," Annie shouted out, all quick and loud and hot. "Just quit it!"

And no one said nothing to that.

Under her straw, sickly Eliza coughed. "When I am ill I like a story best of all."

"Oh, yes," Mary Bootle sighed, "but Truly Polperro is best for tales. Remember the one she tells about the eel that grew wings. One day it sneezed and flew out the stream and over the Wall and up the sky, and straight through the sky lid into Heaven's Garden. Or what about the mole that liked digging so much it burrowed under the Wall and was never seen again. Or what about the climbing rose, who loved growing, but whose tallest bloom got chopped off when it got to the top of the Wall, which made her so sad her petals turned to tears, and she cried herself into rose water. I think I liked that one best of all."

Which had us even sadder.

"Well," I said, bright as I could, "my throat sure is dry, but I reckon I could remember something of the starting of us. I mean, not as well as Truly tells tales, but I could. And Appendix truth is much better than tales, isn't it?"

Millie Gatwick was crawling up the row, calling out for her rat.

"Well? Do you want to hear it or not?"

"Can you not do the flying eel?"

"No."

"Suppose," someone muttered.

"Suppose?" I said. "I am talking of our truth and purpose and you say 'Suppose'?"

"Well, go on then, Flap-ears, if you're going to bother." Nancy Nunhead that was, squirting over the shit bucket.

"Alrighty, hold on, will you?" I said. I sat up and looked about at the shadow lumps of my sisters, twitching about like grubs in their straw. The night outside was corpse-still. Down in her Hole, Maria was quiet. Next door, the pigs were sensible and settled to snoring. There was still no shifting from Annie up by that wall, and still no noise from poor old Truly on the other side of it. Well, a clear reminder of our purpose was about the best thing we needed on a night like this, it really was.

"This is a perfect tale for the dark," I said.

I cleared my nose on my smock, and settled myself down in my straw. Then I closed my eyes for better remembering the most glorious story ever told—the truth of how we sisters came to be.

C FOR CREATION

In that place before time ever was, the Mother Goddess lived in Heaven and watched over all the Universe. She watched over the planets and She watched over every twitching creature down to the skinniest gnat, and even them insects which are so tiny they don't seem to twitch at all, but they do.

"Well now, after a while the Goddess got tired of watching over everything—which don't sound like much, like the watching Aunty does over us—but, like Aunty says, is a thoroughly draining business indeed. So She plucked off a hair from Her head and bit it in two—for having a hair and a spare. She planted them two ends in Heaven's Garden, and by next morning they had sprouted. One grew immediately All Wise and All Useful, and was naturally shaped as a Daughter. The other grew stunted with pus-soaked blackspots, and most unfortunately into a Sun."

"Yuck."

"Yes, yuck, but don't interrupt. Now you don't need me to tell you, this male hair was pure trouble from the word go. Matter of fact, He didn't like to do nothing other than start up fires. He would suck hundreds of bugs into the sky, and click His fingers to strike up flames and roast them. Which is where lightning comes from, if you didn't know, and the thunder is the sound of their poor backs cracking.

"Course, the Goddess would have squashed this nasty Sun of Hers to death right then, if She could. But being grown from Her, He was immortal. Which was something problematical. So She called Him to Heaven's drainage ditch, where there was a waste disposal lid to the stinking Universe below, and She said, 'Sun, I've made you a world of your own to rule. And isn't that nice and Motherly of me?'"

"'Where, Mother?' Her Sun said, looking out to the Universe, and seeing nothing but black.

"'It's just past this planet,' She said. And She rolled a pebble in Earth and lifted the lid and chucked it out. 'It'll look bigger once you're down there. Wriggle through the Earth to the other side and your own world will be straight in front of you.'

"Which, by the way, is called a little white lie. Which is a most useful tool, sisters, when dealing with demonmales.

"'Off you pop then,' said Mother. And She opened up the waste disposal lid, and shoved Her Sun out of Heaven.

"Once He stopped screaming and falling, it took Him no time at all to wriggle deep into the Earth. Matter of fact, He was very happy down there, tunnelling away and sniggering about all the fiery nastiness He would get up to in His own world, when—BUMP! His nose smashed up against rock. He pushed and shoved, but no matter, He had hit the pebble in the planet's heart. And like all males, He got angry then. In fact, He got Himself so wound up with rage that He couldn't back out. Yes, sisters, He was trapped good and proper.

"And up in Her Heavenly Garden, the Goddess looked down at the quiet Earth. She shut the lid and winked at Her Daughter, and told Her to take over the Universe, while She retired to grow roses in peace and quiet."

"Well, we know all this, Clam."

"Thank you, Nancy. And I suppose you know the poor Goddess Daughter didn't get no peace and quiet for long? Oh no. Because deep in the Earth's Bowels, Her angry Brother had started chomping up worms and millipedes. Day after day He chomped them poor old bugs and beetles, and day after day He grew fatter and hotter."

Down the row, someone sobbed.

"Better huddle up, sisters, because now our story gets proper nasty. One morning, when everything looked to be waking up perfect on Earth, the peace and quiet was disturbed by a sound like pain, sisters, only worse. The ground groaned. It shook. And a mighty ball of hair and grubs and sizzling fire burst out of the soil, and shot straight up the sky. Yes, sisters, it was Him—the Sun, who is also known as Demon and Devil and One Whole Heap of Stinking Trouble— shooting up and crashing into that very disposal lid that separates our sky from Heaven.

"There was a big BANG! and all of Heaven shuddered. But, though the lid shook something terrible, it didn't crack, and thank goodness for that. But most unfortunately, bits of Him—like lumps of burning hair and chewed-up grubs—

flew off from the impact, as it is known, and fell back to Earth. Here they turned solid, and we all know what else they turned into, don't we?"

"Is it demonmales, Clam?"

"Yes, thank you, but I really didn't need an answer, Millie. Nasty stinking demonmales. Set to wage His War on Earth. But we shall come to them in a bit."

"Do we have to, Clam? Only Truly never says on them, in case it causes bad dreams."

"Well, I won't say look where Truly's thinking has got her, I won't say that. What I will say is the Sun shoved at the lid all day, but no matter, He couldn't break through. By evening He was starving, so He retreated to His Bowels, to feast on what grubs He could still find alive down there. And He left a stain of Himself in the sky to mark the spot, like a dog does, and the Goddess Daughter covered up the lid with dark blankets, and tried to forget about Him.

"But the next morning, when She pulled the blankets away, well, He only went and tried again, didn't He? Shooting up for another bash like He hadn't learned His lesson the first time. Which males don't, by the way.

"Course, the lid didn't budge. And it was never going to—what with Him weak from eating only grubs. He needed proper meat to eat. Males do.

"There was nothing to eat in the sky, so He looked down at the Earth. And there He saw those nasty lumps of demonmales twitching to life. And He saw other species staring up at Him, and turning blind from looking into His burning fury. He saw those species that are not protected with fur or feathers, starting to roast from His terrible heat. And what did He think to Himself then? They look tasty. That's what. And this is when He realized His most dastardly plan. Who's crying? Well, who is it?"

"Me. Only Truly Polperro always tells happy stories."

"Well, 'Me,' this will be a happy story when we're done, but first the truth must be told, and this is it—the Sun set His demonmales to grab the planet's furless females and spurt fire inside them, to cook them up for Him to eat.

"So the demonmales set to, and for years they have been using demonic tools called Love and Marriage, to trick females into letting themselves be spurted with fire. When females are cooked enough, inside and out, the demonmales drag them down to the Bowels of the planet to finish them off on a spit. Every night, when we are sleeping, He's busy down below eating female flesh. And every day He grows stronger. And one day, unless He is stopped, He will smash through the lid of the sky and take over Heaven."

"But what about Truly?" a little voice wailed in the dark.

Well, that stopped my telling sure as piss on a matchstick.

"Yes, Clam, what about Truly? Won't she be dragged down to Bowels, now she's gone and been—"

"Well," I said quicksharp. "Well, thank you very much, whoever, for cheering us all up. Now just remember, Truly ain't known to be sure and certain dead yet, is she? No. And even if she was foolbrained to go climbing the Wall without her headscarf, there were protecting clouds about. And His moonstain ain't never as strong as His real burning self. And she did fall in the Wall's shadow. And I'll say it again, Truly ain't known to be dead just yet, so cheer up. Or if you can't cheer up, can you hush up a bit, so I can get on?"

Well, the sobbing wasn't quietening, but I sat up and

raised my voice and said, "Come on, sisters, this ain't sisterly. See, sisters, you aren't the only ones crying. No, the Goddess Daughter also blubbed like a baby when She peeped through the lid and saw what was happening to all the females on Earth. So She tried to think up a plan."

"Is this us, Clam?"

"I am coming to us, if you wait on and let me tell you."

"In your own time, eh, Clam."

"Thank you, Nancy." Mother alone knows why she chose to rescue Nancy, she really does. "Anyway, so the Goddess Daughter pulled out a hair from Her own head. She planted it unbroken, so it would grow practically perfect in every way."

"Mother!"

"Yes, all right, Millie, she don't like her name being shouted out by us. And the Goddess Daughter said to this new Daughter, who is also known as our Mother, 'Pop down to Earth and build an army to take on the demonmales at their own game.' She said, 'I've got just the spot to grow them, it's called North Wales. There's a pretty Walled Garden, and what's more, the Sun doesn't bother with Wales very much.'

"So Mother tumbled down from Heaven. Except, and this is most unfortunate, sisters, a breeze blew her off course, so she landed in an oak tree outside the Garden, not in it. So He sent an army of His foulest demonmales racing to the oak. And all at once the ground swarmed with—"

"Is this the injuns, Clam?"

"Yes, thank you, Millie, and now I'll have to say it again."

"Don't bother, eh."

"And all around the oak, Nancy, an army of fearsome injuns—"

"Ha!" Now I should say this laugh weren't from Millie

or Nancy. Oh no. It was thrown out loud and sudden from the wall by the mending room.

"Annie?"

Weren't like injuns were for laughing about.

She shook her head and snorted.

"Annie, ain't like injuns are for laughing at."

"Sorry, Clam, but Truly Polperro said she didn't see no injuns outside the Wall. That's what Truly said—'no injuns.' "

Well.

Well, I tried not to look at Annie like she hadn't just chucked the whole truth of our Creation into the shit pit. "Annie," I said low and warning, "you ain't to interrupt me."

Annie shrugged. "All I'm saying is, there's something peculiar here."

I started up again quick. "And all around the oak, them snarling injuns—"

"But Truly didn't see no injuns. Didn't you hear me, Clam?"

"With them ears, eh eh eh!"

"Shut up, Nancy."

"Yes, Nancy, please be quiet a moment." Annie hunched up before me, flashing her green eyes right up in my face. "Clam, listen. I know that the Appendix says injuns are prowling outside the Wall, waiting to rip off our heads, course I know it says that. But listen, Truly told me she didn't actually see no injuns out there. Not with her eyes."

Well.

Well, the hiss that escaped me then was hotter than steam. "Blasphemy, Annie. That is utter blasphemy you're speaking, and you better get it scrubbed clean out of your head."

"No need to shout, eh, Flap-ears."

"Well, yes, Nancy, yes, there is need to shout," I said,

38

shooting her a look and then shooting my eyes straight back to Annie. "You scrub out that blasphemy right now, Annie St. Albans. Right now. Right now. Right now."

Course, when I look back, I see I should have crushed Annie's blasphemy like I would a snail in petals. I should have torn out its body, and split its casing under my heel, before it set about devouring the whole crop. That's what I should have done. But I only had words, see. And Annie wasn't ever one for hearing my words.

But now it wasn't just Annie. Now Dorothy was up and grasshopping her bones all hot and bothered about the dorm.

"It is peculiar," Dorothy said. "There must be a reason why Truly saw no injuns out there. Caterpillars turn to pupas, and pupas to butterflies. Algebra. These are things of perfect reason. Where is the reason in what Truly didn't see?"

I rolled my eyes. "We have better than reason, Dorothy, I am very surprised to have to tell you. We have the *Ophelia Swindon Archives* to listen to, the Showreel to watch, and our very own Appendix to read and treasure and to consult at any point, Dorothy. And if I could run out now and get it from the schoolroom, I think we'd find *I for Injuns—red-skinned, feather-skirted, whooping demonmale warriors, set to prowl about Outside the Wall and tear wandering females into pieces with machetes or arrows.* However, I will give you three perfect reasons, if you want, and you can choose any one of them to chew on. Number one—maybe Truly didn't climb all the way up the Wall—it is a long way. Number two—maybe the injuns were sleeping—it was night. Number three—maybe they were sick, so they couldn't whoop."

"Like me," sickly Eliza Aberdeen whispered from her lump.

"Like sickly Eliza. And here's another reason. Number

four—it was dark—happen Truly couldn't see proper. Or happen they were hiding. Or busy killing things—numbers five and six."

No one said nothing to this sense.

Except then Aunty did. And I will always thank her for that.

"Poo," Aunty said, pulling the bolts and swirling daylight into the dorm, in a shiny dressing gown, with yellow hair and her living eye painted up silver. Nosy bluebottles came zipping in behind. "Pooey. You've created quite a stink in here, haven't you, dear hearts?"

Aunty held her nose. She was still wearing her night-time moisturizing gloves. "Nancy, Mary, Millie, run these slop buckets to the latrines before my skin is impregnated with fecal odor. Im-preg-nate, nieces. It means ruin beyond hope of repair. Do avoid it, nieces, if you can. Shake a leg, darlings, before I'm overcome."

Aunty moved out of the door to let them pass. She grabbed Mary's plait. "Split ends, Mary Bootle, I won't warn you again. Nancy, show me the belly. Dear oh dear, we are a little doughball, aren't we? I can see I'm going to have to start weighing you, niece. Millie, how's that T-zone?" Aunty pinched Millie's chin and dropped it quick. "Quelle horreur, white spots! We must act without delay! All nieces are to hose down immediately and apply an oatmeal scrub and buttermilk all-body conditioner. Only then may you take breakfast and proceed to general Garden duties. Lessons and fight prep will be held after lunch. And darlings, do remember to soak your hands for the full ten minutes, before you even think about guzzling the milk. No milk for you,

Nancy dear," Aunty shouted out the door, "until we've ditched that podge."

Aunty's eye looked over us, and her mouth snapped open in a full-teethed smile. "My eye, but I've missed you, nieces. It shocks me to say it, but I really have." Mr. Stick went counting down the row one by one, and bounced on the belly of Adelaide Worthing. "But where was I? Oh yes, I was saying there's a wonderful surprise waiting outside. Oh, but hush my mouth, I don't want to ruin it. Chop-chop, girls, head-scarves on, and out with you!"

Well, first off out, like the dorm was burning, was Annie St. Albans. "Aunty, is Truly well? Can we see her now, please, Aunty?"

"Yes, please, Aunty," I whispered. There would be some clear and common reason why Truly saw no injuns, which she would want to say to us. Most probably—Truly being Truly—at some length. Possible she was looking the wrong way. Yes, it was possible that was the most sensible reason of all. And I ran out to tell my sisters this. And I bumped into Dorothy's back.

"Something's missing," she said. She was stopped dead in the eaves' shady safety. "Something's gone missing."

I looked quick round the yard.

Schoolroom, beauty parlor, kitchen on the left. Our dorm and the pigs behind us. The fence and the gate to the roses in front. Hen coops stinking out chickenshit on the right of the yard, and behind them, the cowshed and the hives. Latrine shed and standpipe in the top corner, the hosepipe curled and ready on the latrine wall like it should be. Trestle table and bales stacked against the dorm wall, like they should be.

Hens flapping round the sundial in the middle of the yard. And Maria banging away in her Hole below. Everything looked the same as any other morning of any other blessed yard day.

"What could be missing, Dorothy?" I said. "What is it now?"

Dorothy didn't answer me. She pulled her scarf end over her nose and ran off to the sundial. She squinted up at the sky, then down at the dial. "That's it! There's no Sun!"

"Bingo!" Aunty shouted from the yard gate. "Well spotted, Dorothy, you are a smarty-pants!" She swirled around. "Take a look, would you, nieces."

There weren't no Sun, because out past the roses, the meadow and the bog, the Wall of Safekeeping had grown taller than ever. Fat red bricks were piled on top of the old yellow ones. It stood up higher than the High Hut, higher than the plum trees. And on the Wall's high rim, glass pieces sat twinkling like the prettiest of teeth in a gum.

I looked up at our Wall, and it was all I could do not to shout "Bingo!" with Aunty, it really was. Instead, I gave Nancy a happy pinch. "See, Aunty's too clever for Him and His games! There ain't no way no hiding injuns are ever going to sneak over that!"

"Quite something, isn't it, nieces?" Aunty pointed Mr. Stick at the Wall and started to spin faster than a Poppins umbrella. "I don't mind telling you, I broke some of the bottles myself. You see, you, my precious little pennies, are just too priceless for Mother and myself to risk any more midnight mishaps. Isn't that just lovely to know? And here's my thought for the day—greasy skin lets boils in. À bientôt!"

And Aunty spun off through the yard gate, slamming it so happy she was probably off to see Mother.

Course, Annie went chasing after, "Aunty, please, please, can we see Truly?"

But Aunty was already spinning off into the Glamis Castles, swiping at buds and bees, and singing about there being somewhere over the rainbow, way up high, where there was a place that she'd been to, once in a lullaby.

MAKING A BODY
BEAUTIFUL

Bees make beauty. This is a truth known by everyone, but not by you, Doctor Andrea Doors. Which is what is written down and clipped on your coat, in case you forget who you are, being so busy nosying after me.

You come in this stinking room, like you do most days, and you come on over, and read these pages I have worked on most of the night, even though I didn't say "Please do." And your forehead cracks up, and you say you'd like to learn a bit more about this Goddess Daughter, if I wouldn't mind stopping writing for a minute.

Well, sorry, but I do. There's a lot needs setting straight before Jane Jones comes back. And then there'll be a lot to get started on.

"She sounds interesting," you say. "Making night and day and rainclouds."

It's us that make the clouds, Doctor Andrea Doors. But if you don't know that, I ain't telling you.

You flip through my pages a while, and I do some jab thrusts at the ceiling. And over on the chair by the wall, that lump of female that is always sat here lets off a moan. And you turn and smile at her and turn back to my pages, and then you frown. Which don't help those cracks of yours at all.

"Were you locked up in the dorm for one night or two?" you say.

And I don't say nothing.

And you say, "You know, Calamity, in my work I've met a lot of girls who have experienced bad things. Girls who felt confused and perhaps a little bit afraid, and who didn't want to talk, because they felt it might be best to keep those bad things locked up inside. But in the end, many of them decided it helped to share their thoughts with someone. They decided it didn't seem so lonely that way."

Well, all you have to do to stop loneliness here is set loose my sisters.

"I know you're writing down your memories, which is a wonderful start—"

And I ain't saying nothing till Jane Jones comes back.

"—and there's no rush, Calamity, you must take your time. I'd just like to suggest a little game for tomorrow. Do you think you might think of a word you like? A word you might like to say out loud? Would that be worth a try?"

Well, I reckon I'll have a spit now. On your shoes. Which will shut you up, I reckon. And it does. See, I ain't saying nothing till Jane Jones comes back to talk protection, and that's the truth. But I am going to write you a quick book, Doctor Andrea Doors. I think I am going to do that. From the look of you, it is clear you ain't acquainted with beeswax, and it just might help fill up your lines. It might keep the demonmales from noticing a while. Though I ain't promising nothing. Bees make beauty, but beauty can't ever stop you cooking up once you've been started. Nothing can stop that, Doctor Andrea Doors.

And I ain't promising nothing for that lump of female that you are always smiling at and calling Mrs. Waverley, and that has been here so long her bottom's probably grown itself into the chair in the corner. Course, it ain't like she does anything but drip from her nose and cry, which Aunty always said—and is also mentioned in the Appendix under *S for Secrets, Snot and Skincare*—"is most unfeminine, and ruins the tear ducts and turns your eyes to pissholes, and if a lady still has her eyes, well she's a damn sight luckier than some, and shouldn't ever forget it, nieces, nor should she ever use them for pissing either!"

Course, an egg white poultice might help Mrs. Waverley with her bloated tear ducts, but like Aunty also said, "I want the best for you nieces, but heavens above, I'm not a miracle worker."

So here it is.

A BOOK ON HOW TO BE BEAUTIFUL (UNLESS YOU'RE TOO COOKED ALREADY). BY CALAMITY LEEK.

BASIC RULES TO MAKE THE BEST OF WHAT YOU HAVE
Bind back what sticks out. Push up what hangs down. Don't squeeze pus spots.

TOOLS
THE STANDPIPE—HOSE DOWN YOUR BODY ONCE DAILY AFTER MORNING LABOR (BEFORE LUNCH AND LESSONS). SOAP AND LATHER TWICE. USE A STONE TO MASSAGE.

THE TOOTHBRUSH—USE WITH PASTE AFTER EVERY MEAL.

THE COMB—APPLY ONCE DAILY AFTER THE STANDPIPE. CHECK ANOTHER'S HEAD FOR LICE. ALL HAIR THAT IS GROWN LONG ENOUGH IS TO BE PLAITED UP. NOT TOO TIGHT TO BREAK THE ENDS.

SUN-PROTECTING LOTION AND HEADSCARVES—TO BE WORN AT ALL TIMES OUTDOORS.

FACE—WEEKLY TREATMENTS (APPLY BEFORE BEDDING DOWN).

HONEY MASK—FOR A SOFTENING EFFECT.

OATMEAL/BUTTERMILK FACE MASK—FOR A DE-GREASING EFFECT. WIPE FACE. SMEAR ON TREATMENT. AFTER TEN MINUTES, WASH OFF. OATS AND GRITS IS BEST FOR BLACKHEADS.

HANDS—SOAK HANDS DAILY IN A MILK BOWL AT THE BREAKFAST TABLE FOR TEN MINUTES. PLEASE NOTE—IT IS ALLOWED TO DRINK OFF THE MILK AFTERWARDS—IT BEING GOOD FOR WHITE TEETH. (N.B. GLOVES TO BE WORN AT ALL TIMES DURING GARDEN LABOR. NAILS TO BE CLEANED OUT AND FILED DOWN NEAT).

HAIR HELP—YOU CAN'T BE TOO CAREFUL HERE, YOU REALLY CAN'T.

HONEY, CURDS, EGGS MIX—APPLY ONCE A WEEK, UNLESS YOU'RE A TANGLED BUSH-HEAD LIKE ANNIE ST. ALBANS, IN WHICH CASE YOU NEED TO DO THIS EVERY *TWO* DAYS.

ADDITIONAL MEASURES—

EGG YOLK CONDITIONING IS GOOD FOR GREASY HAIR LIKE NANCY'S, AND MIGHT ALSO BE GOOD FOR MRS. WAVERLEY, IF YOU WANT TO TELL HER. UP TO YOU, DOCTOR ANDREA DOORS.

<u>VINEGAR AND WATER</u> IS A PERFECT FINISHER FOR A MOTHER IS COMING TO LUNCH! DAY.

BODY—HEAT UP BEESWAX WITH WATER AND FLORIBUNDA ROSE ESSENCE FOR CREAMY MOISTURIZING EFFECT. APPLY WEEKLY TO FULL BODY, NIGHTLY TO HANDS, FACE AND NECKS AFTER CUSHION LABOR. <u>!!!!!!!!!!!!!!!!!!!</u> THIS FILLS IN ALL KNOWN <u>CRACKS, DOCTOR ANDREA DOORS</u> <u>!!!!!!!!!!!!!!</u>

AND HERE'S THE APPENDIX'S QUICK *B FOR BEAUTY REMINDERS—*

BEAUTY ISN'T A PART-TIME JOB—IT'S A FULL-TIME COMMITMENT.

BEAUTY ISN'T A GIFT—IT'S A WEAPON.

Hope this helps, Doctor Andrea Doors. I wouldn't bother with your hair, seeing as it is dead, but do try rubbing beeswax in your face cracks. But like I say, it ain't a cure and won't deceive them demonmales for long. Sorry, but you're too far cooked for that.

By Calamity Leek. THE END.

SPITTING IMAGE MARIA

Annie hadn't budged her bottom from the mending room door.

She was squatting there after breakfast, knocking on the wood and waiting for Truly to knock back, when I went to rinse my teeth at the standpipe. And she was stood there, picking at the lock on the bolt, while us other sisters were gathering to read the duty list on the dorm wall. Never mind that duties were to be done, the list said, *without any distractions from a certain body in a certain room, if nieces know what's good for them. Out of sight is out of mind, ladies.* Never mind all that, because even while we ran about preparing for duties, Annie was still glued to the mending room door, picking at the bolt and calling "Hello, hello" to Truly through the cracks.

I dragged Maria out of her Hole, and over to the standpipe to give her a hosing down. Maria wasn't ever listed as being a capable working body, but I reckoned that didn't mean she couldn't learn something by watching us, did it?

"Annie, you coming on over to the Boules now?" I shouted, keeping one hand on squirming Maria. "I reckon those sorry old Boules need some fair old TLC, and you're listed with Mary and Millie and me to do it."

But Annie didn't say nothing for dropping herself belly down in yard dirt.

"Annie?" I said. "Well, don't mind Annie," I said loud and clear to Maria, releasing her to run herself screaming dry in the yard, "because there's them that are bothered about harvesting petal protection for all, and there's them that ain't. And besides, Maria, happen we might just pop by the Sacred Lawn on the way, and ask Emily for a miracle for Truly, happen we might."

Course, Annie's head popped up at this. But then she shrugged and turned back down to start on talking to the crack under the door.

We did stop off near the Sacred Lawn. Me, Mary Bootle and Millie Gatwick, and Maria, course. We had to be quick, the Lawn being Out of Bounds In All But Exceptional Circumstances, and Emily needing her space. But then I reckoned Truly was exceptional, wasn't she? And Aunty was still off in the north with Mother.

Still, I kept all my toes in the Glamis Castle soil on the south border of the Lawn and all off the grass. I kept my head ducked out of the Crème de la Crème climbing rose arch, which we had growing at every entrance to the Lawn circle—north, east, south and west, most probably so Emily could have a nice view from where she was stood in the middle, and nice smells too. Course, I couldn't see more than Emily's toes from outside the arch, but never mind, I closed my eyes and stuck my nose in a low-down Crème de la Crème and sniffed up its sweetness, and I asked Emily if she was listening in there to please help Truly get better, I really did.

Mary Bootle finished first and turned and set off stomping down the barrow path east through the Silver Anniversaries. Mary was swinging her plaits something cross, and never mind them plaits were the longest in the Garden, they were bashing petals off the fullest Anniversaries as she went.

I shouted for her to wait up. But Mary didn't hear me, being too busy shouting on about the duty list always letting the Pontefract twins take care of the second-wind toddlers, and not her, and it wasn't fair, was it? And that's what Emily should really sort out if she was going to sort anything, and matter of fact, that's what she asked her to do first, so there.

So I shouted to watch the roseheads, please, Mary, and that she could wipe Maria Liphook's bottom if that's what she was after. Because not one second after I'd got her head pointing straight down the Anniversaries path, I am sorry to say, Maria had turned and run off grub-hunting in soil.

"Nancy says she doesn't know why you even bother learning a mashhead," Mary said, swinging her plaits all scornful, "'Why does Clam even bother?' That's what Nancy says."

"Well, Nancy can go talk to her pigs," I shouted up. "Happen she's learned her manners from them. *Every niece in the Garden is a Valuable Asset*—that's direct from page N of the Appendix, Mary Bootle, in case you forgot it—*every niece*. If Maria was allowed in our lessons, happen she'd be less of a mashhead and more of an Asset."

"Well, Nancy says you've gotten loonheaded yourself, for bothering."

Millie Gatwick came panting up the path behind us with the barrow, Gretel rat sitting up on the shovel handle, her white belly out. "Bothering what?"

"That rat's gotten herself fat with riding about all these days," I said. "I am only telling Mary how Maria Liphook was once reckoned to be as brimful of brain fiber as Dorothy Macclesfield before."

"Before what?"

"Before she started hitting the Wall. Hitting her head on it so hard that Aunty had to mend her. Aunty had to—Maria being the first rescued and first meant for unleashing. You can't go to War all covered in bruises."

"But Sandra Saffron Walden says she's off first."

"That's what she thinks, but don't forget, Maria Liphook was rescued a whole year before Sandra. It wasn't months after Emily returned to Heaven, that Mother got Maria. 'My Miracle Baby,' she called her. And you know why she called her that?"

"Spitting Image," Mary flung back from where she had swung off into the Icebergs. "Everyone knows that."

A red admiral flapped past. Maria Liphook dived off after it.

"But what about Sandra?" Millie said. "Ain't she Emily's Spitting Image? She says she is."

I watched Maria crashing through Iceberg bushes, petals falling off wasted as latrine paper scraps, and I shook my head. "Fact is, it was Maria who started the most Spitting Image of all of us. She was some years older than us when she was rescued. And she wasn't grown in the yard—not for months, she wasn't—no, first off she lived up in Mother's Glorious Abode. But when Maria started with the Wall-banging, well, Aunty realized the mistake right there and then. Never mind that Maria was a Spitting Image of Emily, happen her brain was already fried up from having lived too many years Outside. 'Over-cooked with Outside ideas' is how Aunty said it. Least a hundred mending room days it took for giving Maria a little more heart and a little less head. And in some ways it worked out. I mean her heart ain't questionable now, is it? Come on, Maria." I went in after her, squeezing my tummy careful between the thorns, and pulled her out by her smock bottom. Don't ask me how, but she had a snail oozing in her fist. "Wipe off that poor creature, Maria, it can't play with you now. Just you follow the bug jar, Maria. Follow the bugs."

That most nasty piece of work named the Sun had finally dragged Himself over the new Wall top, and was sizzling angry by the time we got Maria to Truly's Boule bush. And it was a sore sorry sight, that bush, it really was. Truth be told, and as I did tell Mary and Millie, taking the pruners from the barrow to get straight to work, "This is about the worst place Truly could ever have chosen for landing. Must be ten heads lost, maybe even the whole bush." The perfume of them ruined blooms was leaking sweet as honey tears. I plucked one of Truly's hairs off a thorn and sliced the cane three inches below, "But if we take cuttings from the strongest, we may get some re-growth next year. Millie, you'll still be around for that harvest. What do you reckon to that?"

Well, seemed no one was for answering me but a passing bee.

I popped up and squinted about. Maria Liphook was

53

squatted down stroking a dead beetle, an Outside plane was roaring all high and mighty above, but there weren't one snip of my sisters' tools going on.

Then I heard it, the eastern Wall, wailing.

Except Walls don't wail, do they? Only one kind of body does that. I dropped my pruners and hurried over.

And sure enough, there were Mary and Millie at the Wall, sitting their bottoms beneath Truly's scuffle marks, busy with nothing but crying.

"What are you two fussing about here for, when there are bleeding Boules to care for?" I said.

Mary looked up, her blue eyes dripping. "Golly, Clam, as if you didn't know."

Now babies-on-the-brain Mary was known to turn on the waterworks most days. So I said I didn't, actually. "Dry up, sisters," I said, "and come on back to your work. Aunty's over in the Glamis Castles. She's heading back to the yard."

And she was.

Twenty-four-seven, three-six-five, that's how the Appendix sets down the size of Aunty's Tender Loving Care for us. And like Dorothy will tell you about numbers, they ain't never wrong.

But Mary didn't budge a finger. "I ain't getting up just because you tell me to, Clam. I'll jolly well sit here and cry if I choose so. And I do so. So there." And she wedged the end of her plait between her front teeth and sawed it about, like that was a way for a Heaven-intended body to behave.

"I see," I said, though I didn't. "And what about you, Millie Gatwick?"

Now, like I may have said, Millie's got the wobbliest eyes ever poked out of a face. Some said there were frog parts gotten in there, but that weren't really true. Except when she was crying. When she was crying, you'd think she lived under water. Millie shook her head at me and two tears plopped out at once. "I'm sorry, Clam, it's just I keep on thinking about Mother. Oh Clam, if Truly goes and dies, Mother might have to rescue another sister. Like after Carmen died from the flu and Mother went and rescued all the second-winders. Only what if she goes out and—and—"

Gretel rat came scrambling up Millie's smock, and set to licking up her tears.

I sighed. "Happen I don't know, Millie. But Aunty does say the second-winders were an unnecessary acquisition. So why would Mother want to go out for more?"

"But Clam—"

"Yes, Millie," I said, thinking on Aunty's telescope, sat out on the balcony of the High Hut, sweeping round and finding our lack of labor, thinking on saying, "Hurry up the water-works, Millie."

"Oh, Clam, me and Mary were thinking—"

"What, Millie?"

Mary Bootle wailed so loud her plait popped out from her teeth.

"Oh, Clam, what if Mother does go Outside, and she's gone so long we leave for War, and well—and well—and well—and well—"

"HEAVENS, Millie!" I gave her a slap before she drowned herself, and never mind the damage being done to her tear ducts.

"Oh, Clam, what if Mother's gone so long that we're sent to War, and we never get to see her eyes."

Well. Well, I sighed out slow as a dying dog before I could

answer that one. "Listen, Millie, I don't know nothing for sure. But I do know that Mother, being Motherly, she will probably want to be around to see us making our goodbyes. And being Motherly, she might not say no, if we ask her to show us them eyes on our way out."

"Is it promised in the Appendix then?"

"I'm afraid I ain't ever read that in there for sure. But her last goodbyes to Emily, now they are written down, aren't they?"

Millie gulped and a tiny smile crept about her lips.

"And I'll tell you what, they went on for years, them goodbyes. 'Years and bloody years' is how *Ophelia Swindon Volume V: A Country Diary* says it."

Mary wiped up her eyes with her plaits. "I remember."

"And I'll tell you another thing. Look up at the Wall rim. See them glass jewels sparking off His heat. Finer than *My Fair Lady*'s tiara, I'd say. Would Mother have topped off the Wall with what looks like her own jewels, if she didn't want to say 'I'm going to stay around to say goodbye'? I think not. So come on, dry up. Them poor Boule heads ain't going to heal up themselves, are they?"

Well, I'd just about heaved my sisters to standing when the communicating post at the top of the Boule row hissed. A magpie sitting on top yelped and flapped off.

BING BONG, the Communicator said, *BING BONG*.

I went to land Mary a punch, but happen it wasn't us being caught dawdling on duty. It was an announcement.

"An announcement. Eldest nieces—that's Sandra, Dorothy, Annie, Calamity, Nancy and Mary only—may run along to the mending room to visit their dearest sister and their loving Aunty's loveliest charge, Truly Polperro, who is currently lying in the recovery position. One never likes to tempt fate, but this does sound like promising news, doesn't it? This offer is solely for eldest nieces. As a consolatory treat for the rest of you, your loving Aunty has generously agreed to perform a little ditty. It's called 'How do you solve a problem like Maria?' Answers on a postcard, please!"

Mary jumped up, "Supercalifragilistic!"

I laughed and spun her around in a dance. "Expialidocious!"

The Communicator started on Aunty's ditty. And Mary and me kissed Millie Gatwick farewell, and raced ourselves back to the yard before Aunty's offer ended.

HEAT

Afterwards, when we had left Truly alone to receive Aunty's Tender Loving Care, I tried to keep my snivelling stoppered up inside me. I did try.

Nancy flicked my ear as we walked out into the yard. "Nearly did it again, eh? Sister Sneak," she whispered. "Very nearly."

"Leave her alone," Annie said, coming up behind and giving my shoulder a quick squeeze. "Clam didn't say nothing."

"No, Annie, I didn't." I wiped my nose on my sleeve, and I headed for the standpipe and calming water. It was a tricky enough job to keep my words from breaking up. "But *you* should have, Annie. You really should have said something."

Annie shrugged. She came along after me and leaned against the latrine wall and started kicking at a loose clot of yard concrete.

I pulled off my headscarf and jammed my head under the tap to let cold water drown me out. But all I saw was Truly lying deadmeat in straw. Truly looking so ready for her shroud, that when Mary Bootle opened the mending room door, she screamed, "She's dead! Truly's jolly well gone and died, and a demonmale's going to come and drag her down to the Devil's Bowels any second now!"

I shivered, but I kept that water pouring its cleansing chill on me. "You should have said on the injuns, Annie. For Truly's sake, you should have told Aunty."

Annie flipped the concrete out of the ground with her toe. She spun round and kicked it hard at the latrine wall.

Wham.

"Sit down, if you're staying." That's what Annie said, when me and Mary stopped dead at the mending room door, our happy giggles turning to screams. "Sit down and hush up."

Annie, Sandra, Dorothy and Nancy were all squished along the wall next to Truly, who was all clean for once, in a fresh smock in fresh straw. Annie was kneeling by Truly's head, stroking Truly's hair which was laid out all neat. She wasn't taking her eyes off Truly's closed ones. "And don't talk on dying, because she can hear you."

Sandra looked up, her pretty pink cheeks puffed damp. "Truly is crying."

"And deadmeat never manages that," Nancy said, jabbing at a wart on her toe. "Left eye. Take a look."

Well, sure enough, the eyelashes on Truly's left eye were wet. And even though her eyelid was shuttered up, a tear slipped out of the corner and rolled sideways over her cheek, and plopped off into straw.

"She's been at it since we came in, and who knows how long before."

I whispered the only thing I could think, "Is she turned Liphook?"

"No!" Annie hissed.

"Well, Annie—" I felt my own eyes filling up, watching Truly's left one pop out another tear, "—well, I am very sorry, Annie, but this carcass lump don't look much like our giggle-mouthed, bendy-boned, non-stop-chatterbox sister to me."

"Well, that's where you're wrong, Clam," Annie flashed back. "All wrong. She can hear me and she can answer me. The only thing she can't do yet is talk. Which she will do soon enough."

I looked at Truly, who weren't saying nothing to this, nor looking like she was even bothering thinking it. Nor bothering thinking any other blessed thing for that matter. "But Annie—"

"Take her hand."

"But it ain't doing nothing, Annie."

"Just take it."

So I squeezed myself up the other side of the room, and took up Truly's hand from where it was laid on her belly. And though its palm was warm, I am sorry to say her fingers were about as lively as stale bread.

Annie's eyes sizzled at me. "Now ask her if her name is Truly Polperro."

I looked around my sisters. Dorothy nodded.

"Go on," Annie said. "Ask her."

"Very well, Annie."

And I tell you this for bone marrow truth, next thing happened was Truly's fingers started to curl up round mine. Sure, they went at it slow as slugs shifting a leaf, but they did curl up. Felt like I felt the tiniest squeeze before they fell loose again.

"Now ask her another question," Annie said. "Ask her the *other* question."

Well, my mouth dried to dust at that.

"Ask her."

I kept my eyes on Truly's hand. "Truly Polperro, listen to me carefully. When you went climbing did you see injuns outside the Wall?"

Not a finger budged. Not one.

It was all I could do not to gasp. "Are you sure, Truly? Are you sure?"

And Truly's fingers stayed flopped.

"Oh, Truly!"

"Now you know," Annie said.

"But Annie, that ain't possible," I said. "Look at her, how can she know what she's saying?" And my own eyes fogged up, and happen I didn't want to look on our deadmeat sister no more, with her flopped-out fingers, and her eye full of tears. I didn't want nothing more than fresh yard air pouring into me. I laid down Truly's hand on her belly and I scrabbled for the door.

"Going somewhere, niece?"

Aunty, that was, arrived behind me, so I near enough fell into her shoes.

"Morning, ladies. What a pleasant surprise to find you all here. May I say it makes for a very touching scene. Act one. Scene one. The death bed. Or should I say sick bed? What do you think, nieces? Death has more drama, but with sickness there's always the hope of a cure."

Aunty wasn't in her gown no more, but dressed up in

61

white, with a belt like a tire gripping her tummy and shiny black tights holding on to her legs. She had taken off her moisturizing gloves, and she held the *Reader's Digest Home Medicine Manual* all careful between her creamy fingers. A cherry-red smile was painted where her lips used to be.

"You seem to be in a hurry to leave us, Calamity. Not a fan of sick rooms? Perhaps you'd like to pick yourself up out of that draughty doorway and get back inside toute suite. That's spelled S-U-I-T-E, nieces. Think Hyde Park Hilton, Nancy, rather than those nasty sugary things that pile on the pounds. You others, budge up. It is a tight squeeze in here, but trust me, ladies, you'll always have room for a small one."

I shuffled back in next to Nancy, and wiped off my eyes.

"Come along, Calamity. I said 'Going somewhere?' It's your line. Need a teensy prompt? Very well, you were about to shed some light on what provoked this emergency exit of yours, how about that? After all, any information is useful when we're fighting the Devil's heat."

Annie's green eyes flashed up, "Is that what you think Truly's got, Aunty?"

"Why, niece? Don't you?"

And Annie shook her head for yes and then for no, which was something muddling. And quicksharp, I looked over at her, and I thought, "Tell her now, Annie. Tell Aunty about the injuns, and Aunty will sort it out. Aunty always sorts it."

But Annie didn't.

Aunty said, "Curious child," and turned her eyeball back on me. "So where were we? Oh yes, darling little Calamity here was going to get the ball rolling by spilling the beans. Because it really is time we got to the bottom of what happened to poor old Truly, isn't it, and I just know you girls

have your sister's best interests at heart. And you, Calamity—
my most compliant of dollar dolls—have clearly got something to get off your chest. A nice, clear voice now, because a
lady should always annunciate, articulate, implicate." Aunty
smiled at me. Her top teeth row was creamed with cherry.

Well Well, what could I say?

See, Aunty's eye was joined by my sisters' ones, and every
one of them eyes was pinning me down, until it got to seeming it wasn't the mending room I was stuck in, but a roasting
corner of Bowels. But instead of demonmales with skewers
for the spit, it was Aunty waiting to tear me one way, and
my sisters another.

Well, my eyes were gushing and my nose was gushing,
and all I could hear was words gushing out of me, "No, no,
I don't know. It ain't fair that it's always me that has to say
things. Annie knows, Annie knows, ask Annie."

"Annie? Annie St. Albans?" Aunty sighed. "I might have
known. Well then, Annie, my sweetie-niecey-pie, do stop
picking holes in the plasterboard, straighten that spine, and
let's be having it."

And Aunty stared at Annie, and Annie looked straight
back at Aunty and shrugged all her bones at once. "None of
us knows anything," she said. "We found Truly on the bush
and Truly hasn't said a word since."

And Aunty went, "Nothing? Not a squeak, not a peep,
not a sausage?"

And loud and clear and cold as water, Annie said,
"Nothing."

I looked up quick, and there was Annie looking straight
at me. And there was Aunty's eye starting its swivel over us,
one by one, steady as a crow after the first twitch of a worm.

"Any thoughts on the matter, dear unfortunate Dorothy? You didn't eat Truly's voice box, did you, Nancy? Calamity Leek, for heaven's sake, wipe that nose. Snot is unsightly in anyone, and nothing less than nauseating in nieces. Thank you. Now I'm going to give you all one last chance to add illumination to Annie's bobby-dazzler of an explanation. One very last chance, nieces."

Only one thing moved, which was a dribble from Truly's left eye.

"No?" Aunty said. "Dear oh dear, how very disappointing. So, my flap-eared friend, there's nothing at all to report?"

I didn't need to look up to know Aunty's eye had fixed itself on me.

"Nothing you'll regret later? Because a lady should never have regrets." And Aunty bent low and whispered into my ear, "Well, not to worry, ma chérie. Tête-à-tête, à deux, peut-être?"

Then Aunty thunked me on the head with the *Digest* and said, "Oh do quit snivelling, child. If there's one thing I loathe, it's a sniveller." And then she shooed us all out of her sight, and told us to get back to work or target practice or something, because we were clearly useless at even the most elementary of role plays, and Truly needed her spoonful of sugar to help her medicine go down in the most delightful way.

Out in the yard, I turned off the standpipe.

"Why didn't you, Annie? Why didn't you say the truth to Aunty?"

Annie stopped kicking at concrete. "It's only words, isn't

it? How can telling those words to Aunty make Truly better? How can words be medicine?"

"But what about the danger? We should tell Aunty in case them injuns are off planning a surprise attack by sneaking up someplace else."

Annie said nothing. She watched me dry off my face with my headscarf and cover up safe again. Appendix words came into my head then. This is what they warned in *S—*

Did you know, a niece with a secret is like a dog with a chicken bone—seems tasty, but BEWARE! Gobbled down in private instead of shared with Aunty, it'll snag in her throat and choke her to death.

I began to say this wisdom to Annie, when she burst out laughing at me.

"Annie?" I stepped back from her. "Annie, this really ain't a time for laughter. We really need to think about the dog with the chicken bone."

But she just shook her head, laughing.

"What?" I said. "What is it? Because getting your throat choked ain't funny, Annie, it really ain't."

"You're right," she said. "Sorry." She tried to shut up her smile. Then she shrugged, "Sorry, Clam. Only, I've just been thinking, and it's plum simple, it really is. Truly's getting better. You felt her hand, it was moving. And when Truly is strong enough to talk, well, then she'll tell us exactly what she saw Outside. In fact, Truly being Truly, we'll never shut her up, will we? And then we'll know what to think about injuns and everything, and how to tell it all to Aunty. Fact is—" and every one of the speckles on Annie's face jumped up happy like I hadn't seen since Truly fell down, "—fact is, Truly can

65

tell Aunty herself, soon enough, all we actually have to do is wait!"

I blew my nose on my smock and I thought about the sense of this.

Annie grinned. She turned and squeezed me up in one of her bone-squeak hugs that she really does better than anyone. "Come on then, race you back to the Boules."

And we ran through the gate, and up the barrow path holding hands, which is nice to do, even if it is a bit tricky on the bends. And I looked at Annie, with her curls bouncing out under her scarf, and her nose turfed up high, which is how Annie always runs through roses, since she and Truly and me were little and they ran along laughing and shouting out behind, "Come on, Calamity Slow-Feet, catch us if you can!" And I squeezed Annie's hand and I said to her, "Catch me if you can, Annie!" And her eyes fizzed with laughter. And my own heart flipped happy. And I thought again about her words, and I thought, yes, happen we will just have to wait for Truly to explain what she's seen. Aunty will make her all better soon enough. Aunty will sort it. So we will all just have to wait and see.

NO WORMS

My sisters' voices are echoing something busy in my ears
tonight. Not just Truly. Annie, Dorothy, even the
second-wind toddlers are going on at me. But I'll put them
away for a little while, because here I am, ready and waiting
for you, Jane Jones.

Course, I expect you won't come till it's safe black outside. I understand that. But it's gone dark beneath the blinds,
and this room's gray as mold now Mrs. Waverley's scraped
her bottom off the chair, and the lights went off after her. Is
it nearly time?

Do you know there ain't a single pipistrelle bat in this
room, or one harvest spider sewing up the ceiling, or even a
woodlouse poking nosy out of the floor. You wouldn't think
one woodlouse would be a problem, wriggling about next to
a bed-stuck body, or even hid under the bed out of the way.
You wouldn't think that.

Happen I could open that window and call up a tawny.

Eliza had a tawny once, she said, flew in and sat under the eaves to watch over her them nights she felt most sickly. But I ain't heard one owl here. I shut my eyes and the only sound is a far-off rushing moan, an unhappy one that never dies off. Might be it is females being dragged down to Bowels. Might be, I don't know. Do you know, there ain't the breath of a crow, a cockerel, or even one old itch of a dog's bottom to be heard anywhere here.

Do you know, I sure would like to hear a word. Not even a word. Just a truly scrumptious giggle from Mary Bootle would do it. Or I would like to see a flash of Annie's green eyes. Or I would even take a thump from Nancy without even seeing her, I really would take that.

I could press on the button to fetch someone in, course. That's what they say. But it won't be Mary Bootle or Millie Gatwick, will it? Won't even be a worm popping up for a rest from turning the soil.

But I'm not going to think Garden thoughts now. You won't come in and find me blubbing in the dark, Jane Jones. No, you won't do that.

HAPPY BIRTHDAY, EMILY

As it happened, Truly never did get to explain anything to us. Because, I am very sorry to say it, the next day, she was dead.

Now, I also have to say, Truly didn't die straight off. No, it took a while, because it was a very busy day. It started in the night with Millie losing Gretel, and it went on in the morning with tea with Aunty. It finished off with Emily's birthday party. And it was only after all this that Truly's death was what Aunty called "certified." And in case I didn't say it, it was a complete and utter accident. Yes it was.

You don't need to know much about Millie losing Gretel, only that it happened. Morning came rainy, and though Gretel weren't ever one for getting her tail damp, she still hadn't shown up by porridge time. Evita called us to breakfast, and Millie's face grew as wet as the Goddess Daughter's tears that were battering the yard, and she had to be stopped from running off to the Sacred Lawn to ask Emily for a rat-finding miracle.

But even frog-faced Millie wasn't wet as Annie that morning. Annie who hadn't come to sit on her bale for breakfast under the eaves. Never mind that I was reading out *M for Mother* and *M for Miracles*, which are some of the best pages there are. No, never mind that, because Annie wasn't no place other than the mending room door, squatting in the rain, waiting for Truly to call out that she was better and fancied a chat.

"What do you think Truly's first words will be?" Annie shouted over to us.

"Hello, fat rat, what you doing in here?" Nancy said, and we all had to laugh at that. Except Millie didn't.

We were still laughing when the Communicator in the eaves bing-bonged, and said due to inclement weather conditions, after breakfast all nieces would proceed to the schoolroom, to copy handwriting from a *Digest* of choice—and then nieces might as well get out the pigskins and revise belly-bayoneting, seeing as their Mother kept going on about it. All nieces—apart from Calamity Leek, who was required upstairs immediately on a private matter. Over and out.

Well.

Well, I hadn't moved an inch from my bale when the Communicator bing-bonged again and said, "Terribly sorry, but your absent-minded old Aunty has actually forgotten to communicate the most exciting news of all." She was just terrible with dates and it couldn't be helped. But as soon as nieces were done jib-jabbing their swords, they might like to think of a gift idea. An apple would do, or one of those straw dolls everyone was so crazy about these days. After all, it

wasn't every day of the year that a certain someone cele-
brated a B-I-R-T-H day. And who knows, it might be the last
B-I-R-T-H day some nieces would witness. Which reminded
her, shoes did not grow on trees, and if Sandra Saffron
Walden wasn't fully shod for the occasion, there'd be trouble. Come along, Calamity Leek, oh and bring up the Appendix, would you, sweetie? Over and out.

Now, I'll start it by telling you this. I ain't ever had the clearest remembrance of my visit to Aunty that day. No. There's
them of my leftover sisters that would say otherwise, because
of all the sadness that happened after, but I'll tell you once,
and not again, they weren't asked there for tea, were they?
They don't know nothing.

It was eight metal steps up, then a turn, then eight more
steps to get to the High Hut, which, like I say, was handily
built right on top of our dorm. A viewing balcony ran all
along the front. When a body stood there, well, you could see
it was no bother at all for a single eye to keep an eye on the
yard, the roses, the Sacred Lawn and the yew path north
to Mother's Glorious Abode. And from the balcony you got
the best view of all, course—of our gray stone, yellow-brick,
red-topped Wall, jewel-toothed and twinkling, and belting us
into perfect safety.

When you walk through a storm
"—shake a leg, Calamity—"
—don't be afraid of the dark.
"—in the bedroom, Calamity, chop-chop—"
Walk on! Walk on! With hope in your heart—
Holding tight on the Appendix, I hurried up, the wet steps

clanging under my feet, my sisters chattering busy about birthday presents down in the yard, and Annie's face frowning up at me through the rain. Beyond the end door I could see Aunty sitting bareskulled at her mirror with the light bulbs round it, humming and painting purple over her leftover lips.

When my sisters asked me what Aunty's room was like, I always said it smelled sweeter than a jam pan and looked busier than if the Showreel's Twelve Trapped Princesses had just woke in a hurry and were throwing their clothes about trying to get out and dance. Hair for every occasion hung off nails on the wall. Pants and stockings were spilled out of drawers. Medicine bottles and toffee wrappers lay about on the carpet, and one bluebottle or another was usually sniffing about. Toto was back-flipped on the pink bed, snoring. And like the Appendix says it—*E for Education, Education, Education,* so Aunty always had the Showreel playing on the television in the corner.

And I don't mind telling you here, the Showreel is the cleverest lesson there is, which is Aunty when she was still *Ophelia Swindon, Operatic Opal of the Black Country! A.k.a. Divinest of Divas, Apotheosis of Athena and Isis Incarnate! A.k.a. the People's Pearl, born with the Visage of Venus, the molding of Marilyn, and blessed with the direct genetic inheritance of Queen Cleopatra's most wonderful, witherproof skin!*

Which words always made Aunty have a little sigh and stroke of her fingers when they came up all quiet on the beginning of the Showreel. They stayed there long enough for us to read them all out, and for Aunty to have another sigh when we did, before the Showreel got on with Aunty *show*ing us all the *real* terrible ways females suffer Outside, "So

72

you'll know exactly what you're up against, nieces, when you pop off to War!"

Right now on the television, Aunty's Operatic Opal self was showing us a lunatic female called Sister Maria, who ran away from Walled safety.

Aunty popped in a row of top teeth. In the mirror her eye winked at me. "Welcome, dear heart, so good to see you in private. Rather elemental out there this morning. Do be an angel and keep the rain out."

I shut the door, and sugary air flew up my nose and sprayed out in a sneeze.

"Heavens, child! Snot is easily prevented by those who care to care about these things. Blow your nose and get over here. And do try not to drip on the Appendix."

Aunty's eye swivelled off to the television screen, where her Opal self was running crazy at the Sun and singing about following rainbows till she found her dream. Aunty hummed along to the end of the song. And never mind there weren't nothing left most wonderful, witherproof but her hands, Aunty's voice couldn't ever be melted away from her, could it?

All about her dressing table were pots of cream and sticks of color. A tub of pink jellies sat next to a bottle of orange medicine. Aunty had a jelly all ready and waiting in her hand, but her eye was fixed on the television. "You know I never got the habit of that habit, Calamity. Ten times in one performance at Wolverhampton Apollo, I came a cropper over that blinking hem." Aunty sighed and popped the jelly in her mouth, "And that was back in the days when I had twenty-twenty vision."

It is a tale as tragic as any in the Showreel, how Aunty lost her left eye. It really is. But you don't need me, you need

Ophelia Swindon Volume IV: In the Eye of the Storm to tell you that. And even if the *Volumes* were unlocked from their case, well, I'm sorry but they'd all be burned to nothing now.

Aunty sucked jelly off her fingers. "My eye, but that's delicious." She held the tub at me and winked. "Go on, sweetie, I insist. Calorie-counted, cellulite-lightened delights. Just one, mind."

It tasted like rose perfume and bone jelly and honey, all melting up together.

"Yes, I thought you'd gobble that down without needing to be asked twice. You are looking a tad off-color though, sweetie. Tell me, everything all right with you? Still pinning back those flappers at night?"

I tried not to look in the mirror. Aunty had herself some medicine from the bottle on the table. "I don't mind telling you, Calamity, sometimes I wonder whether your Mother actually bothered to stop and check over any of you, or whether she just panicked and snatched the closest thing to hand. Of course she denies it. She would. But there's you, there's boz-eyed Evita, there's Tombstone Mary. Heavens, I shudder to think about Dorothy, I really do." Aunty went for a jar and threw rose water at her chins. "Still, a deal's a deal, we work with what we've got, niece. Let that be a lesson to you, we all do it. We all manage."

I shifted the Appendix about and tried not to look at my ears in the mirror. "Utterly outstanding ears," Aunty once said I had. "Jumbo specimens."

"I'll let you into a secret, niece. Whenever I get to feeling a little low, thinking about everything I used to be, you know who I like to think of, to snap me out of it?"

Aunty went for a long drink of medicine, and I kept my eyes down.

"Dumbo!" Aunty shouted out, laughing like it hurt her, so some jelly bits flew out and hit the mirror. "I think about Dumbo, niece! No one can tell me that elephant didn't make the best of what he had! Who wants to look like Marilyn all their lives? Not me! And if an elephant can fly—well, niece, let's just say, where there's hide there's hope!"

Aunty stopped laughing and finished off all the medicine bottle.

"I will get to go Fight the Good Fight, won't I, Aunty?"

"Have another Turkish delight, Calamity, no need to start snivelling. I'm sure we can unleash you somewhere undiscerning. Luxembourg, perhaps."

Aunty grabbed a stick of brown grease and set to thumping it on her melted cheek. "Not every girl is fortunate enough to be born a Sandra Saffron Walden perfect ten, you know." Aunty went on thumping her eye socket, and her living eye jumped back to the television where, with the Visage of Venus, she was busy getting trapped in marriage. "But don't you worry about Sandra, because it doesn't last, Calamity—"

And all sudden, the grease stick fell down on the table, and Aunty's hands went rushing to push up her melted cheek, and smooth out the lumps of her leftover lips, and press down the spread of her fallen nostril. And she turned her head sideways so the mirror couldn't see her shrivelled eye socket, and then she spun away from the mirror, so she couldn't see her face at all. But in the television screen, her bald head was mirrored bright. Aunty jumped up and ran to the door.

But then she didn't go outside, she just stared at her hands a while. And I reckon that made her happy, it really did, because she stroked her fingers up and down. "Nothing lasts," Aunty said, "nothing at all."

After a bit Aunty came back to the table for a pot, and started to coat up her fingers in cream. "Dream your dreams while you're young, Calamity. Because that's where happiness lives. It's the only place happiness lives in this world." And she held up her creamy fingers, and they waved at her and she blew a little kiss at them. "C'est la vie. One did what one had to. Je ne regrette rien. No, I don't."

It sure was hot in the room, so I sneezed again. So Aunty looked up at me. "I'll tell you what lasts, Calamity Leek," Aunty said, and her finger and thumb reached out and grabbed my wrist in a creamy pinch. "Love, Calamity Leek. Flap-eared-one-eyed love. The love that passes all understanding." And Aunty's one blue eye twitched at me like it had one drop left in it. It fell back to staring at her fingers. "That's the only thing that lasts in the end."

Aunty opened a door into the sitting room.

Now I probably don't need to tell you this was a room made for sitting and watching and drinking tea. But most of all it was a room made for reading, because standing against the back wall was a fat bookcase with glass doors, where the *Archive* was locked safe inside in five square brown *Volumes*. A group of chairs huddled round a table in front of it. On top of the table there was a new brown *Volume* lying open. A purple ink pen was waiting on a half-written page, and I gasped out loud to see it. So Aunty smiled and said, "Yes, indeed, my dear, *Escape to Freedom!* we're calling this one. However, now's really not the time for our little book group."

And she shut up the *Volume* all quick. More medicine bottles and jelly boxes were thrown about the carpet here, also a *Reader's Digest* on something called *Spanish for Starters!*

"Naturally, a southerly aspect would have been preferable," Aunty said, heading to the glass wall that opened onto the viewing balcony, and snatching the telescope from its hook by the communicating microphone. "Face the meadow, catch the evening sun and so on. But mustn't grumble, apple crumble, we make the best of what we have."

The rain had stopped. I could see my white-scarved sisters down in the Icebergs, crawling about like new-hatched maggots, snipping off deadheads and harvesting the year's last blooms into barrows. A most perfect view, it really was.

Aunty swung the telescope down. "I make that eight. Plus two in the kitchen with the lunatic, and Nancy with the pigs. One in the mending room, the most efficient Pontefracts with the second-winders, you up here. I think that's all our little piggies safe in the bank. Excellent, we can all relax."

Aunty turned and pointed at one of the chairs. "That one there will do you nicely," and she took the Appendix off me and went to the table and opened it up. "My it's getting hefty! That's the weight of wisdom for you!" And she flipped the pages and sprung open the metal hoops and added a new page. "*N for Nosiness*, Calamity. I'm putting it after *Nieces*. Be a sweetheart and read it out twice daily for a week or so." Aunty snapped the metal hoops shut. "You'll take some tea."

Aunty went off. The chair swallowed me up in softness. On three television screens on the unglassed walls, the Showreel was playing. Three perfect Operatic Opals were busy laughing and singing happy.

Aunty came back in with a tea tray and the pink rose

cups. "You can see what they saw in me. It's not often a star that bright shoots along. I'll let you into a secret, Calamity. I once understudied at the Slough Palladium. It's common knowledge that HRH himself sent me a bouquet after that. Imagine him! Imagine that!" Aunty sat down and poured out the tea. "Goodness, Calamity, just having you up here makes a person jolly, it really does."

She leaned over and tapped my ears. "And entre nous, about these danglers, don't take it to heart. I shall make sure you're taken care of, all the way."

I felt my ears starting to heat again.

"You know, I always knew you were the one for me, Calamity, right from the get-go, I knew. Naturally, I adore all my nieces as equally as pennies in a pot, but sometimes with a person, there's a certain je ne sais quoi. Affinity, I'd call it. Instant and bottomless. And when your Mother brought you in after another of her forays in the Potteries—and heavens, Calamity, you never knew what to expect when she hit the road—could be a mink, a cabbage, or a toddler—any manner of uselessness. It's a sickness she tells me. Born of neglect, she claims. Like she's the only one. Like we didn't both suffer the same. But never mind, when she brought you in, all damp and pongy from the road, and I saw those ears of yours, well, right then—once I'd got over the shock, of course— right then I thought at least it's an honest face we have here. And an honest face can be more useful than roses, can't it, Calamity? It certainly can be a better friend."

My ears were about red enough to drop off now, they really were. "I was held by Mother?"

"Such a forthright face, right from the start. And you've

been nothing but a forthright little treasure ever since. No trouble—unlike others you and I could both mention. Anyone to mention today? Heavens, I do believe you're blushing. Well, don't, my treasure. Take some tea and think about it."

I tried hard to remember being held by Mother.

Aunty sat back, her eye on me, and took a sip from her cup. "Goodness, that's grim. Now, Calamity, I don't mind telling you, I'm going to enhance my beverage with a little medicinal compound." She reached into the cushion behind her and pulled out a medicine bottle, and poured some in her tea. "It's such a shame you're too young, it really is extraordinarily efficacious—powers the neurons, brightens the eyes. It probably flattens the ears right back, who knows!"

I looked at the bottle, all shining golden and sloshing pretty.

"I expect you're wondering what it tastes of."

On the television behind Aunty, her unmelted self had been winched in Cinderella's peachy clothes and was busy being swirled senseless by a demonmale.

"Go on, have a guess."

"Is it honey, Aunty?"

"Interesting." Aunty sipped thoughtfully, "One might say there's a certain hive-ish aftertaste." And she sipped her cup all the way down to the bottom. "One might say that." And she licked her lips and prepared herself another drink. And her eye went up and down and up from the medicine bottle to me. And Aunty leaned forward, "So, Calamity, what do you think?" And she winked her eye.

On the television, the demonmale was stepping up to seal the deal good and proper with poor Cinderella, or, how they say it so females should know to set off running, if they haven't already started, *Forever and ever OUR MEN.*

"Do you know what I think, Calamity? I think we're having such fun that it would be jolly mean of me to have all this medicine on my own. I think I'd like to share it with a friend. I might just say my best friend."

My eyeballs stung hot as my ears at that.

"Now, who do we think my bestest friend might be?"

They started to water. I kept them watching on my rosy teacup.

"My eye, what a modest little niece I have. Come now, Calamity Leek, let's have an answer from you."

Loud as I dared, I whispered, "Is it me?"

"Oh, my darling shy-but-forthright niece, yes, of course, it's you!"

And I could have cried a bucketful of tears at this. But I didn't, because Aunty got busy pouring medicine into my cup. She looked at her watch. "We don't have much time, I'm afraid, so drink it down quick. I'll warn you it may taste a little grim initially, but you'll soon get used to it. You have to be brave, Calamity Leek. Only the bravest girls get the flattest ears. Are you willing to be brave?"

Now, happen if Aunty had said, "Are you willing to pop outside and jump off the viewing balcony onto yard concrete, Calamity Leek?" I would have done it, such was the love smashing up my heart for her. But she didn't, course. So I took up the cup and drank it down at once.

The medicine smashed into my stomach and flipped it into a nest of spiders that came leaping back up my throat. I got my hand to my mouth and swallowed them down.

Aunty looked at her watch and looked at me. "Is your

head feeling a little dizzy, darling? It looks it. Tell you what, you should see how your ears are shrinking, you really should. Can you feel them?"

"Every second, Aunty." And I really could. Every second they shrunk up smaller. And it weren't just my ears that were busy changing, the medicine was melting every bone in me to butter.

"What did I tell you?" Aunty poured more medicine into her cup. She sat back, sipping thoughtful. She looked at her watch and looked at me. "I'll tell you what, though. I reckon we could get them even flatter."

"You reckon?"

"Ho, ho. I reckon, Calamity, I reckon."

So Aunty poured me another cup—of purest medicine this time, because she said tea would only get in the way. On the screen, her Cinderella self was back at the start of the Showreel. Happy and demonmaleless, she was sweeping a kitchen floor and wearing a comfy smock. Two big sisters watched on lovingly, sharpening their knives.

My stomach flipped over at the smell of this cup, but Aunty twisted tight on my nose and held my jaw until it all stayed down. She clapped and said my ears sure were flatter than a worm's, and that was a clear medicinal triumph, and we just had to wait a bit for the full effect. And she found herself a cream pot under the chair and started coating up her fingers. I hiccuped and was about to say I was pleased to hear it, when I heard myself moan instead. See, right then, the sitting room spun about, and Aunty's fingers turned to rose stalks, and her empty socket popped out a new eyeball. But that weren't just it. "Aunty, the medicine has turned my tongue into a fish."

"That's excellent news," Aunty said.

I tried to lift my sorry flopping tongue to say, "It is?"

"Oh yes, it is. And I know just the cure."

"You do?"

"A talking cure, niece. If you talk long enough, we'll have you restored in no time at all. Remembering is best. Things that have happened recently. And mind you tell the truth and nothing but the truth, otherwise you'll spawn fishy babies in your belly that will burst out and kill you. You'll start by telling me everything you know about Truly's transgression of Garden rules. Now, did she say whether she managed to climb high enough to see anything outside the Wall?"

And that is about all I remember of sitting in Aunty's High Hut.

Yes, it is.

TALKING WORDS

"Mother," I say.

"I never forgot you," Mrs. Waverley says. Her hand comes for mine before I can shift it off me.

"That's wonderful," Doctor Andrea Doors says. "That's really wonderful, Calamity."

But it ain't, course. There ain't nothing wonderful in this female's grip.

THE NEXT DAY

I never gave up hoping," Mrs. Waverley says, throwing out her hand.

"Aunty Ophelia Swindon," I say, keeping my own hands under my bottom.

"Every day I, I, I—" Mrs. Waverley says.

"Easy now, Mrs. Waverley," Doctor Andrea Doors says. "Deep steady breaths."

"I-I-I thought about you every single day."

"Anything else, Calamity?" Doctor Andrea Doors says when Mrs. Waverley has dried up. "Anything else you'd like to say?"

I think I would like to say, "Where is Jane Jones? Tell me what has been done to her. Is she still protected, or has she been taken, like every female is taken in the end? Where is she? It's been three days."

I would like to say this. But I don't.

THE DAY AFTER THAT

Maria Liphook, Sandra Saffron Walden, Dorothy Macclesfield, Annie St. Albans, Truly Polperro, Nancy Nunhead, Mary Bootle, Eliza Aberdeen, Evita Thrupp, Millie Gatwick, Odette Pontefract, Odile Pontefract, Fantine Welshpool, Cinderella Galashiels, Adelaide Worthing, Toddler Thurrock, Toddler Pease Pottage, Toddler Gordano, Toddler Gretna Green, Toddler Watford Gap, Toddler South Mimms, Baby Sainsbury's," I say.

Mrs. Waverley says nothing.

Doctor Andrea Doors says nothing.

I think I hear a Bootling scream. It might be six walls off. It might be more.

"Mary Bootle!" I shout. "Supercalifragilistic—" I shout.

Mary doesn't expialidocious.

Mrs. Waverley starts to drip into a tissue.

Doctor Andrea Doors says nothing.

"All right," I say. "Where is Jane Jones? What have you done to her?"

Doctor Andrea Doors looks at me. "I think Nurse Jones is taking some time off this week. So you're interested in Nurse Jones, Calamity? I'm interested in that."

I think I will pop myself under the sheet now.

Shrouded up in peace and quiet, I move my potted toes about and flex my throttling fingers in and out to fifty. I think about Jane Jones. If one of His army overheard us talking, and something bad has happened to her—which now looks sad but likely—seems I must get back to preparing for War on my own. I must not waste any more days. No, I must not.

THE DAY AFTER THE DAY AFTER THAT

C alamity, can you hear me in there?" Your voice presses up to my sheeted ear, "It's Andrea Doors. Please could you come out, there's something important I need to talk to you about."

Well, I might come out, Doctor Andrea Doors, but if I do, I ain't playing at talking in turns no more. Sorry, no. Still no Jane Jones about, so care needs taking. If I come out now, it is only to keep an eye on you. That is all it is. My eye, it is.

"Thank you," you say. You are sitting by my bed with a smile fixed neat on your mouth. "We've made some good progress these past few days, don't you think, Calamity? You've been such a brave girl since you've been here. So I'm just wondering how brave you're feeling today?"

Course, I ain't being fishhooked to speaking easy as that.

"So, Calamity, what do you think?"

No, I am not.

"I'm asking because there's someone Mrs. Waverley would like you to meet. Someone who loves you very much, and who has been waiting to see you for a very long time. Now, I want you to remember you're perfectly safe. I'm not leaving, and this person is not going to come anywhere near you, they'd just like to pop inside the room for a few moments. So what do you think to that? It's all right to say no, Calamity."

Well, I shut my eyes tight, and I don't move one bone in my body to say, "Yes, all right then, Doctor Andrea Doors."

But never mind me, because you're saying, "OK, Mrs. Waverley, but just as we agreed—inside the door, absolutely no further."

So Mrs. Waverley is ripping her bottom off the chair and clomping to the door, and the door is opening, and I can feel the air in the room shuffling round a new breath.

I pull the sheet over my head to wait till it's gone.

I wait.

I wait a bit more.

Course, the only reason I pop an eye out of the sheet is to see if it's gone. That's the only reason I do it.

Except it hasn't, has it? No, it is standing over the lump of Mrs. Waverley, gripping her shoulders, four steps away from me. Its mouth is black and hairy. Its ears are square and red. It sees my eye popping out of the sheet, and its arms fly out at me.

"Oh my—" it whispers. "Oh my—"

It is the demonmale. Come out of my dreams for me.

And there ain't no sheet going to stop a demonmale. There is only one thing for it.

I kick off the sheet and I jump off the bed to make a run for it out the window.

Only I come off something crooked, and my potted leg goes crunch on the floor, and everything else goes black.

A PIG IN A BARROW

C lam! Clam, wake up!"

    "Are you a fish too, Truly?"

"Clam, it ain't Truly, it's Millie, Millie Gatwick. Clam, you've got to wake up and get in this barrow if you ain't for walking. It's Emily's birthday, and we're doing a pig and everything."

"You ain't a fish, Truly?"

"Mind my smock, Clam! In the bucket, Clam, oh please puke in the bucket! You got took sick at Aunty's. But hurry up, will you, because Mother's coming for it, Clam, we're doing a pig for her, and Aunty says she is sure and certain coming!"

EMILY

Now Truly Polperro was still not certified dead when Emily came to the Sacred Lawn for her birthday party that afternoon. Matter of fact, for most of the afternoon, Truly was alive, and lying quiet as a fish in her barrow next to mine.

But you probably don't want to hear about poor old Truly just yet. Not on Emily's birthday. So let me tell you about my sisters, who were standing in line, neat as a fence, facing the empty plinth in the middle of the Lawn. My sisters, with vinegar-rinsed hair and painted eyes, and their toes pressed against presents in soft Lawn grass. Never mind that I was puking in a bucket, in a barrow next to Truly's barrow. Never mind that we were both parked up down by the toddlers' trolleys, on the most important day of the year. Never mind all that if you can, because eleven of my sisters were rose-scented and looking, just like Aunty said, "Hot to trot and market-ready in every way."

Danny Zuko waited on the butching sheet, shuffling his piglet thighs in readiness. Aunty waited in a shiny red cloak by the empty plinth in the middle of the Lawn, a chimney pot hat jammed on two yellow plaits that stuck out like broke chicken legs. Maria Liphook waited, grub hunting under the southern Crèmes. And up above us, heavy-bottomed clouds waited, stacking themselves protective across the sky.

Aunty straightened her hat. "Wherever is she?"

A screeching sound started up in the yew path north of the Lawn.

"There she is," Aunty said. "ETA—thirty seconds. Voices at the ready." Aunty swiped Mr. Stick along our line, "A-one, a-two, a-one-two-three and—"

We're leaning on a lamppost, at the corner of the street, we sang—

In case a certain little lady comes by.

"Belt it out!" Aunty yelled, *Oh me! Oh my! I hope that little lady comes by!*

And we did belt it out, and Mother did come. Her electric chair screeched through the northern Crèmes and bounced onto the Lawn. It skidded down to the empty plinth and died. And Mother plugged her ears and waited for us to finish up singing.

Course, you're wanting to know how she looked, aren't you? Well, all wrapped up in black blankets, Mother sat skinnier in that chair than any of us sisters. Her head was shawled in black, though one or two Heavenly hairs poked through. She wore black glasses on her face to shield her Heavenly eyes from us, but stretching down to her chin, for us all to see, were two plates of skin—pure and witherproof as washed bone. There was her teensy mouth and her shrunk-up nose—she had all that like normal females—but it was that cheek skin I always kept my eye on. And I'll tell you this for nothing, that was Heaven-grown skin, right there.

We finished off her song and saluted, Aunty curtseyed and Mother unplugged her ears.

"Miss Swindon," Mother said—and I don't mind telling you her voice was purer than kettle steam screeching off to Heaven—"one will never understand this insistence on inflicting these common chorus-line caterwaulings on one's ears. One feels one should not have to persist in reminding you, an army is forged from steel not sentiment."

Aunty stood up from her curtsey and threw a kiss at the air near Mother's cheek, "Forgive me, Gennie darling, old habits."

Mother knocked Aunty's kiss away with her glove. "Your breath, Miss Swindon. One also deduces that you have ballooned. Around the midriff."

Aunty laughed happy. "Dearest Gennie, our very own Ladyship, and one true Leader. Aren't the weapons looking gorgeous? The eldest ones are almost ripe and ready for it, I'd say."

"And one would answer, but are they hungry for it, Miss Swindon? What is the size of their appetite, Miss Swindon? One knows all about your appetite, but are they hungry for it? Are they hungry for War?"

Aunty turned to us and sang out, "Piggy, piggy, piggy!"

And we jumped in the air and shouted back, "Kill, kill, kill!"

"Just a little routine we've been finessing," Aunty said.

Mother looked back at the yew path. "One hasn't got all day," she said.

"I thought you'd like it," Aunty said. She went over to Danny and started a big old curtsey, "Ladies and your Ladyship, the time has come—"

And Mother's voice screamed so kettling Heavenly, happen her throat was near boiled dry, "Bloody well get on with it, if you're going to bloody well do it, Frumps!" Mother stopped and her perfect voice near split my ears in its Heavenly wail, "One need not remind you how the sight of blood upsets one's angel!"

Aunty stood back up and straightened her hat and turned around and spat at the southern Crèmes. After this she put a fresh smile on her face. "Off you go, Nancy dear."

Keeping the blade behind her back, Nancy stepped up to the butching sheet.

Danny Zuko snorted and whirled his tail. Nancy sniffed and wiped her eyes and threw Danny Zuko an apple. Danny chewed it up. Nancy brought out the blade, and stuck him in the throat. Aunty waved Mr. Stick in the air, and we all cheered. Apple chunks fell out of Danny's screaming mouth. Nancy wiped her eyes and stuck him again.

"Piggy, piggy, piggy!" Aunty sang out.

"Kill, kill, kill!" we shouted back loud.

Danny went over on his spotted side. Mary ran to help Nancy drain him into a bucket. The air filled so hot and plummy, I puked. Nancy sniffed and wiped her eyes and started the blade on Danny's windpipe. Aunty waved Mr. Stick and we cheered Danny's head off.

"Well? What do you reckon to that for hunger?" Aunty said.

Mother turned her face back to the yew path. "Oh, my own true angelkins, wherever are you?" she said.

Aunty stared at Mother's back a few seconds and then she made a smile at it and said, "Would her Ladyship care to inspect the weapons while we're waiting? They're clean."

"Angelkins, coo-eeeee," Mother said.

"So good of you to express an interest," Aunty said to Mother's back. "Anyway, how the devil are you, Ophelia? Not too lonely down here on your own? No? That is good to hear. Goodness, is that a new frock, Ophelia? Well, it's just your color."

Aunty called out loud to Mother, "Wasn't that what you always said on our Sunday Best days, Gennie, do you remember? Those awful cast-offs we got given to wear. 'Oooh, lilac's just your color,' you'd say. 'Lucky you, Fifi-Frumps, wearing lilac nylon from the rubbish dump.'"

"Coo-eeeeeeeeeeeeee," Mother said.

"Wasn't that what you said, Gennie? Not that Father Tony gave cast-offs to you, with all your special privileges."

"One's eyes do not deceive me, Miss Swindon, you really have puffed up all round," Mother's voice said, never mind her Heavenly eyes were still fixed on the yew path. "Five or six inches one would estimate. One shall have to contemplate a reduction in your allowance. One's always erred on the over-generous side."

Aunty turned away from Mother's chair and spat at the Glamis Castles.

"If her Ladyship doesn't fancy inspecting the weapons, and she doesn't want to admire my frock, why doesn't she have a squizz at the Little Chefers while we're waiting?" Which was the name Aunty sometimes gave to the second-wind toddlers, who had started up bawling in their trolleys past Truly and me. "One might surprise her. I'm not saying Spitting Image, but why doesn't her Ladyship take a look?"

Mother watched Annie running off north into the yews, and her perfect black-gloved finger pushed up them glasses that kept her Heavenly eyes safe from us. Eyes that weren't made a common Garden blue or brown, but, like the Appendix says it—*are thought to consist of twenty-four carat gold.*

"Come to Mummy," Mother said, staring off into the yews. "Mummy's waiting."

I don't mind telling you something of Mother's tragic dilemma now. Course, you ain't forgotten how she was sent down to raise an army, only—and it is explained more fully in *Ophelia Swindon Volume V: A Country Diary*—how was she ever going to raise an army on Earth, when her only beloved daughter got killed off by a demonmale?

Well, the best answer she came up with was to rescue other daughters already part-grown Outside, ones something imaged like her daughter—if something less than perfect—and to grow them like her own. So that's what Mother did.

Aunty looked at the second-winders bashing about in their trolleys and gave off a merry tinkle, "In any case, something has got to be done with them. They're crawling now."

Mother's voice said, "It would appear your face is retaining water as well."

"Her Ladyship knows they're not part of the Deal," Aunty tinkled.

"As one recalls, slimness was never your forte, was it, Frumps?"

"Argentina is waiting," Aunty kept on. "South America is crying out for my music. What with the peso plummeting, facial reconstruction rates won't remain low for long. Rhinoplasty's already shot up two hundred percent—"

And then Aunty stopped tinkling and started staring at Mother. Aunty stared, because Mother wasn't looking up the yew path no more, her face was turned back to Aunty, and Mother's face was smiling. All up her cheek plates I could see her smiling.

"One almost forgot," Mother said. "One received a telephone call from a pleasant chap this morning."

Aunty stared at Mother. "And?"

Mother stretched her smile wider. "Frightfully pleasant, if a tad plebeian. Claimed to be from the Llandudno *Gazette*."

"And?"

"Just a few questions, he said. Frightfully sweet, considering. Quiet news season, he said. The Unsolved Crimes file gathering dust, he said. That sort of thing."

Aunty's hand went up to her mouth.

"Recent reported sightings, that sort of thing."

"Recent sightings?"

Mother smiled, "One said that's what he said."

"But what did you say?" Aunty whispered. "What did you tell him?"

"Oh, one was discreet, Miss Swindon. There was not a peep from me. One's no sneak, Miss Swindon. One was never the one who ran about bleating 'Father Tony, Father Tony, Gennie's been stealing again.'" Mother hissed perfect Heavenly, "One was never the one for that."

Aunty's eyeball fixed on Mother like it had got stuck.

She fell down to Mother's chair and set about kissing all over Mother's hand.

"It would seem you shall have to rely on one's possession

of discretion." Mother took her hand away. "Perhaps it's your turn, Frumps, to see if someone can hold their tongue. But one shan't speak further on this. It's Emily's special day, not yours. One does hope there's games."

And then all sudden Mother spun her chair about and cupped an ear to the yews, and screamed in Heavenly delight, "But hark! One does believe one's angel cometh!"

It was actually Dorothy and Sandra who came out of the yews first, heaving on a yoke. The cart came next. Annie came last, pushing from behind.

"Aaaaaaaaah!" Mother said, spinning circles in joy. "Here you are, angelkins. Mummy was beginning to think she had lost you forever."

Aunty was having trouble standing herself up. She crawled about and got herself up at the plinth. She turned to us and straightened her hat, and never mind her voice was something shaky, it was good enough to shout, "Here we go, girls. A-one, a-two, a-one-two-three and—"

We sang out "Hopelessly Devoted to You," and Sandra and Dorothy dragged the cart to the plinth. Sandra unwrapped Emily from the plastic and they heaved her upright. And like she did every year, Mother jumped out of her electric chair and ran to Emily's toes, and kissed every one of them.

Aunty once told us it took Mother six months to make a new Emily. She rescued the statues from demonmale marriage-trap churches, sawed off unnecessary wings and repainted the faces into Emily's plump prettiness. On Emily's seventh birthday, if you're interested in knowing, Mother used Sandra for being what is called "a live model." Sandra was six, and still something imaged like Emily then—particularly her nose—and it was looking good for her, it really was.

Four days she stayed in Mother's Glorious Abode, with us all thinking that was it for Sandra—life with Mother and a direct pass to Heaven without War. But on the fifth day, Sandra's nose grew too fat, and she was sent back to the yard. Though having as much sense as a snowdrop, Sandra still thinks herself special.

But never mind Sandra, because eighteen-year-old Emily was stood steady on the plinth, all ready to watch over us now. She wore a blue cloak and yellow hair and was something heftier than her seventeen-year-old self. She didn't have a lamb nudging her knee this year, but a little robin was glued on a finger of her left hand. Course, under her white headscarf, Emily's blue eyes were lifted up something sorrowful, most probably in remembering her tragic end of life. But on her lips she wore the prettiest smile—like she really didn't mind nothing now that her skin was varnished perfect. Tears ran off my face to see that smile, and I promised to fight my hardest for her when I went to War.

Rain began to fall down on us from Heaven. Straight down heavy.

I looked over at Truly. She was sleeping, course. Her smock was blotching wet.

Aunty looked at the sky lid and said to it, "Don't suppose there's any chance at all her Ladyship could keep this brief?"

But Mother didn't hear Aunty. Mother was dancing round Emily on her plinth, her Heavenly knees jerking, her back crooked angelic. "Come to Mummy, come to Mummy, come to Mummy," Mother was singing as she danced. And everyone, even Aunty, had to wait quiet now.

We held our breaths, and I checked on Truly in her barrow, in case she felt like starting a moan and ruining everything, but

99

she still lay quiet as a fish. And I looked up at eighteen-year-old Emily, and I sent over a request. If she was planning on doing any miracles this year—which might be nice for us—well then, what about starting on her very own birthday and sorting out Truly?

Mother started some kissing up Emily's shins, and Aunty spat in the grass and pointed Mr. Stick at us. "Let's get on with it, nieces, before we all catch our deaths."

Two by two, my sisters went up and laid down their strawdolls and apples at the base of Emily's plinth. Nancy went last with Danny Zuko's head. And up in Heaven, the Goddess Daughter sure was sad about something, because the rain kept on coming.

We were in the middle of singing Happy Birthday to Emily, when I heard a thumping noise next to me. It was Truly's heels banging in her barrow.

"Aunty—" I said.

"Games," Mother said, turning round. Rain was stuck on her black glasses like dead tears. "Emily says she wants party games."

"Aunty—" I said a bit louder.

"And they'd better be bloody good ones, Miss Swindon."

"Then bloody good games Emily shall bloody well have!" Aunty yelled out cheery. "Musical statues all right with you, Emily? I'll sing the music."

"One will judge the statues."

I watched Truly's heels rattling busy next to me, and I tried to catch Aunty's eye. But she was busy starting on "Hopelessly Devoted" again.

I tried to catch the eye of Odette Pontefract, but she was being a statue patting a toddler in the trolley. I tried to hiss at Fantine Welshpool at the bottom of the row, but she was busy being a one-legged statue praying to Emily. So you see, I did try.

"STOP!" Mother shouted.

And I thought that was good, because now everyone would hear Truly's heels. But the barrow was quiet, so I reckoned Truly must have stopped rattling and started joining in with statues. Which would be easy for her this year, wouldn't it? And I had a little smile, thinking about Truly at last year's birthday party—trying to keep herself upside down in a one-handed cartwheel statue. That was Truly Polperro for you.

Emily won the game. Mother kissed her pink toes. "Well done, my angel," Mother said. "What's that, my angel? You want more?"

Hailstones came jumping down onto the Lawn. It sure wasn't just Truly feeling the cold now. But Mother flung off her black shawl to go skipping about, her hair flapping Heavenly in excitement. "That one's out! That one's out! They're all out! Well done, Emily! Marvellous! Again?"

Sometime in the next game, Maria Liphook screamed like a proper loonhead, and went running off to the yard. But Mother didn't mind because Emily was winning, and Aunty didn't mind because she was holding tight onto a big smile at Mother. After ten more games, Mother got back in her chair and sat patting on Emily's feet. There sure weren't no cold in the rain for our Heavenly Mother.

Then it was time for us to clear the area to give Mother and Emily some Quality Time. Which weren't such a bad idea, because my sisters' eyes were bleeding paint down their cheeks. Their lips dribbled red off their chins and onto their smocks.

I climbed out of my barrow with my sick bucket, and helped Nancy and Mary heave Danny's corpse in. Annie ran up to take Truly's barrow.

It was when she went to tuck a fur over Truly that Annie jumped back, her finger pointing at Truly's lips, her mouth moving without words.

I went to look closer and gave out a yelp—least Nancy says I did, because Nancy said, "What is it, Clam?" and came to see, and went, "Oh no."

Dorothy ran up and blinked ten times, and turned away.

Sandra barged down the line to us, and, course, she screamed it loud, "Truly's lips are blue!"

So everyone came running, and Aunty came too.

Aunty jabbed fingers in Truly's neck. "Cold as cod," she said.

She kept her fingers dug in, turning her head like she was listening for something. "Nope. Nothing doing," she said.

"What?" Annie whispered.

Aunty took her fingers away. "Nothing doing, I said."

"Can we not try wheeling her up with Emily?" I whispered.

"Rather too late for miracles, niece."

"I don't understand," Annie said.

"Hyperthermia," Aunty said.

"What?" Annie said.

"You heard me." Aunty prodded Truly's tummy. She put her ear to Truly's heart, and shook her head. "Hyper-thermia. Overheated insides."

Eliza Aberdeen fainted off into the Glamis Castles.

Aunty slammed her hat down low. "Well, that's ten grand down the spout, I'd say. That's a new top lip flushed down the pan." Aunty fixed her eye on Mother, but she couldn't put a tinkle with it. "Nancy, pick up Eliza at once, we don't need any more casualties." Aunty spun round and stomped off south through the Glamis Castles, spitting and thwacking roseheads off bushes as she went.

Well.

Well, we stood round Truly's barrow, dumb as worms.

Annie tried to shake Truly's shoulders awake. She tried Truly's arms.

The rain slowed. Annie tried Truly's legs.

The sky lid went dark.

The rain stopped. Dorothy stopped Annie's hands.

One by one we turned the waterworks on.

Only Annie stayed dry-eyed. "No, this ain't so, Truly. No, come on, Truly, quit fooling," Annie said, like she was waiting on someone to shout out it was just a demonmale dream we were all in, nothing more.

Mother had driven her chair down the Lawn to us before we heard her. She stopped a safe distance off, and waved her handkerchief in front to keep her Heavenly eyes double-safe from us. "Attention, weapons!"

We swallowed our tears and saluted.

"The weapons are making an obscene amount of noise," Mother said. "Emily abhors crying on her birthday. The weapons had better get back in their box at once, before Emily's afternoon is completely ruined."

Mother spun her electric chair about and drove back up the Lawn, to get back to kissing Emily's toes.

We roasted Danny Zuko's head on a spit in the yard that night. We ate him with Evita Thrupp's best rosemary loaf, and he tasted good. Nancy had herself three helpings, which might be why she is more pig than sister. Annie St. Albans didn't eat nothing. She kicked away the ear I saved off Nancy for her, which everyone says is the best bit.

We left Truly with Emily on the Sacred Lawn, it being late and all the sky being emptied of rain.

X-RAY

It is heavy, this new pot. And I am pinned in it, which roses
never are. That is because there is now a compound frac-
ture inside. That is what they say. Doctor Andrea Doors
shows me the photograph.

"That's an X-ray," she says, "of your femur."

Only it isn't really me. It isn't good and proper me, like
the photograph Aunty took against the schoolroom wall a
few days after Truly died. The one which meant we eldest
would soon be flying over the clouds to War.

"Line up, line up, heads up. No sloppy fringes, double chins
or cheeky grins for Her Majesty's Government," Aunty had
said. "One at a time."

She went as far as Eliza Aberdeen.

"Millie Gatwick, you'll be advertised in the next batch,"
she said. "Those boobs'll take a touch more ripening before

you're ready, so there's really no point hanging around here. Goodness, it's exciting, isn't it?"

After that, Aunty measured us for what she called our burkas. Of course, we wouldn't be wearing them to fight in, they were just for flying us to War. Because we had to get there safely, and Aunty said we'd be pleased to hear there wasn't a demon body alive could touch us in these things.

"Ta-dah! Get a squizz at that, nieces!" She flicked her wrists. "Call me a genius! One hundred and ten percent protection, I'd say!"

What floated down wasn't black like the one Aunty puts on when she has to go Outside sometimes. It was blue, like Emily's cloak. "Actually, this one's an old tablecloth I begged off your Mother," Aunty said, "but I've cut a slit for your eyes, so it'll give you a fair impression of the real thing."

For the rest of that day we elder nieces had turns in it round the yard. Course, Mary spun about and made herself dizzy, and Dorothy tripped over the hem, and Annie—who had already started with her "Why this" and "why that" nonsense, and which we didn't know was only going to grow more dangerous, the more sad she got about Truly—well, Annie kicked up yard concrete and said she didn't want to put it on at all. But I'll tell you this, I ain't never ever felt so safe my whole life. And I'll tell you this too—my ears didn't even touch the sides.

But, see, it ain't so bad, this new pot on my leg, because even if I can't run off and start things just yet, it meant a few of my leftover sisters came to see me. I wasn't the most lively of the lot, seeing as I was mostly sleeping. But I remember they did tiptoe in, my sisters. I remember them smelling good and proper of themselves—of straw and compost, beeswax and pigs—a smell settled too deep in their bones for this new world to scrub out. Annie left me a pretty Milli Vanilli shrub rose in a pot. And that wasn't all. There was a purple wire-worm hiding under the mulch. I put him on my finger today, when no one was here to see. I am going to name him Danny Zuko.

SHOWREEL

W e buried Truly in the plum orchard, which was always her favorite place.

Aunty said, "Put her where you like, as long as you dig it
deep enough."

Annie said she'd probably like to lie under the tallest Victoria plum tree and feel them fruit bombs dropping on her.

I said putting her in the middle of the orchard was a good
thing, because if she sat up out of the soil one night, there was
no way she'd be able to see the Wall and feel foolish about
climbing up it and dying off so careless. Course, I said that to
get a smile from my sisters, who were busy sobbing and sticking strawdoll Trulys in her grave, and whispering about her
possible ascension to Heaven, like happened to Emily. But it
wasn't the bone-marrow truth, what I said about Truly sitting
up. No, the real truth I read from page *D* of the Appendix the
night after we buried her, while we sat stuffing petals into
"Home Sweet Home" cushions in the dorm.

"I am sorry to say it," I said, "but today there's a new page stuck in *D for Deserter*—saying Truly has most probably been dragged straight down to Bowels. It says, 'Just you remember this, nieces—no one ever gets to Heaven without fighting the Good Fight first on Earth. Which is what Deserter means.'

"Isn't that set down good and clear for us, Annie?" I said, looking where she wasn't stuffing her quota of cushions, because she was lying face down in Truly's straw.

Annie said nothing.

"So, Truly's being cooked up for Him right now?" Millie whispered.

"Most likely, I'm afraid."

Which was very sad news for her, and for three days the Goddess Daughter threw gray sheets over the sky lid and cried non stop. And we did too. And after this Aunty said, "No use crying over spilt milk and ruining valuable tear ducts. Time to accentuate the positive. Eliminate the negative. A.k.a. dry up."

So we did.

Days went by. Winter snuck into the Garden. Trees dropped their leaves and died off. The last of the roses died off. Grubs did too. The duty list doubled. Close combat sessions tripled. Our weekly cushion quota increased to sixty. There was harvesting to finish, the yard fence wanted painting, and the latrines disinfecting. Cloth had to be stitched into winter smocks for those who would still be around to wear them, and rabbit traps needed setting for skins to patch up our old fur coats. Like this, more days went by.

To our lunchtime ablutions, Aunty added Exfoliation with a fistful of gravel in straw. To evening moisturizing, double beeswax portions were given to us eldest. "It's the Final Countdown!" Aunty said. "Don't cry for me, Argentina! Reading, writing and arithmetic will be scrapped forthwith for all eldest nieces. Mother herself has requested afternoons to be dedicated to Fight Revision. Action stations!"

We elder sisters practiced Snogging, Slow Dancing and Groping, like Aunty showed us, because that was how demonmales would expect the Fight to begin when they met us Outside. Then we did Judo and Jabbing-of-Blades-in-Bales, like Mother ordered, which is how we'd finish them off. Seeing as Truly weren't here, Aunty said Annie should practice snogging with me. Which was nice, I told Annie, because she really had the softest lips of us all. And never mind that she didn't say much to me saying that, nor didn't bother shifting her lips much either, she really kissed nicest of all.

Only after all this Revision did our younger sisters join us on the schoolroom floor in front of the television screen, to listen to Aunty's daily Tale from the *Archive* and watch a Showreel lesson on the Outside World.

Now, like I've most probably told you already, this Showreel lesson was made special by Aunty to *show* us sisters the *real* truth of women's tragic lives on Earth. So, though it starts off happy, with Aunty showing us a female called Cinderella and her loving sisters sharpening knives, quicksharp Aunty shows us another one called Sleeping Beauty, waking up all dozy from a good old sleep, and getting snogged straight off. Before she's even washed her face or changed her smock, she's been trapped in marriage. After this, the Showreel gets worse, with injuns fighting poor old Calamity Jane,

and demonmales fighting poor old Fantine on the barricades. And after all this, it's worst of all, because brave Aunty
actually meets the Devil. Yes, poor Aunty has to pop off the
stage and ends up running through the Earth's Bowels, because
the Devil has stuck on a cloak and mask and is chasing after
her, saying he only wants to sing once again with her a strange
duet.

Course, the Showreel ends happy, thank goodness, with
Aunty and that fleabag dog travelling safe over the rainbow
to a pretty Garden like ours. And thank goodness for us all
for that. And like Aunty always said, and like I'll tell you
now, that Showreel lesson was sixty minutes of the purest
education on the Outside, and we always ended with a sing-
song. And about the best song we ever sang Aunty called
"Never underestimate a woman's touch." And sometimes she
winked at me as we sang it, and in my head I promised I
never would. And those demonmales better watch out.

But never mind me telling you all this, what I only meant
to tell you is Annie weren't interested in a happy sing-song
no more. No. Ever since Truly died, Annie weren't interested
in nothing but the Devil and His Bowels, which she always
crawled up close to the screen to see when He appeared. She
said it was to keep an eye on the cloaks and masks He uses
when He takes on human form. But I knew it was really
because it gave the best view of Bowels. Annie was watching
to see if Truly would pop up anywhere down there. But she
never did.

More days went by. Nights turned colder. Maria Liphook
stayed unbothersome down her Hole. Aunty taught us a new

song about demonmale seduction-through-dancing called "Singing in the Rain," and a cat came to live with us. We called her Kathy Selden. Though Millie tried on drowning Kathy Selden down the latrines, seeing as Gretel rat still hadn't turned up, and though Annie was more interested in sitting under plum trees than talking to anyone most days—not even them sisters who went to sit with her—it really wasn't a lie to say proper peace was returning to our Garden. Yes it was.

GRETEL'S BABIES

"You know, sometimes of a day, I forget her," I said to
Annie.

We two were in the vegetable field, west of the yard, spending the morning pulling up turnips for winter storage. It was
nice to be two, except that Kathy Selden cat had followed
along, because, I am sorry to say, she didn't like to do nothing better than turf up worms.

I planted my fork and wiped my nose, keeping my face
hid from a most uncommon Sunny day. "I mean, with us elders getting ready to be unleashed for War. And now that
Baby Sainsbury's is here."

Mother had brought her in three days ago.

"One wasn't able to resist it," she said to Aunty when she
drove into the yard, the baby all tucked up in a blue basket on
Mother's lap. "It was parked up in frozen foods, like it had
one's name written all over it. There was something, just

something, in the shape of the cars that one thought might develop."

Aunty pointed at the purple blotch over the baby's left cheek and smiled and asked Mother how her Ladyship thought that might develop? After that, Aunty said "Excuse me," and she curtseyed at Mother and turned and spat on the yard and climbed back up to the High Hut, because she felt sick and she was also something lost for words.

Mother left the basket by the sundial, and drove her chair out the gate.

And on the viewing balcony, Aunty watched Mother go off north, and then she found her words.

Too many risks were being taken. At a time for lying low and making final preparations. This was yet another one above and beyond the Agreed Deal. Mother was Damaged. Disturbed. Dim. Did you forget about the Llandudno *Gazette*, Sieve Brain? Never the Sharpest Doll in the Dorm, were you? What pretty little Gennie wants, pretty Gennie always gets. Not this bloody time. You can bloody well take it back before The Bloody Cops Come Knocking. Aunty was not speaking to Mother until that happened. No Bloody Way, José, she wasn't. Otherwise Aunty would chuck it over the Wall and Don't Think She Wouldn't! Oi, Klepto! Take it back! Oi, a Deal's a Deal!

Those were Aunty's words.

Aunty went into the High Hut, slamming the door.

And Mary Bootle scooped up Baby Sainsbury's basket and ran off out the yard.

Baby Sainsbury's was sleeping in Nursery Cottage now, in her own cot because she was too small to join the toddlers' mattress. The Pontefracts were taking care of her, which had

Mary Bootle sucking her plaits something sour—when she wasn't sneaking over to the Cottage to sing "Hushabye Mountain" through the window to it.

One morning, when I had a barrow of Icebergs to take to the supplies barn, I went along to have a look myself. Not the healthiest place to live, weren't Nursery Cottage, with the air trapped up against walls of solid brick and windows of glass. Still, I popped my face to a window and watched the second-winders playing on the floor with our old dolls, and Baby Sainsbury's sleeping in her cot in the corner. It was clear and certain she wasn't ever going to grow into Emily's Spitting Image—not with that purple blotch on her cheek. But never mind that, because she was rescued now, and she would grow safe and uncooked to fight the Good Fight and ascend to Heaven.

And secretly—though we were supposed to wait for Aunty to choose her first name, and it might be a while, because none of the second-wind toddlers had been given one, because Aunty said you didn't name a dog you were going to take back to the park—I named her after Calamity Jane's friend, Katie Brown. She had the same black eyelashes. "Never underestimate a woman's touch, Katie Sainsbury's," I whispered through the window. And her sleeping eyelashes flickered back at me, like she was answering, "OK then, Clam, fine with me, Katie Sainsbury's it is."

I didn't see Baby Sainsbury's much after that, because like I said, we elders were set to harvesting, and the Pontefract twins were taking care of her. And now me and Annie were in the turnips, and Annie's green eyes were fixed hard as the sky lid on me.

"Who, Clam? Some days you forget who?"

115

"Well, Annie, happen you know who."

JAM! went Annie's fork in the ground. All morning she hadn't been so much digging up roots, as spearing for soil fish.

"I mean, Annie, all I mean is some times of the day I don't think on her. That's all. Is that bad? That the gaps in my head are filling in so soon? Only I looked all through the Appendix and it don't say nothing on this."

Annie crouched down to pull a turnip off her prongs, her headscarf sliding back from her brow.

"Annie?"

She snorted.

"Annie?" Weren't like our sister dying off was one for laughing about.

"I bet Maria Liphook hasn't."

"What?"

"Forgotten her."

"Can she? Can she remember not to forget? Staying in her Hole so long?"

Annie's eyes crackled. "Why do you think she's staying in her Hole?"

JAM! went her fork in the soil.

"Watch out, Annie!"

But it speared a baby pumpkin that wasn't for harvesting yet.

Annie threw down her fork. "Stupid pumpkins! Isn't like they do anything but rot off. Grow up and rot off."

And with that nonsense said, Annie was stamping off down the crop row, faster than a flat-foot duck. Kathy Selden looked up from trapping a sorry little weevil in her paws, and bounced off after her.

"I'll see to the rest of the row on my own then, shall I, Annie?"

But happen Annie St. Albans's ears weren't best-shaped for hearing me, because she just kept on.

I watched her go, her headscarf flapping loose behind. At the end of the field she didn't turn left down the path back to the yard, but stamped off for the plum orchard.

"Wait up, Annie," I shouted.

But she didn't.

I thought to catch her at Truly's mound, rearranging strawdolls or the Boule blossoms stuck up in the soil. Either that or tidying off dropped plum leaves, or leaving a fresh plum near Truly's mouth, or straightening the pebbles on the tricky Os of the words she had laid out along the mound— TRULY POLPERRO IS HERE.

"Annie?" I called, running through the trees. "Annie, where are you?"

But Annie wasn't about.

No, Annie had stamped herself all the way out of the orchard, and was heading off west through that nasty nettle patch known as nothing nicer than Sting Alley. There weren't but an acre of stinking bog ahead.

Well, I thought, watching from the orchard, that'll be an end on it.

But Devil melt my eyeballs if Annie didn't pop out the other side of the nettles, and go plunging her feet into the bog, where there weren't nothing but fizzing horseflies and rotting ferns. Where there weren't nothing to stop a sister being sucked down non-stop through bog to Bowels at any second. That's where Annie went—stepping her feet into most

117

dangerous bog. Without tying down her headscarf. Without even lifting up her smock. With a striped cat bouncing after.

Well.

Well, weren't nothing for it now. I pulled my headscarf low, and hurried on after.

"It weren't true, Annie," I shouted out. "What I said about Truly. Only in the first half of a breath or a swallow of pig-stew, I ain't thinking on her, Annie. I miss her something sore night-times. Come back, will you, Annie? The bog ain't no place to go stamping. The bog's Out of Bounds, ain't it? Ain't it, Annie? Annie, please come back."

But Annie didn't hear me.

A pair of crows flapped past, laughing loud. And I stopped and scratched my knee of a nettle sting, and I watched that skinny body stamp off through the wild bog, and I thought, well, when has she ever heard me? I thought backwards, and I couldn't think of one time. Even when we were new-rescued and busy crying, and Aunty brought toys for us, so she got some peace and quiet for ten minutes, well, even then, Aunty said she remembered little Annie didn't think nothing of ripping up her sister Calamity's doll to see its insides, no matter that her new sister was crying, "Please don't, you've seen inside the others, please not this last one too."

That's the truth that Aunty said to me *in confidence* after I started seeing her for tea and book readings. And the truth was and always will be, Annie St. Albans was made with ears that would hear nothing but just what they wanted. And a mouth that would sing different words to a song if it chose. And she had a body that never went nowhere without Truly Polperro. And that was the bone-marrow truth of Annie St. Albans.

I watched her elbows chopping the air. Seemed she wasn't heading for nowhere but the western Wall. With not one cloud cushion above and only the skinniest rind of Wall shade about. Well. Weren't like we needed anyone else going up Walls, was it?

So weren't nothing for it then but for me to race on over through that stinking bog, jump for Annie's headscarf and get it tugged safe over her brow.

Annie hit me off. "Don't!"

"Well, all right, Annie."

She jerked her head back, even though I weren't touching her no more. "I said don't."

"Well, Annie, I only—"

"Just don't."

"Annie?"

I thought to say, "It ain't sisterly to drag me—and that cat too—deep into Out of Bounds stinking bog with the winter Sun still something dangerous above, and then go hitting me when I try to protect you, Annie." But then I didn't say that. "Don't think I haven't noticed you not talking to me these last days, Annie," is what I said.

She looked at me. "Oh yes? And you never think on why I don't?"

"I know you miss Truly something sore."

"You never think on why I don't talk to you?"

"Happen I don't. Should I, Annie?"

And she spat. But not at me. Down into the bog.

I watched her toe stir that spit in deep, and my eyes started to fog up. "Annie?"

She sucked a breath in, and let it slide out without one word on top.

119

"Annie?"

And she looked up from her spit to me, and her eyes were bright as ice. "Never mind, Clam." She shook her head. "It's just something Nancy said."

"What did Nancy say?"

Annie swiped at her eyes. They were spilling over.

"Annie, what did Nancy say?"

"Never mind." She swiped her eyes. "It's too late now. Everything's too late now."

I stepped up close, and I re-wrapped the ends of her head-scarf and knotted them firm under her chin. And that felt good to do. "I do miss Truly, you know. I miss her something sore."

Annie looked at me. "How sore?"

I had a think.

"Maybe like an ulcer. But not in my mouth. One round my heart. And every time my heart jumps, it hits the sore and rips it open. Maybe something like that."

Annie swiped at her eyes. She nodded. "I don't miss her like I've lost an arm or a leg or something like that—because you've always got another spare. No, the way I miss Truly is more like in the middle of me is nothing but a hole. It's like a well hole where you can't see the bottom, and no matter how much porridge goes in, it won't fill up. No matter what I eat, I can't stop feeling hungry for Truly. Something like that."

She smiled bright and hard at me, like she didn't know she had tears jumping off her chin. I waited for her to offer me a bone-squeeze hug, but she shrugged and said, "Well, come on then, seeing as you're here."

"What?"

"Aunty's always saying you got the best ears, Clam. Come and press them here."

Annie walked right up to the Wall. She closed her eyes and shoved her left ear up against solid bricks.

"All right then, Annie," I said slow. "If that's what you want."

I went up next to her and counted out a minute. My ear started to itch. I unstuck my face from the Wall and said, "I can't hear nothing, Annie."

"Exactly."

"I said I can't hear nothing."

Annie smiled and nodded. Her eyes were still closed.

"Annie? Are you OK, Annie? Maybe you caught the flu from all the rain. It can set winds whirling in your ears, you know."

"Exactly. That's exactly it. You can't hear nothing."

"Can you, Annie?" I tried to speak soothing. "Can you hear something?"

"No. No, of course I can't!" And all sudden, she was wide-eyed and laughing, going at it loud and unsteady, like she'd just learned the taste for it.

I asked her gentle to come back and take some marigold tea.

But she just turned to try her other ear. "Nothing!" she laughed. "Nothing at all!"

So I shook my head and hitched my smock up high, and said I'd let her be. Them turnips weren't going to dig themselves up, were they?

Except I didn't get to do any more thinking on Annie, because when I got back to the turnips, Millie Gatwick was in the furrow, jiggling a pitchfork, and looking so excitable it seemed her jelly eyeballs really might pop themselves out this time. Which was about all I needed now.

"Gret—Gret—" Millie started.

"Don't bother," I sighed. "Come on, Millie Gatwick, seeing as I'm spending the whole blessed day running about, why don't you show me what's flipped you so dizzy. Won't be much more than hot water in the turnip soup tonight."

Millie tugged me back to the yard and into the mending room. Truly's straw still lay flat on the floor, and it wasn't like I wanted to see that. But Millie pointed up at the roof beam. "Look! She ain't dead. Or been eaten by that sneaky cat!"

It was Gretel, course. Poking her ratty nose out of a red satin shoe.

Well, I had to whistle at that. "Didn't I say she was a clever one? Wait till Sandra finds out that's where her shoe got to!"

Gretel rubbed her whiskers, and Devil take me if she didn't wink at us before she turned and popped back inside the shoe.

"Looks thinner for it," I said, laughing.

Millie giggled. "But Clam, you mustn't tell no one. Promise on Truly's bones. That ain't just it. Stand on the bucket and look in the shoe. She won't mind you. Look at what clever Gretel's made."

Well, I felt so perked after seeing Gretel that, while I was washing off bog at the standpipe, I started thinking about Maria Liphook. For sure she might like learning about rats. So I got the bug jar from under the fence—three horned beetles had crawled on a dandelion inside it—and I ran to the Hole door.

Maria was hunched in the dark coalbag corner, nibbling her toenails.

"Pooey, Maria, you growing mushrooms in here?" I said.

It was a minor miracle how our sister could stand the smell of the Hole without her nose collapsing, it really was. One time we left her with a bucket of Margaret Merril roses to help with the stink, but it only got knocked down in the dark so they rotted. Which was a shame. And more of a stink. And Aunty said it was a sweet idea, but a wicked waste of valuable petals, and not to be repeated.

I waggled the jar into the dark. "If you come on out, Maria, happen I've got something to show you. Horned beetles, Maria, are better tasting than toes."

Well, weren't one flash of an eyeball to say for her hearing me. Maria swapped a leg to her mouth, bending it up like as she was all made of dough.

A drop of water fell on my neck. "Fair enough then, Maria." I left the jar on the first step and turned around, listening out for her to lunge like always.

But she didn't.

Annie's speckled face popped in my head. I turned back. "Say, Maria, you ain't hiding, are you?"

She nibbled off a rim of toenail.

"You don't think after the Devil took Truly that He's coming for you? No, course you don't. Don't know why I said it. He ain't, anyways. I mean, don't take this wrong, Maria, but He's after the strong-minded first off. Well, fair enough then. I'll leave the bugs here. Be kind and eat them up quick, they ain't got much crawl left in them."

I shut up the Hole door, and was busy thinking about what a long old way it was back to the turnip row, and was considering on getting an apple from the kitchen for the journey, when Millie blundered out of the mending room and thumped into me, that fishface of hers shaped round a big O of her screaming mouth.

HOW ARE RAT BABIES
MADE?

C ourse, Gretel rat's babies needed killing.

"Vermin is what they are," Aunty said, emptying Sandra's red shoe into a brown paper bag, "and I will not have
you crying, niece Gatwick, over contagion-carrying, pestilen-
tial dog-torturers."

Gretel was sat on the mending room roof beam, snapping
at any hand that came near her. I kept a steady hold on Millie's shoulders while Aunty kicked Truly's straw to the side.
She dropped the bag on the concrete, and set to bashing it
with Mr. Stick. "I said shut up, Millie darling, if you want
supper. And as to why that cat can't do its job properly, I
don't know. Are you girls feeding it?"

I turned Millie away. Mr. Stick had been very busy since
Baby Sainsbury's arrived, and there weren't no telling who it
might swing on next.

"Speak of the devil," Aunty said, stopping her bashing to
stare at the cat that had come padding in. And coming to

lean against the door frame behind it was none other than bog-drenched Annie. "Poo. Speak of the Devil and He'll bring His stink." Aunty's eye fixed on Annie, "Where've you been, sweetie? Swimming in latrines?"

Now every blessed body with a mouth knows it from the very first Appendix page that *An Aunty's question requires an answer*. Every body ever grown knows that. Except, as it happened, my sister Annie St. Albans. My sister who didn't answer nothing on her bog-wandering ways, but said this instead, "Aunty, how are rat babies made?"

Aunty didn't do nothing for a few seconds but look down at the twitching brown paper bag on the concrete, where pink juice was starting to leak out the bottom. "I'm so sorry, Annie. Did you just ask me a question?"

"I understand rat babies need killing. I just wondered how they are made, is all. Only I've been thinking—"

"Thinking? I don't remember writing that on the duty list today." Aunty winked at me and leaned the correcting stick against the wall. "I'll just pop Mr. Stick down to give him a breather, in case he's needed shortly, Annie, and in the meantime, I'll give you one last chance. I said, 'Poo, have you been swimming in the latrines'—and you, my sweetest of peas, were going to answer—"

"Annie hasn't been feeling well," I jumped in. "She has flu."

"Thank you, Clam, but I feel fine actually," Annie said. "I was just wondering if it's like us in the rose bushes? Are the babies seeded in buds Outside, and then rescued by Mother and brought here to grow? Because how could Gretel bring them in, if she didn't know how to get out? I mean she couldn't get over the Wall, could she? I mean perhaps she

126

could have got out through a rabbit hole, that's what I was thinking. But how would she find the same hole to come back in? And wouldn't she get eaten up by injuns on the way, Aunty? And was it rose buds, Aunty? Or, I was thinking, would rat babies actually be seeded in something smaller?"

Aunty, Millie and me stared at Annie. Kathy Selden stopped licking bog off her paws and looked over. Even Gretel gave up snapping for a second to blink. But did Annie let go of her question? Annie who probably wouldn't know when to stop sticking a headless pig? Oh no, Annie shrugged her shoulders and said, "And Aunty, I was also thinking, what about the baby pigs, and all the milk cows, and the hens that come in here? What are they all grown from? Only there isn't actually an explanation in any of our *Garden Growers' Digests*. So will you tell me the answer please?"

Well.

Well, Aunty's eye fixed on Annie like she was nothing more than a trapped rabbit, and Aunty was figuring the best way to skin her. But here's the peculiar thing. Annie looked straight back at Aunty, like if she was a trapped rabbit, well then, she didn't want anything so bad as to be skinned right away.

And no one said nothing, except for Gretel on her beam, hissing her teeth.

And I didn't know what to do, so I thought to whisper, "Annie, you know we have the Appendix for all the answers we need in life."

Except she didn't hear me. And Aunty didn't hear me neither. Her eye had skinned Annie from head to toe, and now it swivelled to the twitching bag on the concrete. "Someone has got themselves a touch too nosy for my liking. Someone would do well to remember what became of a certain too-nosy sister."

Aunty hitched up her skirt and stamped her heel on the paper bag. "Kerplunk!" She ground it down and winked at Annie, "My eye, niece, I can see we're going to have to keep an eye on you." And Aunty winked at me, and she spun out into the yard, singing about anything you can do, I can do better. I can do anything better than you.

"Annie," I hissed, "you know nosiness don't lead to nothing but nonsense. What were you thinking?"

But happen she just scooped up that cat, and skipped off out.

Well, I'm sorry to say, by evening Annie had developed the flu good and proper. Weren't no doubt about that at all.

It was the night after we had swirled round the yard under the burka, so happen I thought she was overexcited by thoughts of War, happen that's all I thought it was.

We had just finished stitching zippers into covers, and I'd read a most happy Appendix page on *C for Clouds and Cushions!* The light had gone off, and we were all curled in our straw down the row, our needled fingers aching for sleep, when Annie broke our peace and quiet with another of her unnecessary questions.

"Where do you think we go?" she said.

I turned to look at her across Truly's empty straw. Even in the dark, I could see Annie weren't corpse-still for sleep. Oh no. Annie was sat up with her fur flung off her shoulders, and that Kathy cat snug like a snail in her lap. Annie had shoved back her straw from the concrete, and was drawing on a board from the schoolroom with a stub of chalk. I sat up and unwrapped my ears from their binding, and I sighed. "What you drawing, Annie? Ain't it too black to see?"

"Only I wondered where it might be, because Aunty hasn't said yet, and it must be soon that we're off."

Up past Annie, Dorothy popped up, rattling her head. "Happen we're waiting to hear from Aunty."

"I was wondering this too—where's Argentina?"

"That's where Aunty's going to fight, I think she said," Dorothy answered.

"Aunty's fighting days are behind her," I said. "That's what the Appendix says. *Aunty's the one female in the world who no demonmale would ever touch now*, it says. *Not with a bargepole*. And the Appendix also says in *W for War* that we could be sent anywhere on Earth. Anywhere at all. Anyway, what are you drawing on that board, Annie, only you didn't say?"

"Bricks."

"Are you sure you haven't got a flu today?"

"Why?"

"Why what?"

"Why will we be sent anywhere at all?"

I sighed. "Because we will, Annie. Because we will."

"Does the Appendix say any more?"

"Well, it's too dark to look in it now. Probably, it does somewhere. Anyway, I don't see why you have to start why-ing everything, Annie, I really don't. These questions are dropping from you useless as diarrhea. Why don't you listen to yourself before you start talking, and hear how foolish they are?"

"And why do we have to wear a tablecloth to travel to

War? I mean, there isn't one female in the Showreel that goes about wearing a tablecloth, is there?"

"I see what you mean," Dorothy said.

So I had to groan then, I really did. See, I knew we didn't need another one raving nonsense right then. Not after Truly, did we? No thanks. "Goddess goodness, it's plum simple, it really is. We ain't like other females, Annie. We are Mother's Weapons, kept safe in the Garden from the Sun's heat and His nasty demonmales. When we are strong enough to leave for War, would we—Mother's Weapons—dress like common-grown Outside females, Annie? Do you see the Devil's injun army wearing common demonmale clothes in the Showreel, Annie, or are they whooping around with only a few feathers on their redskin bottoms? And it's called a burka, not a tablecloth. You sure have the flu bad, Annie. You have forgotten all your lessons."

Annie jumped up with her drawing board and ran off to the door. Down the row, bodies started to rustle and moan.

"What you doing now, Annie?"

Annie shoved the door open wide to the night.

Truth be told, my temper was growing something scratchy. But Annie had the flu and that needed remembering. So I sat up and pulled my fur tight and I kept my eyes on her back, and I spoke out loud and comforting truths for all the young ears I knew were awake down the bottom end, and most probably shivering from the cold Annie was letting in. I reminded them of our fortune, and I spoke of the excitement of the Good Fight ahead, and the perfect roses waiting in Heaven. Then I lay back down.

Annie didn't shove in with nothing else then, she just stared out and started up drawing on her board again.

So I thought to finish it off good and proper. "So, really, Annie, I reckon questions about our clothes are something neither here nor there, are they? Not when we're 'The Goddess Daughter's Army a.k.a. Mother's Weapons—training under General Miss Ophelia Swindon's Command.' Clear enough, Annie?"

"Suppose."

"You do want to go to War, don't you, Annie?"

"Suppose."

"I'm eldest. I'm going first, don't anybody forget," Sandra shouted.

"Will we get to go too?" Millie shouted up. "Me and Adelaide and the others who ain't been photographed yet?"

"You heard Aunty. You're second-batchers, Millie Gatwick, but yes, it is true that none will be wasted."

"And the second wind toddlers and Baby Sainsbury's?" Mary Bootle said. "They'll come and join us, won't they?"

"Most probably in a few years. If none grow into a Spitting Image and stay with Mother."

At the door, Annie kept on drawing.

Outside, all looked blanketed safe black, seamless as a perfect-stitched cushion.

"Are you all right, Annie?" Dorothy called out gentle. "Do you want my fur?"

I crawled up to Dorothy. "Her headscarf was slung back today under His Heat," I whispered. "And she had her feet in bog for hours. Happen He might have started cooking a fever in her. We should keep a watch on her."

I called out, "Dorothy asked you a question, Annie. Are you all right?"

"Suppose."

"We'll be out there fighting soon enough, Annie, don't you worry."

"Suppose."

Well, I reckoned if I asked Annie "Are you a spotted frog?" she'd say, "Suppose." So I said nothing more, but shook my head at Dorothy and crawled back to my straw.

Then I wondered about shunting up to Nancy's fat bottom to get warm. But Nancy had backed herself against Mary. I turned over to my other side, but Truly's straw was stiff with cold. So I rebound my ears and scrunched myself up tight as a Devil's hairball in my own space, and tried to put whirling blue burkas in my head. But it was no use. Not with Annie up and drawing her own Wall on her board by the dorm door. So I counted out skinned rabbits for a while, which Truly always said brought sleep.

I'd skinned sixty-three in my head by the time I heard Annie slide the door shut and patter her feet past me. A rustle said for her curling up against Dorothy and Sandra, and possible she was whispering to them too. And then I heard nothing more.

ROLE PLAY

Now, I suppose it's all right to tell you that life got even busier after that. And I'm happy to say a lot of Annie's questions were answered in our lesson, the very next afternoon. And I don't mind telling you, it was the best lesson we ever had. Like Aunty said, "Watch and learn, nieces, because in a very short space of time, if you do exactly as you're told, all our dreams are going to come true."

Aunty had come along painted up neat in a red uniform, with a little bowl hat on black hair and a neckscarf tied in a bow, and Toto had a red bow too. We kicked out the cockerels from the schoolroom and dragged in bales from the yard, and turned it into a place called an Airport, which is where, Aunty said, we would be flying to War from.

We had to bang the walls and shout bing-bong bing-bong, because, "Airports are noisy places," Aunty said, having a drink of medicine, "and you'd better get used to it." Sandra was dressed up in the burka and Aunty started asking her questions.

"Have you packed this bag yourself?"

"Did anyone give you anything to put in it?"

"Do you have any seating preferences?"

"Do you have any dietary requirements?"

"Enjoy the flight."

And Sandra had to say—"Yes, no, no, no, thank you."

"And even you, Sandra," Aunty said, "can manage that."

Next, Aunty changed her red hat to a black cap, and made her voice hard as a brick. "Passport!"

Sandra had to walk up and hand over a piece of card.

Aunty frowned and looked at Sandra and looked at the card, and handed it back. Then Sandra had to stand with her arms out, and Aunty patted her up and down and went, "Shoes off, miss. Beep-beep."

"And that, my gorgeous golden tickets," Aunty said, "is how you go through an airport."

Aunty sent Mary to fetch a water jug, and we all sat down in two rows on the floor, with our backs against bales. Aunty handed out a tiny pink sweet to each of us. "It might make you feel a little air-headed, darlings, or it might do nothing at all, but let's each try one and see what happens."

"Why?" Annie asked, looking at her sweet like it was a bit of grit.

I held my breath, but even Annie couldn't bother Aunty today.

"Heavens, practice makes perfect, sugarlumps! Just imagine the consequences if you were to suffer an adverse reaction when you come to swallow one for real. It would be catastrophic for all concerned."

"But why do we have to swallow them at all?"

Aunty smiled so wide her top teeth fell down, "Well now, niece nosy face, we have to help the plane get off the ground somehow, don't we? You've seen how big they are. And if I'm not wrong, this will turn you light as a cloud, which, without getting too technical, should make the plane's uplift easy-peasy. Off you go, darlings, down in one."

Aunty sat on a bale in front of us, because she wanted to keep her eye on us while the sweets worked. Us being so valuable to her, she said she didn't want us floating up to the ceiling and banging our heads.

"See, this is how we fly without wings," I whispered to Annie. "If only Truly could have stayed to try this." Because I reckoned it wouldn't take another sweet to send me up to the clouds.

Little Adelaide Worthing spoke out for us all when she said, "I'm floating."

Aunty looked at her watch and smiled at Adelaide, "Well, you just sit back and enjoy the flight, my sweetest of peas." Aunty settled her bottom on the bale. She had a hard brown book in her hands. As a treat, she said, she would tell us a tale from the *Archive* while the sweets got to work. She started digging through the pages.

"It's *Volume Four*!" I tried to tell Annie, though my tongue weren't too keen to budge. "We're getting the Splashback story! For sure we are!" Which story was the tale of Aunty's most tragic Splashback, when she tried to put a poor old female called Penny the Dreariest Diva in Dudley out of her misery. See, poor old Penny was getting cooked up regular by a demonmale called The Director, which not only made her burn nasty inside, but also made her prance about non-stop, snatching all of the roles that really should have had Aunty's name on them. Which was a big problem for the whole planet, because how was Aunty to extend her Showreel to show the Outside's miseries to Weapons like us, when she never got to act them out? So brave Aunty had to finish off Penny's prancing quick with spirits of salt, only silly Penny shoved the acid pot back at Aunty's face when Aunty did it. Which was a very silly and selfish thing to do, because Aunty still needed her eyes, even if Penny didn't. So Aunty—screaming in pain—with just about every demonmale ever grown setting a hunt on her, flew over the rainbow and came home to Mother, to serve the Goddess from the safety of the Garden. It really was about the best story of bravery there was, with the happiest of endings.

Like I say, I tried to tell Annie this, but my tongue had gotten too loose for words. So I leaned against her shoulder, and I flopped my legs onto Nancy's warm belly.

Aunty opened up a pot and creamed her hands, and then she began her tale.

And it ain't no lie to say I heard a Polperroey giggle fly past me then, and seemed I went floating up to the ceiling, chasing after my sister Truly.

THE MEANING OF
ELIZABETH JONES

Well, Jane Jones walks all alive and easy into this room, like she ain't never kept me waiting six days to talk War. My heart jumps up, and I pop Danny Zuko back under the soil, and brush my hair over my ears to look ready and waiting for business.

"Hello sweetheart," she says, leaving her wash box on the floor and coming to sit on my bed. "How are you today?"

I try not to look at her, but her voice makes me. She is still black and uncracked, I am happy to see. "I've been waiting six days for you to come," I say.

"I'm afraid my mother had a fall, so I had to take some time off. But I remember you had some questions for me. We've got a few minutes now, if you like. But what happened to your leg?"

"They brought a demonmale in here."

She looks something surprised. "A demon what?"

"Yes, I know. So I had to run. Only my leg weren't for it."

"I'm sorry to hear that."

"So it broke again."

"Well, we'll have you fighting fit soon enough," she says, smiling at me.

I think about the meaning of this. I can see the sense in strengthening me up before anything is to start. I ain't done a sit-up in must be three weeks.

"I brought something to show you," she says, bringing out a photograph from her smock pocket. "Seeing as you were so interested when we spoke before."

Well.

Well, I nearly drop down dead to Bowels to see it, I nearly do. The photograph is of three black-skinned girls. They are sitting on the ground in the daytime—without headscarves or hats. They are wearing tunics—that is all—and all their hands and arms, and legs and feet, and shoulders and heads and necks are out under the Sun.

"My granddaughters. Elizabeth—on the left, holding up the starfish—she's about your age."

Elizabeth has a pink tunic on, and she is smiling at me. Actually, she is squinting a bit because He is strong up there. But she don't look worried. I look all careful over her black arms and legs and her face. And I look at Jane Jones. Then I look at Elizabeth again, and I realize why she is smiling so happy and headscarfless under the Sun. And my heart starts to flip in its box. Over and over it goes.

Jane Jones is smiling too. "And that's Janine, with the bucket, she's nine. And Lottie, on the left, rolling in the sand, is six. She's my youngest daughter's daughter. A real little mischief-maker."

I look at the three black-skinned smiling girls, and I look

at Jane Jones, and I am smiling, and my heart is jumping like it wants to come out forever. "It is very clever," I say, shaking my head at the cleverness of it. "You are breeding up girls who are protected like you."

"It's not so easy to say who will be protected in life, honey. But I do my best to teach my granddaughters what I know."

I look at Elizabeth Jones again, and my eyes start fogging up.

"What is it, sweetheart, have I upset you?"

But sometimes tears run happy, don't they?

See, I look at these girls who are hatless, scarfless and furless under the Sun, but who are as uncookable as black-feathered crows, and I think something so wonderful I can only whisper it, "Are there other girls like this Outside?"

Jane Jones hands me a tissue from her box. "Millions, sweetheart."

"And they are all black-skinned?"

Jane Jones laughs. "Lots are, sweetheart."

And I'm shaking now. My heart is shaking up my whole body with the joy of it. There is a strip of Him scalding the bottom of the blind, like He wants to nosy in and interrupt us, but what do I care about Him? He's the one needs to worry now!

I can hear Mary Bootle singing through the walls, and when I stop shaking I will shout out, "Mary Bootle, it's OK, it ain't just us. There's millions of girls being bred to fight. If you can hear Dorothy or Annie, tell them this—it ain't just us, there are millions! All with special-protected skin! If you can speak to Dorothy, tell her to compute how many millions all these millions could kill off!"

But I don't shout just yet, because Jane Jones's arms are wrapping me up in Gloriana tea roses. "It's all right, dear. You're quite safe here."

And I know it is all right. Everything is all right. And I want to say to her, "Well, yes, of course it is all all right now."

But I'm wrapped up so nice and rosy, that I don't.

PURPOSE

"What you doing, Annie?" I said. "What you doing hiding in here?"

I tried to make the words slip out friendly, but they snagged in my throat.

The barn door slammed behind me. I pulled off my headscarf and stood my torch on the ground in front of her. "I've been out hunting you everywhere."

"Oh hello, Clam," she said, squinting up. "It's nice to see you."

Which I don't need to tell no one, wasn't no manner of excuse for being found squatting in one lonely torch puddle, in the petal bin corner of the supplies barn, in the middle of the Devil's own night. Scrunched under a rack of drying Margaret Merril heads like a slug under leaves, so I had to look long and hard to find her. With about every gardening tool we ever had, heaped about her, and a pile of sacks too.

No, I didn't need to tell her, there weren't no good reason for this at all.

"Do you mind moving out of my light?" she said.

Well, I did, so I didn't.

"Why are you hunting me everywhere anyway?"

"I didn't say that," I said, sniffing back a string of snot. Cold nights and the smell of drying roses made it pour fast. "I didn't say I was hunting you everywhere, like I was following you everywhere, did I, Annie? Like I wanted to catch you? I didn't say that at all."

She shoved a trenching spade in a sack. And then she spat on a piece of sack and held it out, smiling. "Looks like you've got chocolate on your smock."

"No I haven't."

"Fair enough."

I looked down at my smock. Aunty came spinning into my head, all black and white stripes of her, dressed like she was Showreeling *My Fair Lady*'s races. Aunty, holding a hamper and a red and green rug, just like she had a few hours ago, when I met her in the plum orchard on my way to compost the trees.

Aunty had spun round singing, "Whoooah the hokey-cokey," and fallen on her rug, right next to Truly's mound. "Yoohoo, Calamity Leek!" she called. "What a perfect coincidence! Drop those poo buckets downwind, sweetie, and take a break. Toto, shift over and make room for our favorite niece. It is such a lovely day I thought I'd treat myself to a picnic, and you simply cannot have a picnic alone."

142

"How do you know it's chocolate cake?" I said to Annie.

"I said, 'looks like.' Looks like it was tasty, whatever it was."

"Feast your eyes on this whopper," Aunty had said. She opened a tin and pulled out the biggest brown cake I have ever seen. She winked and chopped it into triangles with a knife, and handed me one on a paper plate. Toto watched on, drooling. Aunty poured out tea from a flask. "Well, isn't this nice, niece?" She sipped her tea and winced. "I do believe I may enhance my beverage with something medicinal. I presume you're going to pass on this occasion? Very wise. How's the cake?"

It was about the nicest thing I ever tasted.

"Goodness, that went down quick, Calamity. You are a guzzle-gob, aren't you? A moment on the lips, sweetie, that's all I'm saying. Well, all right, go on then, take another slice. I promise I won't tell."

This slice melted even more creamy than the first.

Aunty handed me a napkin and winked, so I reckoned on it being safe to ask a question. So I said would there be cake like this in Heaven, and Aunty laughed and said of course, and there would possibly be something very similar for sale in the Outside World, and did I want to go there to fight the Good Fight?

"Very much," I said.

"And your sisters?"

"Them too."

"All of them?"

"For sure," I said.

"That's splendid news," Aunty said, giving her cakey fingers to Toto to lick up. "My pals battalion, led by my number one pal! You know, Calamity, I always knew you were the one for me. Never trust a pretty face, that's what I said to myself. All the trouble in the world comes from pretty faces, Calamity. I shan't mention names. An uglier world would be a more harmonious world, niece, I'm afraid it would. Chacun à sa place. Naturally, I'm telling you this in confidence, and naturally, there are degrees of unattractiveness, niece Leek. In fact, I don't mind telling you, when you arrived, I informed your Mother that for all her derring-do, she could have had the decency to stop off in a lay-by and eject inferior goods. But deliberation was never her style— over-influenced by the ram-raid genre of her youth, I fear. She hasn't changed. Years of pilfering in our dorm and getting away with it, so what do you expect? No one ever changes, Calamity. What can you do? What could I ever do for you lot, stuck in here?"

Aunty had herself a long drink of medicine. "All I ever wanted was to make you girls happy. And tell me the truth, you are happy, aren't you?"

I looked up from drinking down my tea neat and proper like we need to.

"Of course you are. It's the most precious thing in the world—a happy childhood. And when you come to look back on it, Calamity dearest, I think you'll know just how happy yours has been."

Aunty dug about in the hamper for a pot of pills to eat.

"Where was I? Oh yes, when you turned up, I'm afraid I cursed High Heaven. Nothing personal, Calamity, time and money, and you looked a sure-fire waste of both. But then I took a second glance at those flappers of yours—sticking out sideways under a fetching blue bobble hat, if I recall—and do you remember what I said?"

I shook my head.

"I said whoopee! That's what I said. Whoopeeeeeee! Because right then and there I knew we could be the best of friends. You see, niece, I knew there was simply no room for ambition in that pair of ears."

Aunty said, "Cheers," and she swallowed her pills with a big drink of medicine, and leaned over and tickled my left ear, and said would I like another slice? She wouldn't tell anybody if I did, because pals didn't tell. No, pals liked to share things, like cake. She went for the knife. Then she gasped and said she had something else she wanted to share with me. A secret. And it was this—we were all going to have a Trial Run, to get the blood flowing, so to speak. Mother had been going on and on about it for quite some time. And wasn't that the best of news?

Which it was.

A woodlouse crawled along the base of a petal bin. I watched it trying to get up the slippy side. "You haven't said what you're doing here, Annie?"

She shrugged.

"Well. What are you doing?"

"Stuff."

"What stuff?"

"Sorting stuff."

"That all?"

"That's all."

I looked at her. "Annie, you do want to go, don't you?"

She tapped a shovel and laid it down by the sack.

"To War. You do want to go?"

She picked up a spade and ran a finger along its edge. She put it down. She picked up her drawing board and wrote something on it, and then she turned the board and leaned it against the petal bin, its writing hidden away.

Well. Wasn't like I wanted to see her nonsense words, was it?

"I have a secret too, you know, Annie."

"That's nice for you." Annie picked up the shovel and put it in the sack.

"Whoooah the hokey-cokey," Aunty sang. She took a drink of medicine, and waved at the big old Victoria plum. "Whoooah the hokey-cokey." The tree was starting to drop its yellow leaves on Truly's mound. "Knees bent, legs stretched, that's what it's all about!"

Aunty stopped singing and sighed. "Such a pretty spot." She waved a bluebottle away from her nose. "Pals like to share secrets," she said. "That's what pals do." And her eye fixed on the cake as she cut out another fat triangle. "I wonder," she said. "I wonder I wonder I wonder." She placed the triangle onto a plate and lifted it up. "I wonder if any of my pals have any secrets to share."

I said, "I have a secret, Aunty."

"You do?" Aunty gasped. Her teeth jumped all together

in a smile. "What a pal you are! And?" she said, looking at the cake slice and then at me, "And?"

"Truly Polperro flew past me yesterday in the schoolroom."

The smile fell off Aunty's teeth. The slice stayed up in the air between us.

"Well, thank you, Calamity, that is good to know. I have a secret about Mother." Aunty jabbed me with her elbow, "She has halitosis." Aunty laughed loud. "And here's another. She once ran away from her children's home and was severely beaten by Father Tony when she was brought back. Explains a thing or two about her subsequent choices in life." She shook her head and laughed some more.

After a bit Aunty stopped laughing, and the orchard stayed quiet, and the cake slice didn't move, and Aunty's eye swivelled and fixed something steady on me.

So I said, "I have another secret."

"Oh yes?"

"It's about Kathy Selden."

"Oh," Aunty said. "Oh, I see." And she began lowering the plate—its slice all cut up and everything—back in the tin. "Just Kathy Selden?"

"Well, there's Annie St. Albans in it too." Now don't ask me why Annie popped on my tongue just then, but she did. And once she was there, well, she was there.

The cake jumped back out of the tin. "Annie St. Albans, you say? Now that is interesting, niece."

"Yes," I said.

Only then I weren't exactly sure what I was going to say. See, sometimes with me, I ain't even sure what I'm thinking till the words have sprung out my throat and gone off, that's just how it is with me. But I tried to think quick because Aunty was winking "That is interesting" at me.

But the problem was, whatever secret Annie had, well, I'd have to go find Dorothy, most probably, and get it off her. And I weren't sure Aunty wanted to wait while I did. And I weren't even sure whether Dorothy would be up for sharing it. Because when I found her hid with Annie and Nancy in the latrines after breakfast, whispering and drawing on boards, seemed they weren't up for sharing words with no one. Oh no.

Annie was pinging the prongs on a pitchfork. I looked at the back of her board leaned against the petal bin, and I sniffed. Them drying roses sure were making my eyes water bad.

"You know, I can't help it if Aunty likes me most, Annie. I really can't."

Her speckled face knit up in a frown. For two seconds she said nothing. Then she looked up and said, "Do you think Aunty liked Truly?"

"Why are you asking? Truly was a tragic loss to Aunty, you know that, Annie."

"But did Aunty like her? Do you think she feels a hole in her belly or an ulcer round her heart, now she's gone? Do you think she cried for her?"

"What do you mean, Annie? You know Aunty's eye can't cry."

"But does she actually miss her in her heart?"

"I don't know that, Annie, do I?"

A pipistrelle dropped off the rafters and cartwheeled over our heads. Annie put the pitchfork in her sack and knotted it. "But what do you think, Clam?"

I sighed. "I think you shouldn't talk like this, Annie, you really shouldn't. Truly was valuable, Aunty did say that. Valuable as a new top lip. And you can't get more valuable than that."

Annie snorted.

"I don't see what's funny about that, I really don't. Truly's dying was a tragic waste of her purpose, you know that."

Annie looked at me sharp-eyed, "Was it?"

"Of course. Like it says in the Appendix, on the first page of the Ps—*Everything has a purpose, and my nieces have a very special one!* Everything has a purpose, Annie. And we do too. You know that. Even our second-wind sisters know that."

But she just shoved a pickax in a sack.

"Annie?"

"Everything has a purpose, Clam?"

"All right then, take that ax you've got there. What does it do?"

"Everyone knows what an ax does."

"That ain't my point. Tell me its purpose, please."

"Smashing stuff."

"And that hessian sack?"

"You should be with the Pontefracts teaching the second-wind toddlers. A hessian sack holds things. Flour and dried petals, and finished-off cushions."

"Cushions then, Annie?"

"Make clouds to clog up the sky lid from His heat. Everyone knows that."

"And what about the petals inside?"

Annie shrugged.

"They perfume the air in the sky so we ain't all poisoned by His polluting farts. And what about the writing on the cushions—taunting him with it's our 'Home Sweet Home' not yours—all that is pure purpose. And by the way, you need to protect yourself more from Him. When the clouds are busy elsewhere, you really need to be more careful, Annie. Who's to say all this hot and bothered talk of yours isn't your brain heating up from careless exposure?"

Annie didn't say nothing.

The pipistrelle whooshed over our heads and flew back to the rafters.

Annie folded over the top of the sack and pressed it down tight. "So, Truly?" she said all quiet.

"Truly what?"

"What was her purpose, Clam?"

I stood up and straightened my smock. "It is very late and we are Out of Bounds. We should go back to the yard."

"What was Truly's purpose, Clam?"

It took a moment to pull my voice out of my throat. "Well, happen she missed it, Annie. She missed it."

Aunty plucked a gray pebble off the T on Truly's mound. She washed it in her teacup and screwed it in her empty socket. Her cheek scrunched up to hold it in. "Annie St. Albans, you say, niece? I'm all ears."

The cake triangle was sitting out on the rug. A bluebottle was crawling along the top, stopping now and then to have a lick of its legs.

"Annie has been listening to the Wall, Aunty," I whispered.

"Now, that is an interesting secret, niece. Most interesting indeed. And where exactly has she been listening?"

"Well, I saw her do it out in the bog, but all around, probably. She's probably been going listening all round it."

Aunty leaned forward and the pebble plopped out of her socket onto the cake. The bluebottle flew off. "So, tell me, niece Leek," Aunty's eye fixed on me, "what does it say, the Wall?"

"Well, Annie says it don't say nothing."

Aunty kept on looking at me, and her mouth started wobbling this way and that, like she couldn't choose between joy or sorrow at hearing this, and maybe I could help her choose. But I couldn't. But never mind, because happen it was joy that came to her, because her teeth spread wide, and her whole body began to wobble with laughter. "I reckon Annie is turning into a bit of a lunatic, that's what I reckon. Asylum Annie—how's that for a new name for her!" And Aunty laughed till her top teeth fell on her tongue.

After she jammed them back in, she handed me my cake slice. Except when she passed it over, happen she had changed her mind, because her voice came sorrowful and her eye turned towards Truly's mound. "I shouldn't have laughed, niece, that was wrong of me. I don't mind telling you, Annie's mental health is a cause of concern. I know she's grieving, but I'd hate to see her mind get fried like poor Maria, or even worse, her body overheat entirely like Truly Polperro. Dear oh dear, that would be such a waste."

Aunty looked so sad, that I felt sad too, thinking on these possibilities for Annie, and I tried to look as sad as is possible when licking off chocolate fingers.

"Napkin, Calamity, please! But I tell you what," Aunty was smiling now, "I know how we can keep Annie safe."

"You do, Aunty?" Because happen I never did with Annie.

"I do, Calamity, and it's very exciting."

"It is?"

There was a crackling in the trees. Toto looked up and snarled.

Aunty beckoned me. "Come up close, Calamity Leek. Closer, pal. Now you ask—quite rightly—how I'm going to keep Annie safe, and the answer is simple. I'm going to borrow a couple of eyes and ears."

"You are, Aunty?"

"I am. Can you guess where from?"

I looked down at the rug. "I don't know, Aunty."

"Oh, I think perhaps you do." Aunty's elbow gave me a jab. "I'm going to borrow them from my bestest pal. Can you think who that might be?"

Well, my heart blushed to hear it.

"And I'm going to cut her a deal. In return—very generously—I'm going to give her the answer to a secret."

"What secret will it be, Aunty?"

Aunty laughed loud, "Oh cute move, Calamity Leek. Well, as your Mother once made me swear right outside this very Garden Wall, the only secret ever worth its salt is the one you must keep till the end. So think carefully. Go on."

Well, there weren't but one secret a Garden body could ever want.

"Oh, Calamity, I can read that face of yours like a book."

"You can?" I whispered.

"It's your Mother, isn't it? You would like to know the color of your Mother's eyes. Well, don't look so gobsmacked, niece. It's a predictable question. One that I, sadly, never had answered as a child." Aunty opened her plastic pot and threw

152

some more pills in her mouth. She swallowed some medicine from the bottle and then she threw out the tea from the cups, and put the cake in its tin inside the hamper. She shook crumbs off the plates onto Truly's mound. "Don't want the poor dear starving down there, do we?"

I stared at Aunty locking up her hamper. With everything she already knew about us, I sometimes wondered why she ever needed any more eyes.

Aunty winked, "And we certainly don't want any more escaping Houdinis, do we? So you keep those eyes peeled, and those ears flapping, Calamity, and we have ourselves a deal. In the meantime, it's back to the coalface for you and your shit buckets. Off you pop now, and get working off that stodge."

Annie had filled two sacks with tools. She was watching me close. "You look tired, Clam. You should go back to the dorm and get some sleep."

"I am tired, Annie, yes, happen I am." My voice wobbled. "But I came to find you, and tell you the knowledge you missed from the new Appendix page I read out tonight. That's all. That's why I'm here."

She smiled. "Come, sit down with me, Clam." And them words curled round me sweet as heating honey. She shook out a sack against the bins next to hers, and patted it. "I'm sorry I missed your reading. I bet it was a good one."

I blew my nose and sat down. "It was." The bin was cold against my back. "It was a brand-new *L*. It was about loss, Annie. The Goddess Daughter feeling sorry for our loss of Truly."

Annie squeezed me close. "That's nice."

"Yes it is. And the Goddess Daughter said she was sorry Truly got so nosy, because look where it leads to—page *N*—nothing but nonsense." I blew my nose again. "You know, I didn't choose to be chosen to know all the Appendix."

"I know."

"No, I didn't. It ain't my fault I was chosen. And it ain't easy, knowing it all and needing to tell your sisters right from wrong. You try it. It ain't easy being always on your guard for Him, and then missing Him when He came and sneaked nosiness into Truly's head. Which I did, Annie, I missed Him. And now she's off burning in Bowels. And there ain't nothing nice in knowing you missed Him coming."

It is a bit of an unpleasant truth, but I was near drowning us both in snot tears. "I ain't stupid, Annie. I can see you packing tools and drawing bricks, and I can see your brow getting all hot and knotted, and I can hear you talking about there being no injuns out there. Which ain't ever been proven, has it? And all your why and how and what-ing talk means only one thing. All this nosiness in you means only one thing. He's coming for you, Annie, the signs are clear."

Annie rocked us close. "Hush now, Clam. I'm safe, I promise."

But I shook myself off, and my eyes and nose gushed free. "You won't even tell me why you're here. How can I help you if you won't tell me?"

"I'm just sorting out tools for winter is all. I was thinking of Truly and I couldn't sleep."

"That's all you're doing?"

"That's all."

Well, I cried a bit more and then I blew my nose on a sack end. "That's good, Annie. That's good."

Annie smiled and ripped me another scrap of sack. "Truly always said a good cry was worth ten pig suppers."

I was about to say, "Well, I don't know about that," when something crashed in the far end of the barn and smashed my thoughts to pieces.

I jumped up. "What was that?"

Annie shrugged. "That cat. Or the bats maybe."

"Bats, Annie!"

The noise echoed away. "We are stuck in the Devil's own night-time, and something clangs louder than a bucket on concrete, and you shrug and say on bats! I never thought you for being a Liphook fool, but well, Annie. Well."

I pointed my torch all about the dark barn. I listened hard. Dead silence now. The sort of silence that comes from sucked-in breath. Shapes were moving in the dark of the supply shelves—bodies, flashing through the shadows. Metal was flashing. I rubbed my eyes and thought the only thing I could. Injuns. Got sneaky through the Wall to kill us off in our sleep. Playing dead with Truly to spring a surprise on us. I looked at Annie to say this terrible news to her, but she had turned away from me. And then a voice came out of the dark.

"Well, hello there, sister Sneak. Enjoy Aunty's chocolate cake did we, eh?"

THE WALL

It wasn't an injun, but Nancy, course, who came stepping
out of the darkness, a butching blade in her hand. Dorothy
came after, then Mary, Sandra and even sickly Eliza, switching on their torches. Every one of my elder sisters, wrapped
in rope and carrying tools. And standing tall behind them,
with not one lump of potatoness showing on her face, was
our simplebrained eldest sister of all, Maria Liphook. Who
was holding an ax.

Well.

Well, I looked from Maria along each of my sisters' faces
to Annie, and what words I had died in me. Annie stared at
her toes. I looked back to Maria, stood there so bright-eyed
and drool-free, I wasn't sure whether the Goddess Daughter
hadn't just thrown all the pieces of her face up in the air so
they landed shifted into someone else.

I shook my head and shook it again. And my leg bones
turned to jellymeat, so as I had to reach behind me to the

petal bin and slide down. I whispered the only thing left rattling my head, "Maria, you came out without me?"

And for half the start of a second, it really seemed like this Maria-but-not-Maria's lips were shaping to answer me, it really did. But then her eyes shifted onto Annie and stayed there.

Annie shuffled along and squeezed my shoulder. "Sorry, Clam," she whispered. "We didn't tell you because—"

"Because someone would go and have a sneaky cup of tea with Aunty," Nancy said. "Or maybe a sneaky slice of cake. Isn't that right, eh, sister Leek?"

"Golly, is she all right?" Mary Bootle's voice said somewhere. "She's turned awful gray."

Happen Mary was talking about me. Happen she wasn't. But I weren't bothered because I wasn't looking at her. I was looking at a little woodlouse crawling along my sack edge and I was listening to a hissing noise. Sounded like a kettle was boiling itself up somewhere. Which was funny stuff.

"We should put her head between her knees. Come on, Clam, hush up."

"What do you mean?"

"Did she just say something?"

I tried hard to speak without that kettle drowning me up. "What do you mean about the tea?"

"Golly, she really is making ever such a funny noise."

I watched that woodlouse come crawling up. I don't think it was doing the hissing. It was wearing Aunty's face. "Keep 'em flapping," it said. "Keep 'em flapping." It winked and went crawling on past.

Dorothy's eyes came close to mine. Hands pressed on my

157

shoulders. "Clam, listen to me. You need to calm down. Try breathing into this sack."

Where was Nancy?

"WHERE IS NANCY?" Whatever else she did, Nancy Nunhead told the truth.

A voice was shouting, "What do you mean about the tea, Nancy Nunhead? Tell me what you mean about the sneaky tea, Nancy Nunhead!"

All sudden, Nancy's voice was heating up my left ear. "Alrighty, Clam, I will. Truly was getting better. And you went for tea with Aunty. And then that afternoon—well, we all know what happened to Truly that afternoon."

My belly flipped. Brown sick shot out of my mouth onto my smock.

And no one said nothing.

After a bit, I heard myself moan, "I loved Truly Polperro." I said Nancy's mouth was crawling with filthy lies and I loved Truly Polperro. "I loved Truly."

And happen my moans turned to howls, because after a bit Annie said, "Hush up, Clam, we know you loved Truly."

"I can't keep saying sorry for Jean Valjean forever, Nancy, I really can't. Like Aunty didn't already know he was missing. Like Aunty hadn't said, 'Kill off all swinefever piglets at once, before they threaten the whole herd and the sickness mutates to humans, wrecking all your Mother's plans for War.' Like I was to know Aunty would make you do his slaughter to teach you a lesson for hiding him. Like I was to know that."

Nancy spat on the sorry little woodlouse. "Nice piece of cake was it?"

"Can I help it if Aunty gives me cake sometimes?"

No one said nothing.

"It was a piece of cake, Nancy, that's all it was. And it tasted horrible. Anyway who was spying on me?"

No one said nothing.

"That ain't nice. That ain't sisterly, spying ain't."

"You should know," Nancy said.

"Am I the only one here who cares to try and keep Annie out of Bowels?"

Nancy spat on the floor. "Like you kept Truly out, eh?"

No one spoke, and Nancy's words lay there between us like corpse meat, to swell and burst with flies.

I wailed that it wasn't fair, it was hyperthermia, it wasn't my tea. This was just Nancy speaking nastiness because of that piglet. Everyone knew it was hyperthermia, didn't they, Annie? Overheating—Aunty said so. And I loved Truly, and Annie knows that, don't you, Annie?

And Annie said nothing. Annie said nothing at all.

After a bit Dorothy blinked and said, "Well, never mind all that now. We've got to hurry if we're going to get you through it tonight."

"Get who through what?" I said.

Nancy said, "But what are we going to do about her, eh?"

So Annie said, "I expect Clam would like to come with us."

"Where?" I said, sniffing up snot and wishing for a voice to come out and answer mine, just this once. "Come where?"

And Annie answered me then, she did. "Why, to the Wall, of course."

Outside the barn, one brave cloud had flung itself at the Demonmoon. Next door, the stone walls of Nursery Cottage were turned to shadows, the second-wind toddlers and third-wind Baby Sainsbury's safe asleep inside, like I wished I was. I pulled my headscarf low and wrapped my fur tight. Heaven's lights sparked icy through the holes in the drainage lid. So many up there that not even quick-fingered Truly Polperro could have pinch-measured them all. It was a feet-freezing night.

Annie shut the barn door and set off down the path. "Everyone stay close, and go tiptoes on the gravel," she whispered. "Someone keep a watch on Maria at the back."

And my sisters crept off after her, their torches making a yellow caterpillar, their sacks chinking with their steps, their breath puffing out in ice clouds. I watched them head west for the path to the turnips, not one of them stopping to say, "Where's Calamity Leek? Come on, sister, catch us up!" No, I watched them go, and I thought to turn back for the yard where some younger body—Millie Gatwick, say—would be welcoming of a cuddle. Then I thought about Annie. I thought how easy she had said to me she weren't doing nothing with them tools. And now she was heading for the Wall. My heart stopped dead a second. Weren't nothing for it, I set off quick after them.

Deep into the plum orchard, I caught up with her and grabbed her fur.

"You never told me, Annie. I asked you what the tools were for, and you never said the truth."

A brown owl leaped off a high branch and glided over us.

"And that ain't sisterly," I said, my voice shrinking off, so it near got lost in the night. "Annie, it ain't."

But Annie just shone her torch in front and kept on stepping.

We came to the fattest plum tree. Annie swung her torch down on Truly's mound. Dew bubbles shone on Truly's pebbled name. Annie swung her torch over the Boule heads and strawdolls, and the millipedes and dung beetles that were chewing over the soil, and she walked on.

I caught her again in the last of the plums, tugging on her smock to slow her steps. "I didn't send Truly to Bowels when I had my tea with Aunty, you know that, Annie. I would have done anything to keep her safe. You know that, don't you?"

Annie didn't look at me, but she did put out her hand for mine. "Step your feet in my torch puddle, Clam, you'll find it easier that way."

"Only, can you tell Nancy, please? Only, she won't listen to me because of that sick piglet. Which I only told Aunty about for all our safety. And you should know I would do anything to keep you safe, Annie, I really would."

Annie lifted a low branch and ducked out of the orchard. Under His deceiving moonlight, Sting Alley was shaped into soft gray feathers. "Run through here fast as you can, Clam. Stay close in my steps."

We didn't stop running until I felt my toes slide into bog. Out here the black night had melted into the ground, so there weren't no way of telling sky lid from soil. There weren't a sound but that of squelching sisters, clinking tools and my own panted breath.

"You know, Annie, we could still turn back," I said. "They'd all listen to you. Happen this midnight bog-stomping has been fun, but it's been quite fun enough."

Annie's eyes didn't shift off following her torch puddle.

"Thing is, Truly was nosy and look what happened to her.

161

I know you loved her, but it doesn't mean you have to end that way too. And if there ain't any injuns out there, but something worse—well then, it will lead to more than nonsense for you, won't it?" I tried to turn my voice nice and creamy. "I won't tell no one if you decide to turn round. If you hurt your toe all sudden, or get a bellyache, say."

Annie stopped. "But will it lead to nonsense?" She looked round to check on our sisters. I counted the breath clouds puffing out in the dark. Thankful, no one looked to have been sucked down to Bowels yet.

"What if it's stopping nosiness we're at, Clam? What if it's that we're doing?"

"Well, everyone knows you don't stop an itch by scratching it."

"But, see, I've been thinking. Aunty always says we are special—"

"—grown with special purpose, yes, Annie."

"Yes, of course, but here's the funny thing. Truly don't seem so special to Aunty now she's dead. So what if Truly's nosiness—all her wanting to fly, all her wanting to touch the sky lid—what if that was what actually made her special? What if that is what her purpose actually was?"

"Well, Annie, that is such a bottom-up way of thinking it's not even—"

"No, listen, Clam. Truly told me things she saw, and then she died. So I've been thinking, maybe my purpose is to take Truly's words and find out the truth of them. So when I find there's no injuns prowling Outside, we'll all be safe, and my own special purpose will be done."

Well, not even Evita Thrupp's sieve would have been able to sift sense from that. And I told Annie so. I said this way of thinking was just a brain set restless from grief. And she looked at me close then, a frown puzzling up her brow. "Is it really so wrong just to want to see what's out there, Clam? Is that really so wrong?"

"What if you get attacked by injuns?"

"I'm taking Nancy's blade. And I can run fast and climb trees."

"Well, worse then. What if you get cooked like Truly, so you come back with terrible words boiling up your brain, but you've turned dumb and you can't speak them, and you die off dumb as a worm?"

We had arrived at the Wall. I leaned a hand against its cold strong bricks, and I felt something calmer for it. "Please, Annie. Ain't you thought of that?"

Annie laid down her sack. "Happen I have, Clam. And what I actually reckon is this—even if I am dragged down to Bowels, even if, then at least Truly will be there. I will be with Truly. And how can that be so bad?"

And then I saw it—there was no stopping her.

We huddled close and stared.

The hole in the Wall winked back.

"What's it doing that for?" Mary Bootle wailed.

"Keep back," I said. "Nancy, get out your blade."

"It's only trees," Dorothy said, figuring it first, like usual. "Trees waving."

Feathered trees were waving their arms like winks through the little black hole where blind safety should have been. We stared at that hole to the Outside. A hole we hoped was big enough for Annie to squirm her skinny hips through, but shaped too tight to let any injuns jump in and tear us all to pieces. That's what we hoped.

All about our feet were clots of brick. And I looked at that hole we had bashed in our Wall, and I tell you this, it looked about as right as a smile when it's got a nerve-dangling gap instead of a tooth, or as happy as a pig with its intestines pulled out, or as pretty as a rose with a slug-swallowed bloom. Which is to say, it was a sore sorry sight and it turned my heart to pus to see it.

Two jackdaws bounced down on the bog. They hopped over and looked in the hole, and they looked at us, and they shook their silver heads and cracked open their beaks, and they laughed and laughed and laughed.

"Well then," Annie said loud, to shut them up. She stepped over to the hole, Nancy's butching blade in her hand.

"Well then," we said.

"I best be off then."

"Best had," Dorothy said.

"Wait up," I said, going over to Annie. Least I could do was check her headscarf was pulled down safe and her fur was buttoned tight. "You'll just have to watch your feet and ankles and hands and neck," I said. "And keep your ears sharp for whizzing arrows. And night's starting to fade, so don't go for long."

"Well then," Annie said, shrugging me off. She put an ear to the hole to Outside.

"Anything?" Dorothy said.

"Trees shushing." Annie turned back round to us. "You know, I was just thinking. I was just thinking someone could come with me. To help if I get stuck in an ambush. What do you think?"

Well, them clever jackdaws were the first ones to answer. They laughed and laughed and laughed. They bounced up and down and nudged each other, and shook their wings like they were so swelled with laughter their coats didn't fit them proper.

Nancy stepped over and jammed her shoulder at the hole. She didn't even get in sideways. "Sorry, Annie."

Annie looked at Dorothy.

Every bone in our sister's grasshopper body was rattling. Dorothy blinked ten times and pinched her nose, and then she came out with it. "Thing is, Annie, only Eliza's skinnier than you, really."

Eliza coughed like she was about to die off.

And I said, "And if someone is to be ambushed, ain't it better to be just one?"

Annie looked down at the bog, "Fair enough. I just wondered." Then she turned and threw herself at the hole. Her feet waggled like a fishtail jumping into water, and like that, she was gone. She had left Garden safety, our Aunty's purpose and all her sisters. But I had tried to tell her, and there was nothing to be done now but wonder if we would ever see her again.

THE DEMONMALE

I am letting him sit in this room when Mrs. Waverley is in it.

She lets him hold her hand. Which is foolish. But since she must be close to being completely cooked up now, she can't be expected to have any sense left inside her.

You tell me this is "Real Progress"—me doing this "letting him sit." You tell me lots of "Real" things these days, Doctor Andrea Doors. Like how the Real World is with men and women. You say, "This is how it Really works."

I listen to you talking about how it works with demon-males and females. "Men and women," you say, using Outside words all careful like I ain't never had a lesson on the Outside in my whole sorry life. How you reckon men help women make babies. How you reckon bits of men are grown inside all babies, even female ones. I look at him sitting there with his red ears and his hairy mouth, and I think of him living inside a baby like Baby Sainsbury's and I laugh and laugh and laugh.

And you ask me how I think babies are made.

So I tell you about the rose bushes, and us seeded snug in the buds and attached to the petal heart, like a feather to a hen.

"I see," you say. "And where did you learn this?"

Well, even Danny Zuko would know that, Doctor Andrea Doors, and he is a wireworm.

"Or would you rather not say?"

Well, ain't like it's a secret no more, is it? So I say, "In the Appendix."

"To what?" you say.

Which ain't but a dumb worm question.

"Or would you rather not tell me, Calamity?"

Over at the wall, the demonmale is pressing his hands into his knees, listening in to us. Like this is his business. Well, it will be, soon enough.

I say, "In the *Appendix to the Ophelia Swindon Biographical Archive*." Which is its full title. Which I don't expect you to understand, course.

"I see," you say.

Except you don't really see much, do you, Doctor Andrea Doors?

You don't see I am letting him sit in here because it's the easiest way to prepare him. Letting him feel safe. If I were Nancy, I might throw him an apple now and then, while I sharpen the blade.

PIGS

D awn clouds had glued up the sky lid gray as porridge. Off in the yard, the cockerels were shouting for their breakfast. Dorothy called through the hole a hundred times, but nothing answered but waving trees.

I faced my sisters, their eyes boggling cold and fearful. "Truth needs telling," I said. "This is it. If we stay longer, we are sure to be discovered and done for. That's it."

Mary Bootle let off a wail and plonked herself down on a sack. "But it's my turn to be at Nursery Cottage today. The second-winders need me to make breakfast."

"Well, Mary, the second-wind toddlers will have to forget you. Most probably we will all be locked away for mending. Most probably till we are all turned Liphook."

Maria Liphook, who hadn't a better game now than bashing at the Wall hole. Who had no interest in grubs, and had been bashing for as long as Annie had been gone. Who, when we pulled the ax off her, had sat down and stuck her arms Outside after those trees like she was saying, "Yoohoo, injuns, come and get me."

I flicked a look at our slowbrained sister and I sighed. "Happen I don't want to be turned mashhead, Mary Bootle. Do you?"

Dorothy ran to the hole and shouted, "Annie, come on back!"

Her words died off. No one said nothing but the cockerels in the yard. Even those jackdaws had gotten bored of laughing at us and flown off over the Wall.

"Truth needs telling, sisters."

Nancy squinted at the bog. "Spit it out then, Clam, before it chokes you."

"All I'm thinking is we should leave here now."

"No," Dorothy said. "We're not leaving Annie."

Nancy squinted at me. I could see she was working through the wisdom of my words. "Well, Dorothy, it ain't fair that we all get into trouble for it, is it, eh? We could leave Maria here to pull her out."

"If she comes back. If she ain't gone and been got by—" I didn't have the voice to finish it off.

Mary Bootle started up with wailing in her messy way, "Please don't say Annie's been gotten by injuns. Not injuns. No, please, no."

"Injuns?" a voice said loud behind us.

And there was Annie's bushy head, poking through the hole in the Wall. And never in my life have I been so happy to see them fizzing green eyes. "Who's talking about injuns? Come on, sisters, give me a hand and pull me through. I give you my word I'm not an injun."

169

It was in the pigs dorm, Annie told us what she'd seen.

Nancy's idea, the pigs. And it weren't a bad one. "We'll be safe and warm talking with them," she said. "And we can run back quick to our dorm if Aunty comes down early."

So there we were, in with the boars. Nancy was flat on her back, crawling with piglets. We others took one boar each. Aunty never minded us touching the pigs. "Practice makes perfect, nieces," she said. "A male is a male is a male, so you just tickle and stroke away."

Annie sat down by hairy Henry Higgins. I went for Caractacus Potts. Sandra got Joseph, and Mary and Eliza set to cuddling Bill Sykes, whose big old belly could take two sisters working him at once.

"Well?" Nancy said.

Annie didn't look up from where she was stroking one of Henry's front legs up and down the shin.

"Well?" I said.

Annie shrugged and kept on stroking.

"What?" Nancy said. "Come on, Annie. There must have been something."

"Trees," she said all quiet, her hand going up and down. Up to Henry's elbow and down to his trotter. "There really weren't nothing Outside but trees."

"Well, we all saw those," Nancy said.

"We all saw those," I said, "and we didn't go nowhere, Annie."

Annie shrugged.

170

No one said nothing. Then Dorothy said, "Well, what were they like, the trees?"

Annie sat up from Henry and scuffed up a space in the straw and drew a feathery triangle on the concrete. "Ones like that, going on forever."

"Well, we all saw those, and we didn't go nowhere," Nancy said. She kissed the tiddlers one by one and lifted them off her, because Oliver Twist was bashing his snout on the back yard door after getting out. "Happen you must have seen more than that."

Annie circled Henry's elbow, round and round.

"Annie?" Dorothy said. Dorothy was hopping about the straw, her brain rattling too crazy for pig-tickling. "You really must have seen more than that."

"I ran all the way round the Wall," Annie said. "I crossed a road that came out of two black gates tall as the von Trapp gates. And that was all I saw. Trees and two gates. No injuns nowhere. Not a whoop, not a feather, not an arrow."

Dorothy pinched her nose to stop it jumping. "Did you look real proper?"

"I've told you, there weren't nothing but trees." Though Annie's face was shining from being scrubbed off under the standpipe, her eyes had grown dull as mold.

"But I don't understand," Dorothy said.

"What's to understand?" I said, and I smiled at Annie. "It's plum simple, it really is. It being night, the injuns were all asleep in their caves. That's all there is to it. And that sure makes a happy end on it, don't it?"

Course, it wasn't like I was waiting on Annie to jump up and bone-hug me and say, "Well done, Calamity. Sorry for not listening to you in the first place and not inviting you along." No, wasn't like I was waiting on that at all. But never mind. I kissed Caractacus Potts all over his ears, and I smiled and said, "That sure makes a happy end on it, like I always said. Don't it, sisters? Don't it?"

Annie jumped up. "I'm mighty tired," she said, and she went through the gate into our side of the dorm.

JAPAN

Now I hadn't thought I would sleep after all that, but when the Communicator bing-bonged for breakfast, I was deep in a dream chasing Truly Polperro up a plum tree.

It was my nose woke me first, hungry for a whiff of her. I rolled onto her space, sniffing up her straw, hunting a scent of the plum juice she dribbled, or the pigs she rode backwards, or the petals she jammed down her toes—I was hungry for just one whiff of her busy breath and silly ways. There weren't one leftover smell of Truly about. And when I rolled over again, there was a concrete space where Annie and her straw should have been.

I sat up.

Dorothy Macclesfield was sitting up too. Her eyes were blinking at Annie's empty straw, like this time they couldn't ever stop.

There were words chalked out on the concrete—

**BEEN THINKING ABOUT THEM INJUNS' CAVES.
TRIED RUNNING ROUND THE WALL
BUT AIN'T TRIED RUNNING <u>AWAY</u> FROM IT.
WON'T BE LONG.**

"Oh no, oh no, oh no," Dorothy said.

"Oh yes, sister Macclesfield," I said, and I spat on every one of them foolish words, and with my smock sleeve I scrubbed the concrete clean.

Course, it got worse then. Course it did. The Communicator toot-tootle-oot-tootle-oooooooted, which was the sign of a Very Important Announcement. The Very Important Announcement was that a Very Important Announcement was going to be made at lunch, which was going to be a Very Important Occasion, with Very Important People in attendance. Goodness, it was going to be exciting. Anyone who wasn't drying out petals had better be in the kitchen chopping up a feast. Bring forth the patio heaters! Get your glad rags on! Rummage up some butching knives, Nancy, and tether Henry Higgins to the fence! As our dear Aunty was overwhelmed with the Very Importance of the Occasion, she was going to spoil her nieces with a perky little number called "Who will buy this wonderful morning?" "A purely rhetorical song," the Communicator said, "because some things in life are just too valuable to sell."

"Well, that's Annie complete and utter done for," Nancy grunted.

Weren't no one shouting over Aunty's rhetorical to go disputing that.

Mother drove into the yard at twelve o'clock, and must be twenty clouds puffed up to receive her. Sickly Eliza had turned on the patio heaters and Millie Gatwick had set out the trestle table with a cloth, a vase of dried Boules and fresh bread. Evita Thrupp bubbled up Danny Zuko's trotter stew. And I had laid out the cutlery neat and tidy.

The Communicator bing-bonged us into in line, heels against the dorm wall, quiet as church mice, please, to watch and learn table manners from civilized people. The Pontefracts wheeled down the second-wind toddlers from Nursery Cottage. Mary Bootle swaggered along with Baby Sainsbury's in her blue basket. Henry Higgins shook his ears and tugged against his tethering. And Annie St. Albans weren't nowhere to be seen.

"Welcome old friend, welcome loved one, on this most momentous occasion!" Aunty called out, swirling down from the High Hut in skirts wider than a cow, a tiara stuck in curly orange hair, and falling into a curtsey like she was Cinderellaing at a ball again. "Her Most Glorious Ladyship's Army, standing to attention, please!"

We saluted Mother and Mother parked up her electric chair on the far side of the table from us. Right opposite me, she stopped, looking as Heaven-cheeked, black-glassed perfect as normal, thank goodness. She gave Aunty a sorry nod. "Emily would like you to know that peach drains you, Miss Swindon. And one does suspect she's absolutely right."

And Aunty shook her finger at the air above Mother's head, and laughed like something sharp was stuck in her chest. "Ho ho ho. You are a one, Emily! Ho ho ho."

And Mother looked up Heavenly and cheeped like the most perfect chaffinch, "Isn't she just!"

175

And we all smiled, which is what you must do when people are laughing near you. And Henry tugged on his rope and whined.

"Stand at ease," Aunty shouted out. So we did. She clicked her fingers once and Mary Bootle ran up with the wine bottle. "Goodness, this is fun. Mangez à deux," Aunty said to Mother. "What do you say to starting with a cheeky little Beaujolais, while I spill the beans about my Very Important News?"

Mary poured the wine into Aunty's glass.

Mother raised a finger. So Millie Gatwick ran up and poured water into Mother's glass. Perfect dribble-free, she did it, I have to say.

Aunty clicked her fingers twice and Evita Thrupp ran off to the kitchen for the stew. And lined up at ease against the dorm wall, all us others opened our ears for catching something of this news. Aunty said, "Cheers" and drank off her glass, and Mother said, "Will you bloody well get on with it, Frumps."

Aunty smiled. "My contact in Kyoto says that subject to guarantees of virginity, he can probably shift three in the first batch. I assured him it wouldn't be a problem."

Mother jumped up out of her chair, so her water glass fell down on the table. But happen she hadn't made up her mind to go anywhere because she just punched up a fist and whispered, "At last" and sat down. Most fortunate she didn't look to be made wet.

Millie ran off to the kitchen for another glass, and Mother punched up her fist again at Heaven. Aunty sang out, "Three little girls from school are we!"

So as silly Sandra sang on, "Pert as a schoolgirl well can be."

So as Aunty shouted back "QUIET! Church mice are seen and not heard, Sandra."

"This is the best news since I don't know when!" Aunty said to Mother. "Since a teeny promotion in West Bromwich, probably. It's quite something, you know, breeding up a nest and watching them fly. Oh, but I mustn't get emotional, this is not about endings, it's new beginnings! This means a new lip—possibly a nose—maybe even some sort of prosthetic eyeball. It's life! Well, a chance at life at least!" Aunty drank off her glass, and Mary filled it right up. "Three now, perhaps another three in a couple of months! At this rate I'll be in South America in a year! Cheers!"

Aunty looked at Mother, who was smiling at the air. Aunty leaned close, "I was going to bring this up later, your Ladyship, but you know how I feel about the toddlers, and that new one. I know it's a sickness, but please, Genevieve, I beg you, return them now. Fifteen, we agreed, would be all the weapons you required. That's what we agreed. And now your weapons are primed and there are targets in sight, we are ready to go go go!"

Mother's chin tipped Heavenly away from Aunty.

"It's not as if they're speaking yet. You could dump them just about anywhere."

And Mother's voice hissed out Heavenly without her teeth opening at all, "Emily says she likes having them around."

"That's sweet of Emily, but forgive me for wondering, your Ladyship, but is it fair that I squander another decade simply because you have a problem controlling yourself in service stations? A bird born to sing cannot live out its days in a cage."

Mother said nothing but smiled up to Heaven, "Don't

177

worry, my darling, I will make those demonmales suffer like you suffered. Bone for your bone, blood for your blood—"

"South America is crying out for my music," Aunty said. "Don't you even want to know how much we're getting?"

Mother said nothing, so Aunty carried on, "It hasn't been finalized, but I expect we'll get fifty percent up front, and the rest on delivery. I've been told the Japs are top payers. I should imagine we'll clear one hundred K with this lot." And Aunty sat back so happy that she had to sing out "Don't cry for me Argentina" and finish off the wine bottle without Mary even doing the pouring.

I looked at Dorothy and I looked at Nancy, and though we needed to be quiet as church mice, my teeth were itching to start sorting meaning from this. Dorothy would know best if all this talk finally meant we were off to War.

Henry butted the fence. Mother turned to look at him. She nodded. "Good question, angelkins, I'll ask. Miss Swindon, darling clever Emily's wondering how we know they're ready for it. That when they're out there alone, they'll actually—"

Aunty chuckled, "Oh, they're ready all right. Let's do it now shall we? Nancy, fetch out the butching knives!" She drank off another glass, and swivelled around on her bale to face us. "Step forward, Sandra Saffron Walden, Annie St. Albans and Mary Bootle. Congratulations, you are Pick of the Crop! Top of the Pops! Prepare to receive some exciting news! Prepare to demonstrate Full Frontal Throat Slitting! You others, get ready for a chorus of 'Congratulations!' A one, a two, a one, two, three and—HOLD IT!"

Aunty's wineglass came flying over the yard and smashed on the planks above Dorothy's head. "Where is Annie?"

Aunty's bale went squealing backwards on the concrete. "Who has done what to Annie?"

Aunty was up and at us. And what weren't melted on her face was blotched purple. "WHERE HAS ANNIE ST. ALBANS GONE?"

It was "a sorry old scene," that's what Emily said to Mother and Mother said to Aunty, "and it's going to look cataclysmically unprofessional, isn't it, Frumps, to make our first delivery with a third of the order missing."

Emily was right about that, I know that for sure. There we were, stood in line with our arms stretched up to Heaven, praying to the Goddess Daughter to find Annie and bring her back quicksharp. And there was Aunty with Mr. Stick thrashing between our bodies, in case Annie was hiding somewhere in the line. Which we all knew she wasn't.

And I can tell you this—it doesn't take five minutes before this manner of praying seeds pain in a body. First off, your fingers turn to needles, then your blood clots up in your elbows, and after this your shoulders turn to stone. Soon enough, your arms are throbbing like a hundred wasps are stinging them at once. Nancy said this is when your hands may as well get chopped off and taken for pigfood.

Mother's voice came drifting over. "Oh absolutely, Emily, they do blub excessively, don't they? When, really, they shouldn't. Really, they should realize they are extraordinarily lucky. It's quite perfect, this Garden, for minors. Yes, angelkins, Mummy does wish her children's home had been more like this. Oh yes, angelkins, it is absolutely ideal for minors, fresh air, free-range, men-free."

All sudden, the air between me and Dorothy whooshed and split apart. Aunty's eye bulged red and blue and close. Her breath blew medicinal. "Calamity, dearest, I recall you promised to keep an eye on Annie for me. All that cake, sweetie. And our little deal."

Before I could stop them, my eyes went to Mother.

"Yes, niece, it's still up for grabs."

And my eyes looked on Mother's black glasses, and my mind ran away to thinking on them two eyes kept safe behind. Most probably they were gold like a comb of honey. Or gold like Aunty's medicine, or like the yolk spilling from a fresh-cracked egg. One of these golds, that's how Mother's Heavenly eyes would surely be.

Down the line, Eliza Aberdeen fainted, but Aunty kept her eye on me. "So, my little flap-eared friend, what's it to be?"

And I thought about telling the truth right then, and not just because Aunty's breath was rusting in my ear, and not just because I was her bestest pal, and not just because my fingers were ready to drop, and every other body's were too. No, I thought about telling it because everybody knows the truth needs telling, so I got myself ready to shout it. "Annie is gone off to the Outside, Aunty!" that's what I would shout. "Annie is gone through the Wall!" And like I say, I got my tongue ready for it.

Only my brain said, "Stop a minute, Calamity," and not just because Nancy's heel was inching toward my toes. No, see, if I did say on Annie going off Outside, well, Mother would surely spin her chair around and drive off in immediate distress, and nothing would be left but Aunty's voice swelling with rightful anger. And Aunty would say, "Weren't you watching Annie when she went through the Wall?" And

I would have to say, "Not this morning, I wasn't, Aunty. Sorry."

"Dear oh dear," she would say. "Deal's off then."

And she would be right.

And I wouldn't ever know about Mother's eyes, would I? No.

So I kept my face turned down to concrete, and I squeezed up my shoulders and sucked in my belly and bit on my lip, and I waited for Mr. Stick to correct me.

"Fickle as the wind," Aunty breathed in my ear, "that's your trouble."

She spun herself away from me and thwacked Mr. Stick into the Boule vase on the table—crash, bash, smash— shouting out about people letting people down, even the ugly ones. Where has loyalty gone in the world? Where? Where?

"There," Mother said. "There."

"Nowhere," Aunty howled. "That's where."

"No. Over there, Miss Swindon. There at the gate. What is that thing?"

Annie St. Albans, it was, flinging herself into the yard, her smock smeared yellow, her headscarf flapping loose, and a dead hen swinging from her hand. Like that made sense of everything.

Henry jerked his rope and snorted. Mother put a hand to her mouth and hissed like laughter. Aunty shoved up her hair and re-stuck her tiara. She didn't look anywhere but the table, as Annie skidded up and backed into her place between Dorothy and me.

"Nieces, not a word from any of you," Aunty said. "It seems the Goddess Daughter has answered your prayers. You may sit down. You, Annie St. Albans, may not. Get yourself over here. Stand behind me, and I don't want to hear a peep out of you, unless you'd like to receive a sound thrashing."

Aunty click-click-clicked all her fingers at once and yelled at Evita to fetch out Danny Zuko's trotter stew. Aunty didn't bother to look at Annie, because she said she didn't want some guttersnipe ruining her digestion. Only after Aunty had eaten three bowlfuls, did she turn round on her bale. "Niece St. Albans, how kind of you to—"

And Aunty's voice stopped.

For sure, she was a terrible wild sight, Annie was, with Desiree Armfeldt, our top-laying bantam, dangled head-down from her fist. But I don't reckon it was the sight of dead-meat Desiree that swallowed up Aunty's words. Nor was it the chickenshit shining on Annie's smock and hair. No, I reckon it was Annie's eyes that did it. Annie lifted her face and looked at Aunty, and even from the dorm wall, I could see that something had gotten itself trapped inside them eyes. It was like the tiniest splinters of the sky lid had trapped themselves in there, that's what it seemed.

Aunty wiped off her mouth on the table cloth and tried her voice again. "Well, niece, never mind that you missed the happiest news of your life. Never mind that your sisters' hands nearly fell off while they prayed for your safe return. Life is too short for blame, and besides, today I find myself in an uncommonly charitable mood. I suggest you make the most of it. Your explanation for this unacceptable absentee-ism is what exactly?"

Annie's face crumpled, "Oh, Aunty, I am sorry. Please for-give me. And please, Mother and Emily, forgive me. And sisters, please forgive me too." And here's the funny thing. Every word came out of Annie soaked in sorrow, but when she lifted up her eyes to look at Aunty, well, they just danced and danced and danced.

"Get on with it, girl."

"I know I've been foolish, Aunty. It's just I was cleaning the hen coops this morning, and poor Desiree Armfeldt here—" Annie lifted that bird so close, Aunty had to slap it away "—well, poor Desiree Armfeldt was nowhere to be seen. So I went off hunting for her—I mean only because of her being the top layer—any of the others I wouldn't bother over, but three-eggs-a-day Desiree is special. And I'm out in the bog looking for her, when I hear the *wok-wok-wok*ing. Full of fear it was. And I run back to the orchard, and surprise surprise, there's Desiree up the tallest Victoria plum. And she looks awful stuck. So I don't think of the danger and I climb up after her. And Desiree goes flapping to the end of her branch, and the branch breaks and she falls, and I fall—which I know is terrible clumsy of me—and I must have hit the sense from my head in landing, because the next thing I know, I'm waking up feeling something squeaky under me. And, well, Aunty, it seems in landing, I went and squashed poor Desiree Armfeldt to death."

Well. Weren't just Desiree Armfeldt open-mouthed at hearing this tale.

Aunty's eye crept across to the hen, who was looking, to say true, about half the width she was in life. "Let's see."

Annie held out Desiree.

"Your head, niece."

Aunty tugged off Annie's headscarf and rummaged under her curls. "You do feel a little feverish, niece. I guess we shouldn't take any chances if I'm to have you off my hands ASAP. Give that bird to Nancy, and get yourself washed off and into the mending room. I will be along to deal with you shortly."

Aunty's eye followed Annie to the standpipe.

Mother threw a bread lump at Henry's rump. "Good heavens, Miss Swindon, would you do one the honor of finally getting on with the demonstration? Emily says this side of the table has been extraordinarily patient. And one has to concur completely—she's right."

BATH

I ask Jane Jones for a butching knife today. She has taken
me for a wash in a tub. Which I would have said no thanks
to, but I am wheeled into another room for it, so we are safe
to talk without demonmale ears listening in to what isn't their
business yet.

Jane Jones turns on the taps, and under the water's noise
I ask her.

"Oh, goodness me, sweetheart, you don't need a knife,"
she says.

"I don't?"

"What's there to butcher in here?"

I think about the *K* pages in the Appendix, with all the
pictures stuck in—

Keep a knife in your knickers twenty-four-seven, because
you never know when the perfect opportunity will arise.
Mother requests you get one ASAP on arrival Outside. It

needn't be much—a stiletto (see A. below) or even some kind of Swiss Army jobbie (see B.) will probably do.

"Does Elizabeth Jones not have a knife?" I say.

Jane Jones turns off the tap and fixes me with a stare, which she does very well. "No, she most certainly does not!" And Jane Jones huffs and puffs and turns the taps, so they gush the Goddess Daughter's own steam out. And for a moment, I watch her puffing, and I think she's going to go up right now, ascending in the steam, leaving me to start the War on my own. And I think maybe I have spoken of things that aren't to be spoken of Outside.

And BTW, mum's the word about our plans, nieces! Careless talk costs lives!

"I am sorry, Jane Jones," I say quick. "I don't need a knife."

"No, of course you don't." Jane Jones looks at me, and she stops huffing and puffing and smiles. "Nasty things, knives," she says. And then she adds a wink.

So I wink back, course.

Like that, we are understood without careless talk. Just like it is written. And I wonder what sort she will bring me. And how soon it will come.

Though I am dropped in something like a potato in a pot for boiling, I tell Jane Jones I reckon I could get to like sitting in warm water. Special this water. Because Jane Jones has put gardenia oil in it. Because she says she knows how I like roses. And I know when she says that, really she means she's making me clean and perfumed as a petal for what I am going to do very soon. It's very important to smell good, because—

Just as a rose lures the honeybee, a sweet-smelling perfume entices intimacy.

186

Jane Jones presses a button and I am brought back out of the bath. It is like a flying machine. Straight off I think of Truly. Truly who never liked nothing so much as going up high. It is like flying, Truly, I whisper in my head, in this swinging machine.

I listen in my head for a Polperroey giggle. But Truly doesn't say nothing back.

Jane Jones rubs me about in a furred white sheet. "That's you squeaky clean," she says. "Would you like to try some gardenia body cream? It smells divine."

"Yes," I say. "Lots, please. All over."

SAM

That same afternoon of Mother's visit it happened, Annie told us the news I'll remember even when I'm pruning in Heaven.

"His name is Sam Matthews," she said.

And nothing in our Garden was ever safe again.

Course, she had already started talking plenty before I found her. It took me a little while, so the first I heard of it was whispering through the door of the end shitting stall in the latrine hut. And when I swung the door back, well, it weren't just Annie in there, but all of my elder sisters, squished in tighter than a nest of earwigs round the stinking drop-hole. Sisters, who, I don't mind saying, were supposed to be hosing off the yard after a "roller coaster of a demonstration." But were they? Course not.

"His name is Sam Matthews," Annie was saying.

"Who?" I said, batting back the dung flies jumping at my face. "Whose name?"

"Oh, hello, Clam," Dorothy said, her fingers rubbing busy at stains on her smock. "We were just talking."

"About what?"

No one said nothing.

My eyes prickled. "This ain't fair, sisters."

I watched Dorothy look over at Annie, and Annie give a nod.

"About the demonmale that Annie met," Dorothy said.

And I near fell headfirst down the drop-hole at that.

"I'm sorry?" I said.

Annie looked quick at me. She was wedged in the corner, under the ridge of the metal roof. Even in the latrine gloom, I could see her eyes were shining.

"His name is Sam," she said.

"You spoke to a demonmale, Annie? You spoke to a demonmale? Oh, Annie, you spoke to a demonmale?"

FLAP! Nancy smacked a dung fly against the wall. "Ears not working today, eh, sister Sneak?"

"But Annie—" I felt every drop of my blood begin to shake "—but Annie—well, Annie—oh, Annie. Oh sisters, happen we must prepare right away. We thought we would go Outside for War. But it has come in here for us." And I turned to run out fast as I could with this terrible news.

Except I didn't move. A fat hand had hold of my smock.

"Why don't we all sit down in the corridor?" Dorothy said. "There's too much stink in here for all this news."

The corridor inside the latrine hut smelled something sweeter than the shitting stalls, because we kept the floor planks scattered with petal dust and nailed dead bunches to the walls. The light bulb hung low over our heads. It was always a good place for chatting, because one of us could sit

189

her back against the door and stop nosying younger sisters coming in. Which Nancy now did.

Dorothy, Sandra and Eliza slid down the end wall. Mary sat on the bucket of paper rolls, and Annie went cross-legged in the corner by the sawdust bin. Straight off, she started emptying scoopfuls of sawdust all wasteful onto the floor. But I didn't say nothing to her doing that, I slid myself into the corner opposite, and I kept a watchful eye.

"Well then, Annie," Dorothy said. "This was out in the trees, you saw him?"

"The demonmale," I said, my belly sprouting out maggots at the word. "Where she saw the demonmale."

Annie smiled. "Sam Matthews was how he said it. He said, 'Oh, I'm Sam Matthews.'"

"And?" I said.

"And I spoke back to him, Clam."

"But normal demonmales are too scared to wander this close by," I said. "Oh, Annie. Must have been he was an injun. Oh, Annie, you spoke to an injun."

Annie scooped up sawdust and kept her smile at me. "He said he wasn't one."

"Well, we can't believe what a demonmale says, can we? And most certain of all, not an injun, we can't."

Annie sprung her fingers open so the sawdust went draining to the floor.

"We can't, Annie. Did you check him for feathers or redskin?"

"I said he wasn't an injun, Clam." Annie smiled. "He didn't look nothing like one."

"Happen he painted his skin pink and he hid his red feathers to fool you. Oh, Annie, I think your brain is cooking up!"

Annie looked at me and she snorted.

"Annie!" I was jumped up. "Annie!"

Annie shook her head and her snorts grew to laughter.

And horror squeezed my words to screams and my finger to pointing. "Sisters, see her grinning mouth? See her dancing eyes! What does she look like, sisters? She looks like a baby sat in the Sun that's laughing while it doesn't know it's getting scalded, that's what! Didn't I say nothing comes from nosiness but nonsense? Didn't I say that? But did Annie listen, or did Annie go out nosy and get cooked up by a demonmale injun? Didn't I say this would happen? Didn't I say that?"

"Hush up, Clam. Sit down." This was Dorothy, come up to me, pressing the shake out of my shoulders. "We must all think logical now. Slow and logical."

But I couldn't stop. I was spinning about after my terrible thoughts. "It's too late for logical, Dorothy. But, all right then, very well then, here's logical for you, Dorothy. The Devil spotted the hole in the Wall and brought a demonmale to check us out. Except He made this one not look like an injun, so we'd be deceived. And Annie plum fell into His trap. Headfirst, she did. Look at her burning eyes! Oh, Annie, say goodbye to Japan. We will need to fight them outside our very own Wall. They could come any second. They could be here now."

"Now?" Sandra screamed.

"Oh, there is so much to do!"

My face was slapped twice. Nancy, I think it was. Sandra and Mary were wailing. Eliza fainted off.

"Calm down," Dorothy said, never mind her own head was rattling circles. "Can everybody please just calm down."

Only Annie was still smiling unbothered when Dorothy

191

had propped up Eliza in the corner and said, "Now, do we all agree it sounds most frightening, and we will have to do something? Good. But do we also agree we should listen to Annie first? Yes? So, Annie, if he wasn't dressed like an injun, tell us what he looked like, this demonmale."

Annie dug her fingers deep in her sawdust pile, and smiled. "I don't know, really. Like us, but not actually like us. He was young like us, but taller than us, with Sandra's black hair and a drop of gray in his eyes like Clam."

"No," I said. "No, thank you."

Annie let out the sawdust through her fingers. "He actually looked like any of the ones we see in the Showreel. Like one of the ones on the barricade, maybe, but without so much hair, and without the demonic obsession with shooting guns."

"Indications of their demonic obsessions can be well concealed, Annie, but sure as meat makes flies, demonmales have them."

Dorothy nodded to that. "Did you notice any other Demonic Indicators on him?"

"Like a Demon-boil bobbling on his neck?" I said. "Which the Appendix says is the clearest Indication he's jam-packed full of fire. So jam-packed he's storing extra in his throat. That can't be missed, Annie."

"Couldn't really tell."

"Can't be missed, Annie."

"He was wearing a coat, OK, Clam."

FLAP! Nancy jammed a bluebottle on the door frame. "Did you see his Thrusting Tool?"

"No, I didn't."

"Well, good," I said. "Because that needs a lot of care looking. Because if he took out his Tool, it would be only a second or two before he shoved you on the ground and thrust it in you, and squirted his fire in you. And then, Annie, unless you had a knife to hand to cut his throat quick, you'd be certain done for."

"I didn't see it, Clam." Under her speckles, Annie's face was pinking up.

"Maybe this one didn't have one," Sandra said.

"Course this one had one," I said. "Demonmales all have them. It was probably sneaking in his trousers."

"Well, I didn't see it, all right!"

"But there must have been other Demonic Indicators you saw," Dorothy said. "Try to think, Annie."

"Well, course, there are plenty Annie should have seen," I said, doing my best to remember—remembering Aunty, the first time she opened up the big black casing to read out the Appendix to the *Ophelia Swindon Archive* to me. "I'm compiling a file for you girls," she said, pouring out our tea into the rose cups. "It's going to reveal how you lot are as joined to me as an appendix to a gut. Umbilically. There may be times in the yard, my little friend, when questions will come to be asked about the purpose of your existence," Aunty tapped the book's hard edge on my nose, "and it's all here, niece. Answers to everything under the Sun. Digest and disseminate this knowledge wisely. I'm counting on you, my flap-eared friend."

"There are plenty," I said. "*I* is full of Indicators to watch out for. The first is Female Murder, that's the clearest Indication of maleness. Others are General Impatience and Frequent Warmongering. Course, all demonmales have an Obsession with Fire. They like starting Fires—particularly in Sunny weather. They like to roast flesh on the Fires and pretend they're roasting things down in Bowels."

"Evita likes roasting things," Sandra said.

"Also Fornication. I forgot that. Their Obsession with Fornication is constant. And Fornicating Magazines. Which are things they look at while sharpening their Thrusting Tools. Which is what Fornication means, Eliza, if you don't know it yet. It means they are Obsessed with Thrusting. That's all their brains were made for—telling their Tools to Thrust females to death. They would Thrust their Fire inside females all day and all night if they could. Matter of fact, Annie, did you see him walk?"

"Of course, Clam."

"And was there a Thrusting stride to it?"

"Like what?"

"Like a cockerel maybe?"

"No."

"You sure you looked proper?"

"Yes, Clam. He was picking mushrooms."

Well, that took a moment's thinking on.

"Curious," I said. "Certainly cunning. A demonmale's disguise is various and happen it might involve mushrooms. But you said, mighty foolish though you were, Annie, you spoke to him?"

Annie was back to swirling her fingers in the sawdust mound.

"Did he listen up? Only them Never Listening to a Female is another sign."

Annie sighed. "You know, he really doesn't sound like all these things you're saying. I mean, I don't remember seeing one Indicator. First off, he jumped when he saw me. Like he was the scared one."

"But Annie, demonmales are not known for any quick

194

manner of movement unless they are chasing a ball. Are you sure about that? Try to remember it proper."

"From the beginning," Dorothy said.

Annie sighed. "All right. I was heading away from the Wall and not ten minutes out, I stepped into a clearing. There's a tumbled tree with its roots stuck up like chicken feet and a spread of moss around it. Well, he was there, rummaging in the moss and he heard me, and he turned and jumped back and said, 'Jesus! Who the hell are you?'"

"Well, there you go, Annie. An Indication of Demonic Inquisition right there. A clever trick—playing scared—but he gave himself away with this question."

"He jumped back, but I didn't move forward, so he calmed down and called over, 'Sorry, you gave me a shock.' And I shouted, 'Sorry' and, 'Are you an injun?' And he said 'What?' and he began to walk towards me. He walked slow as a cat. And here's the funny thing, sisters, and I can't tell you why, but I wasn't scared."

Annie looked up and smiled. And that simplebrained baby sat in Sunny danger came shooting back to me. And all my skin shivered to think on it. "You let him come up to you, Annie? Are you a total loonhead?"

But Annie kept on talking like she hadn't heard me.

"'Sorry,' he said, coming up—he's quite tall, you know, sisters—'I never expect anyone to come out here,' he said. 'Well, you've come, obviously. Um, sorry, did you just ask me if I was an engine?' And he smiled—it was something nice and neat and wondering.

"'An injun,' I said. 'In. Jun.'

"'In. Jun? What's one of them?'

"So I had to tell him what they looked like, and he said,

195

'Um, do you actually mean In-de-an? And, no, I'm not.' And he seemed to think this was something funny. 'Anyway, aren't you supposed to call them Native Americans now? Sorry, do you actually think that for real? An In-de-an in Snowdonia?' And he still seemed to think this was funny. So I said quick-sharp it wasn't.

"And he said 'Sorry,' and he said 'Wow,' and he looked at his shoes a bit—and then he looked at me—his eyes are shiny as stream pebbles, did I tell you?—and he said, 'You must be from that St. Emily's, right? I mean it's actually your land we're on, so I guess it's me that's trespassing, so—um—apologies and all that. Hi. Um. Hello.'

"And I said 'Hello.' And I felt my cheeks heating up, so I looked away."

"Blushing, Annie. Preliminary Warming of the Body was happening in you."

"Shut up, Clam." Nancy stamped on a bluebottle, "I'm enjoying the story."

"And I'm counting Demonic Indicators," I said, and I licked my finger and drew a number two on the floor. "Go on, Annie."

"I spoke next. I said, 'Who are you anyway?'"

"And that's when he told me his name. 'Oh, I'm Sam,' he said. 'Sam Matthews.'

"So I said, 'You better be careful, Sam Matthews. I have a butching blade under my smock, you know.'

"Except that seemed to make him more puzzled than scared, because he said, 'Wow. OK.' Then he grinned and held up a paper bag, and said, 'You're better armed than me.'

"I said, 'I am Annie St. Albans.' And he said, 'Um, well,

it's nice to meet you, Annie St. Albans.' And he grinned and put out his hand, so I shook it like Aunty told us to. It was quite soft, actually, and cool.

"'So, Annie St. Albans,' he said, 'can I tempt you with a mushroom?' "

"You didn't take it, Annie? Tell me you didn't take it."

Annie stabbed her fingers in the sawdust. "'They're not bad raw,' is what he said. And he took a handful out of his bag. One he turned upside down and said, 'Feel that—isn't it softer than a mouse ear?' One was hard as a hoof. One he called a trumpet, one an ink cap. He said he was avoiding an assignment from hell, and he was waiting for something called opening time at the Crown. He pulled out a red-headed mushroom with white spots. This one was poisonous. But this was what he was really after."

"Oh, Annie!" Dorothy jumped up, rattling all over. "Doesn't the *Digest Woodland Manual* say on mushrooms making bodies sick to death? I'm going to go get it."

"Look at her face, Dorothy, she is redder than a blood boil," I said, jumping up and pointing. "And look at her eyes! I knew there was something wrong with her eyes!"

"He wasn't like a nasty demonmale!" Annie shouted back. "Nothing like! It really is the Devil's own job to tell you sisters anything."

Annie swirled her sawdust a while, and nobody spoke. Then she said all quiet, "He didn't say 'Eat the poisonous one,' OK? He actually said he might 'give it a go with a couple of mates,' because he didn't fancy trying it on his own. He put the mushroom back in his bag, and he laughed and said it sure wasn't one for his Mother's soup, that was for sure. And

I went along and sat next to him on the trunk, and he didn't thrust me neither, not one bit. All right with you, sisters? Good."

And Annie stamped her heel. So I told her I couldn't see what she'd got herself so itchy about—her sisters were only worried for her, when it was clear and certain she was not.

Dorothy sat down. "I'm sorry, Annie. Go on to the end. We won't interrupt you. What happened next?"

"If you don't interrupt."

"We promise."

"Clam, too?"

"Clam?" Dorothy said.

"I suppose." But I kept myself standing between Annie and the door.

"Well, then he said, 'May I tempt Miss St. Albans with another mushroom?' 'Another mushroom?' I said. And it's funny to say, sisters, but that word shapes your lips so funny that we both burst out laughing. 'Mushroom?' he said. 'Another mushroom?' I said. It got so we couldn't even say the word because we were laughing so much. Laughing till I had to hold my sore stomach in. Laughing like it weren't ever possible to stop." Annie grinned at us, "Silly, really."

Well, I looked back hard. "Mushroom," I said. "Mushroom. No, sorry, Annie, it ain't working on me. Try it, sisters. Mushroom. Mushroom. Mushroom. Not a giggle, Annie. Not one."

"Well, it made me and Sam laugh."

"Was there forking on his tongue? Bad breath?"

"What?"

"Indicators, Annie. Oral Stinking."

Annie still couldn't zip up her smile. "I guess. I wasn't close enough in to—"

"Don't guess, Annie! Not with your own safekeeping."

"Well then, no. There was no stink from him. Listen to me, sisters—"

She had stopped smiling. Now she looked round us like she had some terrible truth she needed us to know. It was like we were going to find out all over again that Truly was dead, it went bad as that, Annie's look. "He was nice, you know. He wasn't Demonic. Not at all, he wasn't. I'm sorry, but he was nice. Nice. That's all."

No one said nothing.

Annie swirled her finger in the sawdust mess on the floor.

"Was it nicer than sisters laughing together?" Mary said.

Annie was silent.

"Well?" Nancy said.

"It was different."

"How different?"

Annie shrugged. It was a big snaky S she was swirling in there.

"How different, Annie, eh?"

"Just was, Nancy, it just was."

And round about then, as we were trying to measure the terrible cooking that had started in our sister, the latrine door opened. Maria Liphook was standing on the step, holding out a fistful of dried roses at Annie.

"Go away," Nancy said.

Maria went.

Annie stared after Maria awhile. She shook her head. All sudden, she snorted. "'Mushroom?' he said, and sisters, I laughed till my stomach felt like Nancy had punched it inside out."

"You've told us about the mushrooms, Annie. And we've told you they ain't funny. What happened after?"

She shrugged. "We stopped laughing, and I said, 'I need to go now, my sisters are waiting.'

"He said, 'Which way are you heading?'

"But I didn't tell him this."

"You did well," Dorothy said.

Nancy stamped a fly with her heel.

"I said 'Goodbye, then.' He said 'Goodbye, then.' Then he looked down at his shoes and said, 'Um, I don't suppose, I mean, will you come back tomorrow? I mean I'll be here if you do come. Same time, same place. Um, if you fancy it.'

"I said, 'Sure.' And he went even redder, and he looked up and smiled quick and looked back down at his shoes, and said, 'Well, that's great then.'

"And that's it, sisters. That's him. That's Sam."

Annie had stopped talking and was shrugging her shoulders and smiling.

I gave her a proper iced stare. "But you won't go back, of course you won't. You were lucky, Annie, that it was only Charming he did to you. Happen he was warming you up for his Thrusting. Now, who is coming with me to tell Aunty that a demonmale was wandering so close by?"

Annie jumped up, "No!"

I turned for the door.

And Annie shoved the sawdust bin so it crashed over.

And in the choking dust she came at me. With a roar in her throat. With fingers as claws to rip me. Just one inch away, she tore her fingers into her own hair instead. She cried out,

"No, you will not, Clam, you will not tell no one about this. Please. Please, you will not go for him with blades. He didn't look Demonic, nothing like. His name is Sam. Sam Matthews."

And while I was still crouching from her, she shoved past me, sobbing. I heard the slam of the latrine door, and her sobbing and shouting in the yard for Maria Liphook. Did Maria want to go with her to the orchard to talk to Truly Polperro? Annie had a lot to tell Truly. Annie was off right now.

My sisters coughed and shook themselves of dust. Eliza sneezed.

"You OK, Clam?" Nancy said, turned brown as a fat woodlouse. "I ain't never seen Annie taken like that."

"Mushrooms," I said, "doing that." I shook out my headscarf. "Sisters, listen. Happen the only answer is to get Annie locked up safe, and this demonmale sorted—if he is just one. Who's coming with me to tell Aunty?"

"Wait up, Clam." Dorothy brushed dust from where it was stuck to the stains on her smock. "I can't but think this is something curious, isn't it?"

"A demonmale's Charm working on Annie so she can't see the wood from the trees? That is exactly what the Appendix says happens to the weak-minded female when she meets a male. Exactly."

Dorothy nodded. "Only, I do want to know why there aren't no injuns out there like there should be. I really do want to know that."

"Well, we can ask him before we stick him in the throat."

"Also, I'm thinking there weren't so many Demonic Indicators, were there, in this Sam?"

Nancy stamped her heel at a fly and missed. "Annie sure didn't think so."

"Sam," Sandra sighed. "Funny word, ain't it, Sam?" Like now Annie had swallowed it up, Sandra wanted her taste of it too.

"Well?" I said. "Who's coming with me?"

Dorothy pinched her nose. "Why doesn't this feel right?"

"Because it ain't, Dorothy. Sisters laughing and eating and sitting with demonmales. Nothing ain't right, Dorothy. And sad to say, it ain't been right with Annie since Truly died."

Dorothy nodded. "Still, you know what I think? I think perhaps no one best say nothing to Aunty just yet."

"But Dorothy—"

"Not yet, Clam, not today. Let's just watch Annie for today. Aunty's always saying sleep on things you ain't sure on, and an answer will pop up in the morning. That's what I reckon we should do."

"But Dorothy—"

"As long as Annie is safe, and she will be today. We should cover up the hole to be sure."

"But Dorothy—"

"Thank you, Clam, we know what you think. What about everyone else?"

Sandra said, "I'll think whatever you say, Dorothy, long as I go to War first."

Eliza was woken up and said she thought she was cold.

Mary danced her plaits about and sang, "Sam Sam Sam."

And Nancy, well, Nancy just went off to feed the pigs.

"I'll keep an eye on Annie," Dorothy said. "Let's just watch and see today, Clam, watch and see." And blinking and nodding, she went off after our demon-charmed sister into the yard.

BIRMINGHAM

I counted out fifty rabbits skinned and boned before the
door opened up to me.

Aunty's eyeball peered out, red and something sticky, like
a slug had just slid across on its way to die. "What is it now,
niece Leek? Can you never leave me alone?"

I looked down at my toes on the metal balcony. "Aunty,"
I said, "I've come to tell you about Annie and the Wall."

See, I had tried to talk to Dorothy, I really had. I tried to talk
sense to her after supper, when I found her in the schoolroom
with Fantine, Cinderella and Adelaide. They were sat in a
bale circle under the light bulb. Dorothy had *The Rose
Lover's Digest* out and our younger sisters were copying onto
boards.

Straight off, I said it. "You said you'd keep a watch on
her, Dorothy."

"Oh hello, Clam." Dorothy looked up, blinking, from the sentence she was writing on Fantine's board. "Annie, you mean? Well, where is she?"

"Pulling cartwheels in the yard, Dorothy."

"I see. Is that bad then?"

"Cartwheels, Dorothy. She's supposed to be embroidering cushions in the mending room."

Dorothy pinched her nose and slipped a smile at Fantine.

"And before that, she was playing chase-the-injun in the yard with Maria. And before that, she was giving Fantine Welshpool here a ride on Tracy Turnblad."

"So?"

"She was down on today's duty list for milking Tracy. Milking her, Dorothy. Not riding her. You were supposed to be watching her."

"Well, thankful you did it for me."

"Am I the only one who cares to keep the Garden safe, Dorothy? Am I?"

"Look here, Clam. It's good of you to tell me about Annie, it really is. But, you know—" she pointed at her board "—I am in the middle of a lesson."

"Like knowing how to write out 'The Floribunda prefers a temperate clime' is going to help Cinderella and Adelaide and Fantine when the demonmales have dragged them off to roast on a spit in Bowels."

Fantine started to wail. Dorothy didn't say nothing.

"Well, anyway, I don't have time to talk," I said, spinning about, "I just thought you should know, is all."

See, I was thinking there might be something set down in the Appendix to help us prepare for this Sam Matthews, something I had forgot. So I hurried on over to the bookshelf, where it sat by the *Digests* ever since Aunty said it could stay down here for general reference by clean-fingered sorts only—"A.k.a. you, my dearest Calamity Leek."

And I reckon I might as well tell you, here was where it all started. Right here, seven years ago, Aunty found me hid under the bottom of these very bookshelves, one night after the bedding-down bing-bong had sounded. "We found each other that night," Aunty liked to say. "Flap-eared, one-eyed love."

Course, I had thought to get corrected for being Out of Bounds at bedtime. Especially when there was zipping to finish on fifty cushions. Except Aunty didn't bring Mr. Stick that night—like she often didn't bother with it back then.

"Yoohoo," Aunty had said, her eye boggling at me. She crouched close. "What's up, my little friend?" She was wearing her night moisturizing gloves, and them white fingers beckoned me out of the dust. "Shelves are for mices not nieces, darling."

Except I couldn't say I couldn't get into the dorm for not knowing the right word for opening the door, could I? It was Truly and Annie started it—saying a word which everyone had to whisper down the line at teeth-brushing time. But funny thing was, I must have heard it wrong. Truth be told, right then I couldn't say much, for crying into the bottom of Aunty's robe.

Which was when Aunty took my hand and stood me up. And she looked at me and then she wiped off my face on her robe, and invited me up for tea. And while I had tea in a pink rose cup, she read a story which she said was the first book written about a little girl just like me—a girl called Ophelia, who was also crying. Ophelia was crying because she was

going to dancc a turn at the "Good Shepherd Home's Yule-
tide Show!" on December 18, 1972. Except the shoes she had
been lent were too small, and Gennie and Frannie and all the
other Shepherd girls who had their own shoes were jumping
around her, practicing their favorite song—"Fifi-Frumps,
the dancing lump, a ten-ton truck would make a smaller
dump"—which they reckoned on singing on stage.

I was very taken with this little Ophelia. By the time she
had finished dancing and hadn't tripped up once, I had forgotten all about my sisters and the silly door.

Aunty shut up the book. "I thought you'd enjoy that."

"Is there more?" I said.

"Heavens, yes! I was quite the Pepys of my dorm." Aunty
sighed and stroked the kitten on the book cover. "What a trip
down memory lane that was, niece! We should do it again
sometime." She reached over and patted my knee. "More
tea?"

And simple as that, it started—me having tea in the High
Hut, and Aunty's memories got churning again "after a long
old drought."

"We'll have our own little book group, you and I," Aunty
had said. "And do you know what, niece, I think I am going
to nominate you my official aide memoire, I think I am
going to do that! Because it's good to talk, niece, it really is."

And now I listened to Dorothy hushing Fantine, and I flicked
a silverfish off the back of the Appendix, and without even
opening it to the index, I knew what needed doing.

I left the schoolroom and headed straight up to the High
Hut.

"Aunty," I said, "I want to tell you about Annie and the Wall."

The door was open. A thin slice of light dangled about like fat on hanging bacon. "Aunty," I said, pushing the door, "I want to tell you—"

Except when I went inside, I couldn't finish my words off.

See, Aunty wasn't wearing no more than a brown bra and pink pants. She was drinking medicine, and trying to trap up clothes and hair and teeth inside a suitcase on the bed. Her room was all turfed up, like angry magpies had got in and then got angrier. Toto ran out from under the bed and snapped at me and ran back under. The mirror was smashed on the floor. The television in the corner was dead.

"Are you preparing for War, Aunty?" I whispered. It was about all I could think to say.

Aunty turned from her case, swinging the medicine bottle. "Who the hell are you? How did you get in here? Did you follow me?"

"Aunty," I said, "it's me. It's Calamity. Your pal."

"Did you follow me?"

"I didn't follow you, Aunty."

Aunty drank her medicine. Her eye crawled over me.

"It's Calamity Leek, your niece, Aunty," I whispered to my feet.

"That's ridiculous, girl." Aunty swung away and set to slamming down the top of the case, "I was brought up in a home. How could I have any nieces?"

I wanted to ask her if I had said something wrong. But then I didn't. I thought to ask her if her hands wanted some cream from the pot by the bed. But then I didn't. My feet wanted to turn and run. But then there was Annie. Annie and the demonmale.

It was hard work for Aunty to slam up the case. Sweat seeded all over her skull, and she needed a long old drink when she finished. Truth be told, she looked so ill I didn't want to say about Annie and the demonmale just yet, so I asked her if it was Danny Zuko's stew making her poorly. Which she didn't understand. So I asked if she was going to have a holiday from us, which she did sometimes, for the sake of her health.

Aunty stared at me. "What did you say your name was?"

"Calamity Leek."

Which Aunty found very funny.

"You named me, Aunty."

"I did? Well, I never." And Aunty found this so funny her belly shook about with laughing, and she fell back on top of the suitcase on the bed, and started up singing, "I dreamed a dream in time gone by." And then she sat up sharp and said, "A holiday? You could say that."

Which was terrible news, what with everything with Annie happening. And I knew I really had to try to say about it. And I got ready for it. Except all sudden Aunty let off a wail and said look what was about to happen to her, just when she could almost sniff the pampas grass.

And I whispered, "What?"

And the telephone went ringing on the table by her pillows. And Aunty fell on it.

"Tomorrow morning?" Aunty gasped. "So soon?" And her hand went to her heart.

Words came out in one stringy breath—

"What does he want to see?"

"Forgive me, your Ladyship, I know you don't know, but didn't you ask?"

"Sorry, your Ladyship, I know it's a shock for you too."

"Of course, your Ladyship, I know you didn't snitch."

"I'm sorry, your Ladyship, I would never ever imply you did."

Aunty had to stop to lick up some pills from a heap on the table by the bed.

"Yes, I am still here. Birmingham, I thought."

"The burka, of course."

"Please don't take him upstairs, whatever you do."

"Sorry, your Ladyship. I understand how inconveniencing it is for you."

"Yes, I realize how much you've done for me. Yes, I know I'd be nowhere without you. Nowhere at all."

"Slopping out? I would be, you're very right."

"Thank you, your Ladyship. Thank you for everything."

"Should I call you tonight from the hotel?"

The phone fell out of Aunty's hand and hit itself against the table. Aunty fell back on the bed with her medicine bottle in her hand. Some seconds later she was snoring.

"Excuse me, Aunty," I whispered near her ear.

Aunty jumped up. "What was that?" The medicine bottle crashed down on the floor and Aunty shrank from me, like I'd jumped out of the carpet to eat her. "What the hell are you doing up here, niece? Don't you know to knock?"

"Annie St. Albans," I whispered, my feet starting a twist for the door. "Only, Aunty, I really need to tell you—and never mind if you don't cut the deal with Mother's eyes—only, Aunty, I really need to tell you—"

Aunty clapped her hands over her ears and her body

stiffened. She started screaming. Worse than a gutted pig it sounded, and it glued my feet to the floor in fear. "Get out," Aunty screamed. "Go, like I should have gone. I should have gone. The second she started laughing I should have turned and left. Go, go, go."

Aunty sagged back sudden boneless against her pillows.

I grabbed the cream pot from the table and held it out.

"Not that I had anywhere to go. I told her that. 'The cops are after me, I am ruined,' I said. 'Desperate.' "

"It's Calamity Leek. It's your best friend, Aunty. Your pal. Would you like your cream?"

But she wasn't listening to me.

" 'I have nowhere to go,' I said. 'Will you give me shelter?' And you, Genevieve—always the cutesy one, always the Fathers' favorite, standing at the gates of the home we had all shared, but that was yours now, just yours—you looked at me, disfigured and desperate at your gates, and you laughed. Already full of your plans by then, you looked at my face and you laughed. 'One didn't realize it was Halloween, Frumps,' you said. 'You're looking more grotesque than even I remember.' And I begged you. I got down on my knees and begged you for sanctuary. And at that you stopped laughing, and you looked down at me and then you said, 'One might. But it's going to cost you.' "

I looked at Aunty. And it was some extraordinary manner of miracle, but her empty socket was dribbling out a tear.

"I'm sorry, Calamity. Forgive me, Calamity."

And my feet came unstuck, and I turned and ran out of the room.

———

"Bing bong," went the Communicator on the dorm eaves as we lined up at the standpipe to brush our teeth, stamping our feet, and shivering in the night cold.

"Good evening, nieces," the Communicator said. "Dear nieces. Goodness, how I love my nieces." The words came crawling out weaker than poisoned ants. We stopped our stamping to listen up. "But it is no matter now. Dear nieces, proceed at once to your dorm. Take shit, apple and water buckets, and thirty cushion covers from the barn. Shut the door, darlings, and assume stitching positions in your row. Pontefract twins, if you can hear me out west, do ensure the second-wind toddlers stay locked in Nursery Cottage tomorrow. I have news. Here it is. Your loving Aunty is popping off for a spot of R and R to complete her sixth manuscript, which I know you are all eagerly awaiting. I shall return to you soon, nieces, I swear it. On my life, I shall—I shall return."

The Communicator broke down for a minute.

It came back something dreamy. "In the meantime, take care of each other and be good little poppets for your Mother. And if she comes into the yard with any other body—even a demonmale, nieces, even that—you must promise me, not a peep from any of you. Lie back and play dead, dears. Think of it as Stealth Surveillance for War. Think of your dear Aunty who loves you so very much—think of her, and don't move a muscle. Promise me, nieces. Promise me that."

The Communicator hiccuped. "I would like to sing 'So long, farewell, auf Wiedersehen, adieu,' but I find my heart is not really in it. No, you see, nieces, I had a dream my life would be so different from the hell I'm living—

"Now life has killed the dream I dreamed."

And the Communicator died off.

I looked about my sisters, their faces darkened by the first blankets of night.

No one said nothing. At the standpipe, Sandra kept on with her tooth brushing. When she looked up, her eyes were as wet as my own felt. I blew my nose on my smock.

Millie Gatwick caught hold of my hand. "Is Aunty well?" she whispered.

Well, there weren't no easy answer to that, so I made none.

Inside the dorm, we settled ourselves to stitching seams. Our needles worked quiet under the bulb, and our breath puffed out in wordless clouds, as we turned over the many strangenesses of the day. Seemed even Annie had nothing to say for once, but only raised her head with a smile to ask, "Scissors, please."

Must have been an hour into our labor, the silence was broken by a thudding on the balcony. Spiders fell from their beams onto our cushions. The High Hut's steps clanged like a carcass was being chucked down them.

We left our cushions and ran to peek between the planks of the wall. In the dark night we could just about see that it weren't a carcass that landed on the concrete, but a case, bulging like a bloated belly. Aunty stepped down after it, coated up safe as a crow in her burka. In the High Hut above us, Toto was whining.

Aunty took the handle and dragged the case along the yard. She slid the bolts across the dorm door.

For about the first time that day, the smile fell off Annie's lips. She ran to bang on the planks. "Aunty, I forgot to moisturize myself. Hadn't I better come out and moisturize myself?"

But Aunty had passed on by.

Adelaide Worthing, who was still skinny enough to squeeze in the corner by the door, said she saw Aunty go in the schoolroom and turn on the light.

"She's got down the Appendix," Adelaide whispered. "She's putting it in the case. She's turned off the light. She's coming out into the yard. She's coming for the dorm."

Aunty came close to the door. Then she was too close for us to see anything but burka. But I could smell her. Her voice crawled medicinal through the wood. "Nieces, darling nieces, will you sing with me as I go?"

"Shall we *So long, farewell, auf Wiedersehen goodbye* you?" I called out.

"Thank you, niece—but no," Aunty's voice whispered. "Let's have *I dreamed a dream in time gone by*. Sing as I taught you, girls, locate the tune in the pit of your belly, but feel it in the chasm of your heart."

So we did, and I don't mind saying it was something lovely.

And while we sang, Aunty took up her case and left the yard.

CALAMITY JANE

It has been twenty-five days. That's what I count when I am back in the white room after my bath, and Jane Jones has left me with Mrs. Waverley and the demonmale. And I don't need Dorothy shouting the maths to figure I should have fought lots of fights by now. But have I? No, I have not.

So now I am clean, and something scented, thanks to Jane Jones's gardenia cream, I give the demonmale on the chair a good look over.

He sees me, course, and he smiles and says, "Did you enjoy your bath?"

Happen Doctor Andrea Doors has told him to talk to me every day. Doctor Andrea Doors who says he is my father. Which I had to have a good laugh at, because it meant she reckons there are bits of him in me. Poor Doctor Andrea Doors whose brain is getting so melted, she can't even see the danger she's in, even when it's sat right here in the room with her.

Course, I don't answer him. And Mrs. Waverley blows her nose and asks me if I want her to comb my hair. Mrs. Waverley, who Doctor Andrea Doors says I can call Mother, as if I didn't have a perfect Heavenly one already. Mrs. Waverley is holding his hand. Poor Mrs. Waverley. This is one of the most terrible things about the Outside I need to get ready for—females with more fat than sense.

I don't answer her. I have a poke in the Milli Vanilli soil for Danny Zuko.

And soon enough Mrs. Waverley stops asking things, and settles down to just sitting her bottom still and holding hands with the demonmale and dabbing her nose. Which is all about as exciting as watching lard cool, it really is.

But I will keep an eye on him. If I keep myself clean, there ain't one reason why I can't do it tonight, when Jane Jones has left a blade, course. Which feels good to know, it really does. I flex my fingers to fifty. And I stare at him. And like that, it pops into my head, a cold little thought. What if Jane Jones doesn't bring a blade. What do I do then?

But just then you come in, don't you, Doctor Andrea Doors, and you sit down by my bed and say hello to Mrs. Waverley and the demonmale all friendly, and you turn your smile on me, and say today you want to talk about damage and do I know what you mean?

"Well, yes, you are looking very cracked today," I say. "Are you feeling hot inside your head, Doctor Andrea Doors?"

You smile, and your eyes shoot out cracks everywhere, and you say it's nice of me to ask, and you are feeling very well, thank you.

So I have to sigh at this.

You tell me you want to talk about Aunty, and what might happen when people get damaged as children.

Except Aunty never damaged anyone, and I tell you that.

You tilt your head about, like there's a fly inside needs freeing. "That's an interesting thought. But I'm afraid to say, Calamity, the woman you call Aunty has hurt some people. Do you have an idea who I might mean?"

Course, I have to laugh at that. Because now I've heard everything from you, I really have. But I'm not saying nothing, because you're fishing for what isn't yours to catch.

"What would you say if I said I believe your Aunty has hurt you, Calamity, in ways you might not want to think about?"

Round about now, I pull up the sheet and shroud myself. And even though you bring your head close and ask am I OK, because I haven't done this in days, I ain't saying. Because I am thinking. I am thinking of what Jane Jones said, "Oh, goodness me, sweetheart, you don't need a knife," I am thinking that. And my heart starts battering in its box. And now I start trying for one hundred finger clenches, into fists and out to stars. In and out. In out in out in out. Strong enough for throttling a cockerel. And who knows what else.

After a bit you say goodbye and go.

Mrs. Waverley speaks. She says she has brought in *Calamity Jane* to watch on a television, if I want.

I have a think for a while. "Alrighty," I shout out from under the sheet, "you can watch and learn from her, if you want to, but keep it quiet out there."

Because me, I'm staying safe in gray, because I am preparing myself.

It goes on for about forever, Mrs. Waverley's *Calamity*

Jane. And, course, it ain't the proper one. It is full of shouting nonsense, and I can't even hear Aunty in it nowhere. All I can hear is Mrs. Waverley laughing all the way through. It is a sloppy laugh she makes. Like injuns and snared females are laughing matters. But, like I said, poor Mrs. Waverley is near enough senseless, so it can't be helped, it really can't.

When it is all finished, and the demonmales are carting married-off Calamity Jane and Katie Brown to Thrust to death, I pop back out. Mrs. Waverley is still grinning at the television. Now that she is not snotting, her tear ducts ain't puffed so bad at all.

I am something curious.

"Have you been married off?" I ask.

"Oh yes, darling." She squeezes the hand of the demonmale. "We've been married sixteen years."

He grins. It stretches something demonic from his hairy mouth to his ears.

And for one rabbiting second I think I will scream at her for this stupidity. And I will throw this pencil at his nasty hand to chop it off hers. But then I don't. No, I don't do nothing but turn away. And I clench my throttling fingers in and out, in and out, and I wait.

When Mrs. Waverley unpeels her bottom from the chair and says it's time for them to go, I say it, I do. "You can leave him in here," I say.

And Mrs. Waverley says, "Really?"

And he whispers, "Are you sure?"

I fix my eyes on his. They are filling so wet it makes me sick to see. "Yes."

Mrs. Waverley throws me a mighty smile and hugs him up in her fat. She says goodnight and leaves us.

We are all alone now.

"You don't know how happy this makes me," he says. He is smiling and crying and smiling and crying.

I make my mouth make a smile back at him. And I curl up just one finger.

And at last I say the words we practiced in so many lessons—"Come on over, big boy. Let's get down to business."

A DEMONMALE VISITOR

Now, I should probably tell you this. It was the night Aunty left us that Emily started talking to me.

It was while I was stitching seams on my second cushion cover she started it.

And first off, I should say this wasn't no ways surprising, because she flew about speaking regular to Mother, didn't she? She didn't always sit dumbed up in her Sacred Lawn statue all day long. And who would want to stay there, when you could pop off down to the yard and see how your weapons were doing? And when your weapons weren't doing very well at all, wouldn't you want to go and cheer them up?

And I should also say, it weren't nothing amazing she said to me at first. See, Emily didn't need to squawk like a bantam for the whole yard to hear, when she knew I'd listen up to her good and proper.

It was answers she gave me first.

See, that night as I stitched my seams, I had so many

questions flying about my head. Questions that went crashing at my brain walls like senseless flies, and wouldn't ever settle. I didn't know what to do about them. I had no idea at all, until I felt a buzz in my left ear.

"What's that?" I said, scratching my earhole.

"You'll see, sister," a voice whispered.

"Emily?" I said.

"You'll see, sister," the voice said. Now, don't ask me how I knew it was Emily buzzing in there, but I did. And my heart began to batter in its box. So I asked her quick.

"Aunty isn't going into another Great Depression, is she?"

"You'll see, sister."

"Will this demonmale Sam cause us trouble?"

"You'll see, sister."

"Will Aunty come back soon to help with Annie?"

"You'll see, sister."

"But when is soon, Emily?"

"Emily?"

"Emily?"

But no matter how I shook my head about, that was it for buzzing. So I reckoned Emily had probably gone off back to her Sacred Lawn statue to sleep.

"Will you shut up muttering nonsense," Nancy said, turning off in her straw.

But never mind Nancy, it was a good thing, knowing Emily was alive and well, and ready to help her weapons good and proper. And I settled to sleep thinking maybe it weren't so terrible—Aunty being gone while Annie was in danger—because in her answers to me, Emily would know what to do to help us all.

Course, Annie, I am sorry to have to tell you, spent about

half the night going up and down by the door like a boxed-in rat. The other half she spent drawing. Sat up in her straw, with a torch jammed under her chin, and that cat curled on her lap, she scratched at her board long after the light went off.

I watched her at it awhile, then I rolled over Truly's straw to her. "What you drawing, Annie?"

Annie turned her board where I could see it under her torchlight. A thin face stared at me. Short-haired. Even-eyed. "I've drawn his chin a bit square, and his hair's softer for real, but the rest is about right." Sparks were dancing in her eyes. "That's him. That's Sam."

Well, I rolled away from that board, fast as I could.

On my left, Nancy and Mary were balled up uncrackable as a nut. Down the row, my younger sisters were sighing or fighting demonmales in their sleep. Annie turned off her torch and laid down her board. She turned to cozy against Dorothy.

And all sudden—and maybe it was Aunty leaving us, or Emily popping by, or happen it was just rolling over Truly's cold space—it was all I could do not to cry. I wrapped myself in a furball and tried to put Truly's giggling voice in my head, counting skinned rabbits to sleep. But she didn't come.

In the morning, long after we'd "Home Sweet Homed" every one of our cushion covers, and the pigs next door had given up bothering us for food we couldn't give them, and Annie had just about worn a ditch in the concrete with her pacing by the door, an electric screech sounded outside.

Straight off, Annie glued her eye to a crack in the planks.

"It's Mother! She's driving through the Glamis Castles! She's heading for the yard."

"Remember what Aunty said," I hissed. "We should lie back and play dead."

But Annie carried on like she hadn't heard me. Like always. "Looks like there's a demonmale following her chair! It's dressed like one. Walks like one. And about the right size."

So each and every one of my sisters gasped and jumped up and ran to press an eye against planks.

"Come back, sisters!" I hissed. "We're supposed to lie down!"

Nancy turned and spat back, "And Devil's turd, Clam, if you ain't forgotten we're supposed to shut up."

So there weren't nothing for it, but for me to crawl to a leftover crack near the floor and blow out a weevil, and watch two trouser legs and two feet in beetling black shoes follow the wheels of Mother's electric chair into our yard. I waited for Mother to take out a blade and kill him off. But she killed off the chair. And she started talking.

"Fascinating character, that Ophelia Swindon," Mother started saying. "If one recalls correctly—and one generally does—she was fostered here in our adolescent years. One doesn't mind saying all this news comes as a frightful shock, Inspector. Llandudno, was it, the sighting? Tip-off at the paper?"

The demonmale spoke. His voice was low. Most probably he was trying for Charming, not knowing he had no hope with Mother, who would not be Charmed again by his sort, as the Appendix says it—*Never ever ever in her short-legged life. Not on your nelly. No bloody way José. Nein nicht nie non no.*

The demonmale said something about being unable to confirm anything at the moment. I wanted to ask Nancy, who was standing at a good-size hole above me, if she could see his hands tied up behind his back, ready for the blade.

"No chance it's a case of mistaken identity?" Mother said.

The demonmale said he couldn't comment at this stage.

Mother sighed. "Hers was a deplorable crime, one knows that much. A vindictive, jealous act." Mother didn't mind saying one remembered an envious streak in her, even in the adolescent years. Mother said one remembered reading about that poor actress's injuries at the time. Such a talent wasted. Even Mother, with all she had suffered—and Heaven alone knew how she had suffered—even she knew the importance of not taking the law into one's own hands. And if anyone had just cause, one did, didn't she, Inspector?

The demonmale said he couldn't comment on her case either.

"Well, one assures you, Inspector, one hasn't seen the woman in thirty years. One had heard a rumor she'd fled to the Côte d'Azur, but one assumes you've pursued that lead already. However, one can state for the record, that one is more than happy to oblige with the investigation, in any way one can. As you see, this yard is where the cows are kept. Marvellous for the orphans to foster some sort of connection with nature."

Mother's voice stopped. I waited for the scream to say the blade had stuck him. Most probably it would be in the throat. Or, if his hands were tied behind, she might split him down the belly—chin to tool.

The demonmale asked her about the orphans. He understood she'd taken some in, after her own tragedy.

"Modesty prevents one from harping on, Inspector, but you make a fair point. One's own grief and suffering did become a spur to noble deeds. A Mother's love is boundless, Inspector. It cannot be packed away or bottled up as though it never existed. So one thought, why not? Why not share one's maternal bounty—and this magnificent estate—with those who have none? They're on pilgrimage at the moment. In the Steps of St. David along the Pembrokeshire coast. One hears they're rather loving it, despite the rain."

The demonmale said that sounded nice for them, and his wife had got him a potpourri pillow in Betws. Which Mother answered, "Very good of her to support one's little enterprise. One doesn't like to gripe, but Vatican funding really isn't what it was."

And now there was another pause, and I was sure Mother was going to do it, when Nancy gasped. "He's heading this way."

I watched the demon shoes step closer on the concrete.

Mother's chair raced in front.

I wanted to say, "Don't even breathe, sisters," but my throat had sealed itself up.

"Just the old cow stalls down here, Inspector," Mother said, swerving and parking Motherly between him and us. "An absolute wreck, but the little angels love to come and play, so what can one do? Although one does keep it bolted to try to discourage them."

There was silence. I figured the demonmale's feet weren't more than a pig length away. "What's happening?" I mouthed to Nancy. "Is Mother doing it? Why's it so quiet? Tell me, Mother must be doing it now."

But Nancy couldn't move her mouth. Her eyes were stuck

open like dead pig ones. I felt my own heart frost up with fear.

Down the row, Eliza Aberdeen sneezed. And a pig snorted back at her.

"Pigs!" Mother cried out. "One meant pigs not cows! One keeps the pork stock in there. Gloucester Old Spot. Tamworth. British White. Adorable creatures, one hundred percent organic. Fresh meat gives such a boost to the orphans' diet. Would you care for a chop, Inspector?"

The demonmale said nothing.

A terrible thought came to me. What if Mother hasn't got a knife on her? What if that's why he's running free? I tugged Nancy's smock. "What's happening? Why ain't he been stuck? Why ain't anyone speaking out there? Is Mother safe?"

Nancy unfroze her mouth. "He's looking along the dorm wall," she mouthed. "He's looking at the door. He's looking up and down and everywhere."

In case I hadn't been doing it already, I held my breath.

"Awfully nippy," Mother said. "This time of year."

The demonmale said nothing.

"How do you manage without a decent overcoat, one wonders," Mother said. "Or are you one of these terribly macho types?"

The demonmale said he doubted it.

Mother said she was sure he was being modest. He looked terribly strong to her. Young and terribly, terribly strong. Did he work out at all?

The demonmale said nothing.

Mother said his wife was clearly a lucky lady. Very, very lucky.

The demonmale said nothing.

Mother wheeled close and grabbed his trouser leg. "If one was only a younger and healthier woman, Inspector."

The demonmale moved off.

"Still looking," Nancy mouthed down to me.

And silly to say it, I flung some straw over my head, just in case. But I needn't have bothered, because—thank heavens—his left shoe swivelled away. He began to move towards the corner of the yard, and the steps to the High Hut.

"Derelict accommodation," Mother said, her chair screeching to life and speeding after him. "For the farm hands. No one's lived up there for decades. Condemned. Rather more than one's life's worth to take on the Council. But be one's guest, Inspector. If you've got the Council's say-so, and all the appropriate health and safety forms, then do be one's guest."

Up in the High Hut, Toto must have heard him coming because she started yapping. About the only thing that flea-bag dog ever did right in her life. And Mother's voice set to hissing laughter, "One does beg your pardon, Inspector. One should have said no one except for the orphans' pet lives up there. But that thing's old enough to have been condemned ten times over."

The demonmale shoes stopped by the metal steps. The right shoe shifted up onto the bottom one. "Would you mind if I—"

But Mother screeched her chair around and started it racing for the yard gate. "Would you care for a cafetière, Inspector?" she shouted out. "One's autoimmunity plummets these days, if one's outside for long."

226

The demonmale shoe hovered. All slow, it swung round and came down on yard concrete. "Yes, of course, Lady Llewelyn. You've been most accommodating as it is."

And that's how Mother got that demonmale shutting up with his nosying and trotting out of the yard, happy as a pig following a bucket to his slaughter.

I took Nancy's hand and squeezed it. We could all breathe again.

Well, it weren't too long after, that Mother came back and let us out. Which was a good thing, because I'd decided on writing our own duty list for the day, seeing as Aunty was gone without leaving one. I reckoned we could try for one hundred cushions stuffed before she came back. Nothing cheered Aunty more than sacks of cushions ready to be released.

Now, the first thing I reckoned on doing was keeping Annie safe from harm, and I told her so. Well, actually, I told her I had a secret, and could I tell it to just her? And I just about got all my sisters out of the dorm, and then I slammed the door and bolted it safe, and then I told her so. Actually, I shouted it through the locked door, "No secret, sorry Annie." See, I figured we were preparing for War, weren't we? And as Aunty liked to say, "The first casualty is usually truth."

"For your own safety I ain't letting you out till Aunty's back," I shouted, ignoring her cursing and bashing at the door. "Awful sorry, Annie, but when I come back from the supplies barn, I'll fetch you in some porridge for breakfast."

"Sandra Saffron Walden," I said, grabbing her smock as she went off for the kitchen, "stand here and keep the door bolted while I go get the petals for cushions. Don't you open it up. Or let anyone else. Or else."

"OK, Clam," Sandra said.

Except when I came back from the barn with my barrowful, the dorm door was thrown open wide.

Well.

Well, the Goddess Daughter's own steam hissed out my mouth to see that, it really did.

Sandra stood by the open door, smiling beautiful and stupid as a snowdrop. "Annie said could she pop out because she forgot something. She said she'll be back soon, and she promised not to bother with mushrooms. And there was something else, what was it? Oh yes. And you're not to go getting hot and bothered. That's just what she said, Clam. 'Don't let Clam go getting herself hot and bothered, and special not at Sandra,' she said. Which is me."

Well, I could have spat out my heart into Sandra's black plaits right then, I really could. But, see, I didn't have to. Because just then Emily popped by. Yes, she did and she buzzed busy enough to shake my ear to bits. And it was questions she had now—

"Who's the one really got hot and bothered, sister Leek, you or Annie?"

"Hot and bothered. Hot and bothered. What needs doing, when something's hot and bothered, sister Leek?"

"Will you tell me, Emily?" I said, cupping my ear steady.

"I'll tell you this, sister Leek. Aunty said to take care of each other. Shouldn't you take care of hot and bothered Annie? Shouldn't you take care of her good and proper?"

"Very well, Emily," I said. "If you say so, Emily. Looks

like I'll have to take care of hot and bothered Annie good and proper then."

And I turned away from Sandra, who was staring at me something drop-jawed, and I went to start thinking what to do.

THE GOOD FIGHT

I beckon the demonmale closer.

Soon enough he is right here, standing right over my bed. Blowing his hot breath down on me. "Is this all right with you, dear?" he says.

And I look up at him, and he looks down at me.

And his hands come for me.

And mine go at him.

But before I can get a hold on his throat, his arms grab me.

I am trapped up. Pinned in. Stuck down. So I can only moan.

And he goes, "Shush, darling, shush. Everything's going to be all right."

And his beard is pressing on me. And he is shuddering and sobbing. And I am trapped and moaning.

It is most tricky to kill a body.

Most tricky.

EMILY

Course, my elder sisters moaned when I stood them under Emily's eighteen-year-old statue on the Sacred Lawn, and told them what we were to do to Annie.

It was a sad old winter afternoon. The birds had all gone off somewhere else to keep warm. The rose crops round the Lawn had died down to their bones. Even eighteen-year-old Emily had drips dropping off her pink nose. And I don't mind saying, all our bodies were shivering even before we looked at the petal bin that Sandra and I had dragged down from the supplies barn.

Mary Bootle touched the bin lid and said, "Golly, I don't like this one bit. Sandra, you are our eldest, and Dorothy you are our cleverest, if one of you says, 'Don't do it,' I won't do it. By jiminy, I won't."

Eliza Aberdeen said, "I feel something queasy today with all this cold. If it's all right with everyone, I'll go back and rest up in the dorm."

Dorothy Macclesfield said, "Remind me, Clam. You said Emily told you this was the only way to save us all from the demonmales. How did she tell you? I'm wondering how this is a logical way to save Annie. Does it seem logical to you?"

Nancy Nunhead snorted out snot on the Lawn and said, "We could pop Calamity in the bin instead." And Sandra Saffron Walden burst out crying.

I climbed up on a bucket and looked inside the empty petal bin. We had placed it ten paces down from eighteen-year-old Emily's statue, so she could keep an eye on things, and maybe help out with a miracle if she fancied it.

Course, Emily was too busy buzzing about me to say yes or no to a miracle happening. But I still hoped. Like ten-year-old Emily had once made a miracle of keeping the chicken-pox off our faces, and twelve-year-old Emily had helped Aunty's *Volume III* writer's block. It was sad that eighteen-year-old Emily hadn't helped Truly at her birthday party, but maybe she was saving herself for Annie, because she knew how bad Annie needed it. Maybe that's what she was doing.

Now, I don't mind saying here, I was something nervous myself about what we were to do to Annie, but thankful Emily whispered in my ear, "Come on, Clam, you can't stop now. It's going to take a lot of filling, that petal bin, so chop-chop."

"It's going to take a lot of filling, that petal bin," I said to my sulking sisters. "Chop-chop."

"You're going to need more buckets to stand on for steps," Emily said.

"We're going to need more buckets to stand on for steps," I said.

232

My sisters kicked their feet about the grass and didn't budge.

I sighed. "All right, Mary," I said. "Sandra is eldest, and Dorothy is cleverest, but just remember, neither were spoken to by Emily herself, and told what to do about Annie—Without a Moment's Delay—as Emily put it to me herself."

"Eliza, wrap yourself in an extra fur—that should do you."

"Sandra and Nancy, I would remind you both that Annie St. Albans's unsisterly behavior meant sore arms for all of us yesterday. Not to mention she revealed information about the Garden to a demonmale, theretofore putting us all in danger. Not to mention she said laughing with a demonmale was as nice as being with sisters. And not to mention she's gone off after him again. Any one of these is a sure and certain Indicator that the Devil has got Himself in her and has started cooking her up Hyperthermia, sisters. Just like he did to Truly. And when He's finished with Annie, He'll be after us all.

"And Dorothy Macclesfield, for the last time, Emily herself whispered to me yesterday that there ain't but one way to stop a Fire burning too deep for a standpipe to cure. Emily herself said that. And how she said to do it was pure logic."

I wiped a drip off my nose. "See, sisters, it comes down to one marrow question, it really does. Do we want Annie free of Him, or do we not? Are we her loving sisters, or are we not? Do we want to save our Garden, or do we not?"

I looked around the shivering bunch of them. "Now can we please get on, and get this bin filled up? Let's make a chain from the standpipe. Happen a spot of bucket-lugging will warm us all up."

BREAKTHROUGH

There has been a breakthrough, you tell me. "Well done, Calamity," you say.

Mrs. Waverley is smiling, near to cracking, the demonmale is smiling, near to cracking. You are sure and certain cracking, Doctor Andrea Doors.

Mrs. Waverley rushes over and smothers me up. Ten long rabbiting seconds it lasts, all lard and a stink of lavender. And after her, the demonmale comes at me again. He squeezes me tight and everywhere, like he is feeling for a crunch of my bones, for an easy break.

And you wipe off a tear, Doctor Andrea Doors, to see it. But you don't do nothing to help me. No, you start to talk about "families" and what "home life" might be like. And Mrs. Waverley and the demonmale get going on this too. You all talk and talk, till even Danny Zuko curls up under the mulch and dies from the boredom of it. And then you and

Mrs. Waverley think it might be a good idea if he comes at me again. To get used to each other. Closeness. To get used to that.

And I sit dumb and helpless under his grip. I am dumb as a worm gone and died.

THE DEVIL-IN-ANNIE

We sat by the hole in the Wall, waiting for Annie. The day went off. The Goddess Daughter blanketed the sky lid black and moonless. Down in the bog, we huddled about waiting, watching our breath blow out ice-white. The only noise about was busy bats and night birds, the only light came from the tiny holes in the lid to Heaven.

I stuck up my finger and thumb to pinch-measure them holes, thinking of Truly pinch-measuring and whispering with Annie the night she fell down. And as I trapped them up, seemed like a Polperroey whisper flew in my ears. "Do you reckon when you get up close they are touchable, sit-on-able, climb-through-able?"

"I don't know, Truly."

"Well, what do you reckon, Clam? Want to climb with me and see for yourself, Clam? Want to come too?"

And for just one rabbiting second, I thought it. Yes Truly,

yes I would like to see how our Garden looks from the lid to Heaven. I really would.

"You OK, Clam?" Sandra's voice said. "You stretching off the cold?"

And I stopped my fingers and brought them down quick, and I sat them under my bottom, and I waited like that, watching the bog, till that whisper of Truly faded off.

Nancy and Mary fetched branches from the orchard and started a fire to warm us.

Sandra dropped pieces of battered Desiree Armfeldt in the embers to cook.

Two jackdaws flapped down on a fern stump. Emily buzzed me to say they brought down a message from the Goddess Daughter—"Good luck." So I gave them a message to fly back up—"Thanks."

Eliza couldn't feel her feet, so we put her in the barrow and drove her close to the fire. We all huddled close to the fire. Nancy grew the flames high and hissing, and Sandra turfed up bits of roasted Desiree Armfeldt and passed them round. But no one was rightly hungry. Dorothy poked her head in and out the Wall hole more times than a woodpecker. But Annie didn't come.

We waited.

Moths stopped by to dance in the fire's green and yellow flames. The smoke went worming up into the night. Our eyeballs grew big and white. All about the bog was quiet.

Mary Bootle said, "Do you think it's true you can see the bodies of Bowel-burning females twisting between the flames?"

"Truly would have said so," I said. "Truly would have said just that."

237

Nancy snorted, "Truly said turning cartwheels made you taller. Truly said burping would start a pig growing inside you. Truly said you could live off plums forever like the wasps do."

"She tried that," I said smiling. "I remember."

"Till her farts blew her out of the tree!" Nancy blew a raspberry on her elbow.

Mary started singing all soft and low, "Truly Fartus, she's truly, truly fartus, Fartus as a plum upon a tree."

And we looked into the twisting flames, as Mary kept on, and we all smiled. And our smiles grew fat, and our giggles rose up with the smoke. That was Truly Polperro for you.

All sudden, Mary stopped. Flames jumped in the black of her eyes. "What if Annie doesn't come back? Golly, what do we do then?"

No one said nothing, but an owl off in the orchard. We were all watching Nancy heave another log on the fire, her shadow beetling and big on the Wall.

I looked at the fire, and I looked round my huddled sisters. "She has to."

"She definitely promised me she would," Sandra whispered. "Definitely."

I kicked the log.

Wham.

"She has to."

The wood cracked open and a nestful of earwigs ran out, and ran away to the end and shrivelled up.

Mary bit her lip. "Well, golly, I'm awful sorry, Clam, but I've just thought, even if she does come back, I don't know if I can do it. Not to Annie. I mean, I understand why Emily says it's necessary. But it ain't a demonmale we're doing it to,

238

is it? It's Annie. It's Annie St. Albans, our sister. So, golly, I don't know if I can."

Nancy sat down heavy and stared into the fire. "I agree with Mary."

I watched the spitting log. I watched a tiny red spider rush out and die. I watched the smoke shift strangeness over my sisters' faces. And then I looked up and fixed my eyeballs on theirs, one by one. "Listen up good and proper, sisters, because I ain't saying this again. It doesn't matter whether you say you can or not, you will do it. You will do it for Annie's sake, to get her brought back to us before it's too late. You will do it because the Devil is deep inside her. He is sloshing about in her blood. He is heating her up like stew in a pan. Remember this, sisters, it ain't Annie we are doing it to, but Him."

Mary's bottom lip wobbled under her teeth. "It ain't Annie."

"It ain't Annie, sisters. You will do it, you will do it to Him."

Must have been hours into the night, a scratching noise woke me. I had been dreaming of being swung in a chair by my demonmale, and it took a second to shake his nasty laughter from my ears. I sat up and screamed to my sisters to wake. I turned my torch at the hole, where, sure enough, Annie St. Albans was scrabbling back to us. With a grin on her face hot enough to burn up the Garden.

"Goodness, good evening, sisters," she said, shaking her hair of brick dirt.

I shone my torch at her head. She wasn't wearing her headscarf.

I shone over the rest of her. Instead of a warm winter smock and thick fur coat, she was covered up in Outside clothing—a black jumper and blue trousers.

And I am sorry to say it, but she looked about as right in our Garden as that demonmale did in our yard. She had white laced shoes on her feet.

Annie grinned. "Goodness, Calamity, you look ever so stern behind that torch. Were you all waiting for me? Well, good, sisters, because I have such things to tell you. Is that you, Eliza Aberdeen, here as well?" Annie shaded her eyes. "That's nice of you, I hope you're warm enough. Clam, would you mind lowering that torch? Well, I tell you this, sisters. Either I am turned loonhead or this Garden is, it sure is."

"What do you mean?" Dorothy said quick.

I thumped her. "We said on no talking, Dorothy."

Annie looked at me something funny. "Your torch, Clam? Well, Dorothy, it's just that everything I thought I knew has been turned inside out. Nothing fits right. Like—" she stopped. "Why are you all staring? Is it these clothes? Or is there bad news—is that why you've come?"

"We came for you," I said.

Annie frowned and looked quick round us all. "That's nice, I suppose. Shall we poke up the fire, and I can tell you everything I found out? Then we can decide what to do."

And for one second, it seemed it was plain-baked Annie, throwing back her curls and chattering on at us. For another second, I was watching her skip to the fire saying, "What've you brought all that rope for, Nancy? Pig got loose?"

So Nancy looked at me, and Annie looked at me. And right then and there my heart seams ripped apart in me and cold water poured in the emptiness. So I didn't need Emily whispering, "Stay strong, sister Leek, this is just Him working in her," to see it clear as cleansing water—He'd been working in Annie for weeks.

Ever since Truly fell. He'd got in the Garden then. When Truly lay on that Boule bush and spoke into Annie's ear, He must have ridden that breath and jumped in and started cooking up Annie then. It was clear in everything she said, and everything she had made us do, even though it weren't ever right. And who wasn't to tell me, that rip down my heart wasn't Him jumping out of her and starting in me?

Truth be told, I ain't the clearest memory of what happened next, but I think Emily took over my limbs for me. My sisters say I leaped at Annie, shoving my torch in her face and throwing a fur over her head. "Devil-in-Annie be silenced!" they say I screamed.

Together we crashed on the ground by the fire.

The Devil-in-Annie lay unmoving beneath me—happen He'd banged Annie's head in falling. Off in the orchard an owl screeched. My sisters stood gorming above. And Annie started to groan.

"Sisters, come on," I cried. "Are you Emily's Army or are you useless worms? Look at Annie's clothing, she is drenched in Outside ways. Nancy, bring the rope and tie her quick, before she starts to wriggle."

Nancy stared as Annie's white shoes started to kick about under me.

"Nancy, you worm! Emily commands you to get over here now!"

And then, thank Emily—because who's to say whether she didn't give Nancy's fat bottom a shove—Nancy came. With a scowl that didn't want it, but with her feet waddling to Goddess service, Nancy came. Nancy bound Annie's ankles, and Emily fetched Mary to help me bind Annie's arms down beneath the fur. Sandra helped me wrap her mouth quiet. Dorothy ran off and was sick in the bog, but never mind, because we got the Devil-in-Annie strung up tight and dumped in the barrow next to Eliza. Though He was making Annie shake and moan, so as Dorothy wondered whether Annie could breathe proper under the fur, I listened for a bit and then I stood up tall and said, "It is Devil's breath, Dorothy, and yes, it looks good enough to Emily and me. Eliza, shine your torch out in front, Nancy, take up this barrow, and let's get going."

We set our steps back for the Sacred Lawn.

Entering under the Crème de la Crèmes, Annie's snorts grew worse than a knife-frightened pig.

"Can't we calm her somehow?" Mary's voice whispered in my ear. "She sounds awful scared."

But there was only one way now to calm Him in her, I told Mary. And He should well be scared of it. And here we were, about to do it, stepping our cold feet on Out of Bounds grass, one after the other in the black night. And me walking up front of everyone. And eighteen-year-old Emily waiting in the Lawn center, like she'd always been waiting for just this moment, her kindly smile fixed on us, her sisterly army, below.

I turned back at Mary, white-faced and quivering in the torchlight. "Do you know, Mary, I can't feel the cold in my feet," I said. "Isn't that something peculiar?"

Mary's face wobbled. "Please, Clam, can't we say one thing soothing to Annie?"

"Emily's taken all the cold out of the Lawn grass," I said. "That's what she's done. Thank you, Emily. You can say thank you, Mary, if you want."

But Mary's mouth just fell to blubbering.

And shivering in her fur lump, Annie let off a moan.

I looked down at Annie, and funny thing was, Emily was heating me so much, I felt strong as a steel blade now. And certain of my aim.

"Halt," I said to Nancy. And I walked to the petal bin and checked the water was high and cool. Then I walked up and knelt in front of eighteen-year-old Emily and felt the heat pouring from her kindly blue eyes.

"Never mind me, best get a shift on yourself," a voice buzzed in my ear.

"Best get a shift on," I said loud and clear, looking round my sisters who were mostly looking at their toes. "Eliza, you can stay in the barrow, but shine the torch steady on the bin. Everyone take a piece of Annie. We'll do it just like we said."

In the barrow next to Eliza, the lump of Annie thumped about. My standing sisters shuffled and stared at their toes.

And whether it was Emily doing it, I don't know, but I stretched my hand down to Annie's lump and watched her quieten to my touch. "I feel how she wants it," I said. "She's ready, sisters," I said.

And I trapped every one of my sisters' shifting glances, and let the steel in my stare make them strong. "Longer we hang about, more of her He heats up," I said. "Hotter she gets, more heat He spreads to us. More heat He spreads to us, more of us are going to need Him drowning out of us," I said.

Mary was shaking. But when I put her hand under Annie's shoulder, she kept hold and didn't let go. I put Nancy on the other side. Sandra went down by Annie's knees, and I got Dorothy out of being sick in the Crèmes, and placed her opposite.

Annie kept on moaning. All my sisters were sobbing.

"I'll take her head," I said. "We step up on the buckets together. Everyone ready?"

No one spoke. Except Annie, course, with her moaning.

"How about a song?" Emily whispered in my ear. "How about my song?"

"Let's sing, sisters," I said. "Let's sing out Emily's song to soothe her. A-one, a-two, a-one-two-three and—"

My heart is not the first heart broken—

"Come on, sisters!" I shouted. "Join in with me."

And they did. Slow and mumbling, but they did join in singing. And together we raised our voices to Heaven, and lifted the wriggling, moaning lump of Devil-in-Annie out of the wheelbarrow and up and over the edge of the petal bin, and dropped her deep in cooling water.

I fastened the lid down. It quietened some of the sloshing.

"Verse one!" I called out.

We stepped back off the buckets onto the Lawn, and sang on,

But there's nowhere to hide, since you pushed my love aside—

FISHED OUT TOO SOON

We had made a good start on the second chorus, when a tall body came bursting from the Glamis Castles, roaring like the Devil Himself was burning out its throat.

Our singing died off.

The body came charging up the Lawn in a blur of fur, its hair smashing at the night like the wings of an angry bird.

My sisters jumped down off the buckets.

The roaring body jumped on them and threw back the bin lid.

Bone-white arms shot down into the water.

"Wait!" I shouted. "It's not time yet!" I shouted. "What do you think you're doing?"

But the figure didn't answer, and Eliza had dropped her torch in fright, so I couldn't see.

"Halt!" I screamed at the crazy sploshing sounds. "Stop right there!"

But they didn't, and it didn't matter no more, because all

my sisters were jumping up on the buckets now to join in the fishing.

"Careful!" Dorothy said.

"Quick!" Nancy said.

"Easy with her head," Mary said.

And like that, a wet lump of Annie was fished out of the bin, long before we could have drowned the Devil out of her.

"Well, thank you very much, that's just about ruined that—" I said, scrabbling about for Eliza's torch and switching it on. And I turned to glare at whatever sister thought it was a fine game to come and interrupt our Goddess-given work.

But my mouth dropped wordless. Because stepping back from us, with her face lowered, it weren't none other than our slowbrained sister, Maria Liphook.

Must be twenty blinks my eyes did, looking on Maria, staring at her white face, at her black hair, dangled feathery and long. Old as eighteen-year-old Emily, Maria looked, but smileless. Maria's face was utter smileless. There wasn't one lunatic grin about her lips no more.

Dorothy unknotted the ropes, and unwrapped Annie from wet fur. Annie fell in a gasping ball on the grass. Mary ran to the yard to fetch a smock and furs, and Eliza went for hot milk. Annie coughed out water. Dorothy rubbed Annie warm. Mary dressed Annie in must be ten old furs and another for her head. Then Annie hunched herself up and flinched everyone off her, and coughed and coughed and coughed.

Maria stared at Annie's heap of wet Outside clothes and shoes.

We others stood about.

And there was nothing to be heard but an owl keeping

watch on the Wall, Annie coughing, and our cold hearts battering in their boxes.

Maria looked from Annie's clothes to us sisters. Her eyes
were shining black.

Mary burst into tears. Dorothy puked. Nancy spat on the
Lawn and glared at me. And Eliza curled up in the barrow
and pulled her fur over her head.

"We were only—"

"I didn't want to—"

"Clam said it—"

I looked over their jelly hearts and I thought, well and
good, I'll be the one who speaks the bone-marrow truth,
shall I? "We were drowning Annie of the Devil, that's all,
Maria. She weren't never going to be killed proper. We were
going to fish her out when her heart had cooled down. Emily
said it was the only way. And now you've stopped it, Maria,
the Devil is still cooking her up, and soon He will cook us
all. And furthermore to everything, it's a rotten old trick to
go being dumb for years, and then start up roaring for Annie, after it was me that tried so long to progress you. Even
though Nancy said I shouldn't have bothered." I sniffed back
snot. "It so ain't fair, Maria Liphook, it ain't."

Maria didn't look to have heard me. She turned and
started walking off north, toward the yews. Like that was
that. Like no manner of explanation was needed.

"Wait up!" I shouted. "You can't just go off, Maria, that
ain't fair neither. And that ain't the path for the yard, Maria.
That's the wrong way."

But her feet weren't stopping.

"Didn't you hear me, Maria? Or are you turned slowbrained again, is that it?"

"Maria, please." This was Annie's voice, calling out behind me. Annie's voice, shouting strong. "Will you please come back, just for a minute?"

And Maria stopped then, she did, straight off she stopped and she turned. And truth be told, I couldn't see one drop of slobber on her lips. And I looked up at eighteen-year-old Emily smiling on her plinth, and I had to wonder about miracles then.

"Will you come and sit with me?" Annie said, flinging back her wet hair, her eyes gleaming on Maria, but not on us. "Will you come back and keep me safe from them?"

Course, Dorothy sobbed at that, and so did Mary. But no one said nothing.

And this Maria, who both did and didn't look like our slowbrained sister, turned to Annie and she nodded. Stepping careful like a sleepwalker, Maria did come back.

Annie opened her furs and tried to wrap them both inside. We others stood about watching. Watching so hard and silent, that after a bit Annie sighed all cross and said, "Well, all right, don't just stand there gorming. You can sit down, you know. Only not too close. I don't actually want none of you touching me. Never again, you hear? And I don't want to speak to none of you, never again neither."

"Oh, Annie," Dorothy sobbed. "Oh, Annie, I'm sorry."

Mary let out a wail.

Nancy thumped me.

Annie turned her head from Dorothy's words and Mary's tears, but never mind, we did go up and sit near them, we did.

For a good while no one said nothing.

Annie huddled into Maria and shivered. Maria kept her eyes on Annie's Outside clothes pile. A bat spun a circle about the Lawn border. And we others sat about staring into the cold grass or over at the rose bushes or up into the inky night, and we said nothing.

And truth be told, it got to seeming no one would talk to no one else ever again. Except that then Maria started talking.

Yes, Maria looked down at Annie's clothes and she started talking.

Now, I should say, first off, the words came out of her as soundless as smoke. But after a bit they began to grow stronger and harder, and after a bit more they hatched themselves into full and proper meaning. And what Maria said was this.

"I wasn't cheating you, sisters. Not on purpose, I wasn't—" She stopped to rub her ears, like the sound of herself was something strange to her. "Dumb. Being dumb—" she said and stopped to rub her throat.

Out of nowhere, that Kathy Selden cat appeared, and jumped into Annie's lap. We others inched closer to hear Maria easier. Eliza's torch shone down from the barrow, spreading our shadows behind us like rotten petals from a rotten bloom. Kathy Selden began to purr. And Maria started up again.

"I did—I did lose my senseful voice. For years I did. Locked in blackness Maria got lost to Maria. So—so how was a lost Maria ever to find herself?"

Maria stared at the Lawn and shook her head. "So much in me is fog. Like it's one lonely day, rolling over and over. All fog."

"What do you remember that isn't?" Annie said all quiet, her eyes on her hands that were stroking the cat. "You must remember something clear."

Seemed Maria looked up then and smiled for a second, seemed so. Then her eyes dropped down. "Trees."

"Plum trees?"

"Not plums. Outside. The smell of trees Outside. I remember them."

Mary gasped. "You went Outside?" And for sure, Mary weren't the only one boggle-eyed at this. "You—Loonhead Liphook—went Outside?"

"The Wall wasn't high then. The bees went over easy. I was six. I went over easy. Gray stone is easy to climb. The smell of the trees, I liked that best. Sweet and sharp as a scratch on your nose. I think about that smell. I think about where the bees still go."

"What about injuns?" Dorothy said. "Did you see any injuns Outside?"

Maria shook her head all slow, like moving was new to her and she had to go at it careful.

Dorothy looked at Annie. Annie shrugged.

"So you never hit sense from your head on the bricks?" Mary said.

"Not on the Wall to Outside, no."

"But that's what the Appendix said happened to you," I said. "The Wall bricks damaged your brain, Maria. That's what happened. It's down in the *B*s."

She gave her head the slowest, saddest shake.

Annie laughed sudden and bitter. "That ain't the only question about the Appendix, believe me."

I threw her a look. She flung back her wet curls and stared back steady at me. Steady and hard and iced all over.

"Mother said Maria was a disappointment," Maria said. "No Spitting Image of her daughter. A waste of face and space. If Maria was trying to run away, she should be shut up good and proper. Once and for all. It was Aunty kept

Maria hid. Said, 'Shush, little niece. Call me soft-hearted, but I can't do it. Mother will change her mind one day. You keep safe down here a while.' "

"But things can't grow without daylight," Dorothy said. "How were you to grow in the Hole?"

"Some things do. If they learn to. If they have to."

"Slugs do," I said. "Earthworms and millipedes do. Woodlice, beetles and earwigs like the dark best of all. Did you know you were eating them, Maria?"

Maria smiled so sad it made me wish she hadn't bothered.

"And you did grow tall, didn't you, Maria? Even in the dark."

"Maybe a body wants to live more than you think it does. I don't know. But me, I couldn't think of never smelling them trees again. One time when the memory came strong, when you were all playing noisy in the yard, I decided on killing myself. I reckoned the Devil's Bowels that Aunty told me about would at least have other bodies in the flames to play with. Least it was not the lonesome black that I hid in."

Maria stopped and rubbed her throat. An airplane roared above us, flashing its night eyes at the sky lid. A horned snail snuck along eighteen-year old Emily's toes.

Maria's eyes moved over our faces. Black as coal balls, them eyes rolling over us. "Course we slaughter pigs and cockerels no problem. But see, sisters, self-killing ain't easy. A fly could go mashing its face on a window. A dog might bite its own leg off and bleed away slow. But there ain't a thing on a sister's body to do it for her. And they say we're cleverest in the Garden."

"So you stopped trying," I said. "Well, good, Maria, that's good."

"I screamed for Aunty to help me do it."

"Well, she wouldn't, Maria," I said. "You being an asset to her, like us all."

She looked at me, and this time her eyes didn't move off. "You weren't going to drown the Devil out of Annie. Because He ain't in there. No, far as I know it, He's in lonely bits of time where there ain't no laughter, nor any light to see by. This is what I know about the Devil." Her voice was rusting away. "But enough, sisters. I saw the look in Annie's eyes when she came back through the Wall. I want to go Outside. I want to touch them trees. That's what I want."

Her eyes turned to the north-eastern Wall of Safekeeping, where the Goddess Daughter had just pulled the darkest blanket off the sky lid. Maria smiled at Annie. Then, all careful, one bone at a time, she got up and started walking off for the yew path north.

"Where you going?" I called out quick. "You're not going now, Maria. You can't go now. You can't go up by Mother's Abode, Maria. That's Out of Bounds on Pain of Death, Maria. That's the wrong way. Where are you going?"

But she went off anyway, under the northern Crème de la Crèmes and up the path into the yews. And we sat and watched her go.

Annie started to cry in little dry gasps over the cat in her lap.

I blew my nose on the end of my fur and tried to speak, I really did.

But no words came.

A LETTER

Yᴏᴜ come in when I am alone, don't you, Doctor Andrea Doors, and you tell me you have something for me. "This came for you," you say. "I think you're ready to read it."

You hand me a white envelope. It smells of medicine and rose jelly. It has my name written on the front in purple ink. My name. Just mine.

For the attention of Niece Leek—it says—
Absolutely Private.

My heart flips in its box.

I shove the envelope quicksharp under my pillow until you are gone.

OUTSIDE

"Mother and Aunty love us and do what is right and proper to us," is what I said in the end. "It would be good to remember that."

"I don't know," Mary Bootle sniffed. "Golly, I couldn't lock up a baby even if it was very, very naughty."

"Pigs ain't ever shut up alone, are they?" Nancy said.

The Goddess Daughter pulled a blanket off the sky lid. Eliza turned off her torch. Dorothy stared at the heap of Outside clothes. "What can it mean? Trees around us everywhere, and no injuns nowhere. Maria locked away for years for going Outside. Then there's this Sam Matthews with so few Demonic Indicators on him. This ain't but counter to everything the Appendix tells us. Where is the logic in it all?"

Fast as a flash in a storm, Annie's eyes went at Dorothy. "Do you want to know what I saw? If I tell you, you won't go—"

"We won't go doing nothing like that ever again—to no one," Dorothy said.

"We only did what Emily told me was necessary," I whispered. "We were only trying to get the Devil out of you. Out of cooking you up."

Annie stroked the cat on her lap and looked at those strange-laced shoes in front of her. Then she dropped the deadliest words I ever will hear. "What if there ain't no Devil?"

Well.

Well, try thinking on an answer to that fat lie. Try thinking what to say to someone who says there ain't no sky lid above you, or your hand ain't really on the end of your arm. For long rabbiting seconds I tried, but my mouth didn't move.

Annie stroked Kathy Selden and watched me with a smile that said, "Yes, I am waiting for you." Dorothy's face turned to me with a smile that said, "I am interested." Mary was sucking a plait. Eliza looked to be dozing. And Nancy was stretching an earthworm. "I am waiting," said Annie St. Albans's smile.

"Very well, Annie." I tried to keep the shake from my voice, "You may as well say I'm not here and you're not here, and this torch ain't, nor that cat, neither." My finger pointed to the sky, where soon enough He would be raging and bashing against the lid. "You think He won't be up there today, Annie? Burning down and cooking up every unfurred female on the planet?"

"Well, Clam, what if the Sun is just a thing called the Sun, and it ain't the Devil. And if the Devil ain't the Sun, what is He then? Where is He then?"

"Can't see air, Annie, but you would die without it. The Sun is the Devil, Annie. That's the Sun's purpose. That's His name, Annie. Goddess-given. Her Sun. His purpose."

"What if people Outside don't actually think that?"

"Oh, Annie, what does it matter what demon-deceived Outsiders think?"

So I set down the one reason she couldn't argue against, "If there ain't no Devil there ain't no point in any one of us. Purpose, Annie. If there ain't no Devil, there ain't no purpose in growing us here at all."

I waited for her to see the sense in this, but it was Dorothy who spoke next. She looked up, not a twitch was bothering her nose. "Enough, Calamity. Annie, please tell us everything you learned. Tell it straight and unsugared. We should not decide what to think about Outsiders, until we know whatever there is to know."

Dorothy finished without one blink of an eye. Which I thought to point to and say, "Is that Dorothy's head's normal behavior, Annie, or is eighteen-year-old Emily making some kind of a calming miracle on her, after she made a miracle of loosening Maria's tongue? And if it is Emily at work, well, stop and have a think about who took Emily's life, Annie. Yes, Annie, a demonmale. And who sent the demonmale to do it, Annie? The Devil, you say, Annie? Quite right. Theretofore the Devil is present."

But just as I was working my head through all this, Annie started talking.

"He was waiting for me, Dorothy," she said, "in the clearing where I had seen him before. He was sitting on the fallen tree, cutting at the bark beneath an old woodpecker hole with a knife."

Annie talked on, and I watched her words puffing out into the last of the night, her hands shaping trunks and knives and Sams. I watched her words puff out easy as breathing. And right then I started to realize the truth of it. And the truth was this—Annie had been Charmed by the Outside. Annie weren't bothered with our Garden no more. Even if we drowned her all out with cooling water—which no one would now—but even if we did, we wouldn't ever get this unbothering out. I watched Annie's hands dancing beneath her easy words, and I would probably have wept out all my tears right then, if sadness hadn't frozen them deep inside me.

And unbothered Annie went on talking.

"Sam turned red when he saw me. He said, 'Jesus, you made me jump,' and, 'for a minute I thought you were a ghost.' Which, he said, was a joke by the way. Then he rubbed at his head and said he wasn't sure I would come back, but—'It's cool,' he said, 'that you did.'

"So I asked him what he was doing to that poor tree, and he laughed and said, 'Just, you know, marking my patch. You can't be too careful round here.'

"'Oh yes?' I said.

"'Girls,' he said, 'wandering loose. A terrible thing, you know. Girls.'

"Three letters were scratched into the bark under the woodpecker hole—S A M.

"'Shall I do you?'

"'Do me what?'

"He smiled and said, 'You're all straight lines so you'll be easy. But turn round or you'll make me nervous.'

"Did I tell you, sisters, he has very white teeth?

"So I went off and had a look for mushrooms in the moss

patch. Then I watched a string of ants dragging needles up a mound. Funny thing was, it made me think of us, up and down the barrow path with our tools. Truth be told, I could have watched them busy insects awhile, but Sam called, 'OK, you're done. Wonky but done.'

"A N N I E it said beneath his name. I rubbed my finger across the bark feeling the sharp edges of the cuts and the wet flesh underneath.

"Sam grinned. 'Afraid you're stuck with me now.'

"I looked on them two names. 'Oh, I ain't afraid of nothing,' I said.

"And he said he didn't suppose I was, and he went a bit pink and he closed up his knife and put it in his pocket, and he looked down and shuffled his shoes and said, 'What should we do now? We could go into Betws, if you want. Have you been to the Crown, because I was thinking we could go to the Crown, see who's on. It's Sunday, so if Mike's on, it won't be a problem, you know, getting a drink in. Um, if you fancy it.'

"So I said, would I be safe? So he said, was I asking if he was a perve, was that it? And I didn't know what to say to that word, so I shrugged.

"'Thanks very much,' he said. 'Because I'm not.' And his cheeks grew pinker, and he looked down at his shoes and said, 'I promise you'll be safe.'

"'On what?' I said. 'Have to promise on something.'

"'On my little sister's life.'

"'You have a sister?'

"'Unfortunately.'

"Stop," Dorothy said. "He said he has a sister?"

"Called Lucy."

"How'd he trap her?" I said.

Annie said sharp, "Sam didn't catch her, Clam."

"Is that what he said to you?"

"He said he liked her. She wasn't too much trouble for a girl, he said."

"They all say that. Think on, Annie. It's demonmale lying, nothing more. This is very very very very bad news, Annie."

Dorothy sighed. "I wish this was getting less illogical. But it's only getting more so."

"And more," Annie said. "And more."

"Well," Dorothy said, "well then, you had better keep going."

"All right," Annie said, "I will."

"'Let's go to this Crown then,' I said. I looked about the clearing where there were four or five paths out. 'Which way is it?'

"And Sam rubbed his head. He was staring at me like I had my smock on inside out. 'Like that?'

"So I said, 'What do you mean "like that"? Is it my head-scarf? Because I'm not taking that off. Well, is it?'

"'Yes,' he said. 'No. Well, I mean, for starters, do you never wear shoes?'

"'We will when we leave the Garden for the Outside.'

"'So where are they?'

"I tried not to look at him like he was being slowbrained about it. 'Well, I haven't actually left for the Outside yet, have I? This is me just popping out for a quick look.'

"'So you don't go out much then?'

"'Well, I'm here today, aren't I?'

"'But you go to the shops, right? Or the cinema? So you must wear shoes then. I mean you must have a weekend pass or something.' Sam wasn't stopping from staring at me, so I shook my head. 'No, actually, I haven't, Sam.'

"'Well, you've done Llandudno, at the very least.'

"'Done what no?'

"Sam rubbed his head then and grinned. 'Yeah, right. Very funny. You're taking the piss out of me.'

"'I'm taking nothing out of you and certainly not your piss.'

"He looked me over. 'No, sorry, you're not getting me with this one. Just because you're wearing all this nun stuff. You're from St. Emily's, right? So you've been to church. Come on, admit it, the Church of the Sacred Heart in Betws?'

"'Where?'

"'Very funny.'

"'No it's not. Where is Betws?'

"Sam stepped back then. He was still grinning, but it was starting to drop off the edges. 'Betws-y-Coed. I mean, you know, you have to have been to Betws. Every man, woman and sheep in North Wales has been to Betws. Betws is ten miles away.'

"'Well, I've never been to Betws, Sam. Never. It means not ever, you know. Look, Sam, we are safe inside. We don't need to go out. Now, please stop laughing at me.' Happen I was something angry when I said this, sisters. 'Please stop it now.'

"'Jesus,' he said then. He said it all quiet, looking at his shoes. 'Jesus.'

"'We are grown in safety, Sam. That's all. Is there actually something wrong with that?'

"He didn't answer. He started to rub the sides of his face—he does a lot of this rubbing.

"'You sure there's nothing wrong, Sam?'

"He looked up at me, and he thought a bit, and then he shook his head slow, and said he didn't suppose it was any of his business. And I agreed with that.

"Course, then he decided to look at my feet again like there weren't nothing more fascinating about me than my ten toes. He grinned. 'Hey, I've an idea. Ever been on a motorbike before?' He lifted a branch, 'Actually, it's more of a scooter.' And he ducked out of the clearing and disappeared in the trees.

"Course, I knew it was the opposite direction to the Garden, sisters, but I hurried to catch him."

BETWS

"Well, Annie," I said, jumping in quick, "thank you very much for all that, but I don't need to hear much more. You got Charmed by a demonmale and put on Outside clothes and rode an Outside bike into an Outside town and saw Outside people, and now you will tell us everything Outside is practically perfect in every way, and everything is wrong in here."

Sandra looked at me drop-jawed. "Golly, Clam, how do you know all that?"

"Plain-cooked simple, Sandra, I am sorry to say. Annie is only being what foolish females are like—*bamboozled by demonlies*. That is what Outside females are like—the ones without proper *Education, Education, Education*. Only Annie's had her *Education, Education, Education* in here, so she should know better, she really should."

"All right then, Clam, here's some education for you." Annie stopped stroking Kathy Selden and looked up at me. "Cushions."

"What about them?"

"I saw our cushions."

"I'm sorry?" I said.

"The cushions we stitch, Clam. I saw them sitting in a window in Betws. There were scarves and dresses and bags in the window. And actually our cushions too."

"What?" Dorothy said. "Our cushions?"

"I don't believe you," I said. "Must have been they were demonmale copies of our cushions."

Annie shrugged and went back to stroking the cat.

"I don't believe you," I said louder. "You must have looked wrong, Annie. Them cushions go straight up to the sky lid to provide cloud cover against Him. Everyone knows that, Annie. Ask Aunty when she comes back, if you won't listen to me."

"Well, I'm sorry, Clam, but I know what I saw sitting in that window, and it was Nancy's cushion."

"Eh?" Nancy said, dropping her worm.

"A 'Charity Begins at Home' one. Got your wonky 'e's all over it. So I asked Sam to take me inside.

"A woman stared at me when I went in. Sam said it was my headscarf doing it. See, none of the Betws females were protecting their faces at all, which is something else I have to tell you. But I didn't bother with her. I went straight to the cushions stacked on a shelf by the back wall. There was a tiny label attached to the top one. It said—

HEAVEN SCENT!
Organic rose petal, fair trade silk cushions.
Hand-embroidered by St. Emily's Orphanage
(reg'd charity 09784438).
Fire retardant. Thirty pounds.

263

"That's what it said, that label. I think it was one of yours, Mary, that cushion. It had your cross-stitch kisses all over the seams. But they were all there, sisters—'Home Is Where the Heart Is, Home Sweet Home, No Place like Home, Show Me the Way to Go Home.' Sam asked if I wanted one. So I asked him what they were used for. And he looked at me and said, 'This time you really are messing with me. You're asking what a cushion is used for?'

"So I had to run outside. And when I looked at the sky lid there were plenty of clouds up there shuffling about near the Sun—"

Right here, I am sorry to say, Annie started laughing. Far worse than mushrooms was the laugh that came from Annie.

"—and I asked Sam if those clouds up there in the sky looked anything like the cushions piled on that shelf, and— and—" and Annie ran out of words and into strange, open-throated laughter.

"Annie, Annie, Annie," I said. "We stitch up those clouds for our safekeeping and for the safekeeping of all females out there, so why are you asking demonmales anything? What do you think they're going to say but demonlies?"

But she just fell her head back and kept on laughing.

"Annie, stop that!" I shouted. "STOP! STOP! STOP!"

The cat woke with a cry, and jumped off her lap and ran into the Glamis Castles. I don't mind saying I was something shaky myself then, and my sisters were something dumb. We all looked at Annie, and Annie looked at us, and she shook her head over and over like to say, "Take it off me, please. Unscrew me." She was laughing and crying all together, "Oh sisters, can't you see, we ain't stitching up cloud safety—we're making pads for bottoms! That's what we've been doing every blessed, sore-fingered night—making pads for Outside bottoms to sit on!"

Well, we all watched our sister laugh and cry until she had no more of either left in her. The Goddess Daughter took another blanket off the sky lid.

"You'd better go on," Dorothy said in the quiet after.

Well, course, Annie did go on then, oh yes. Annie went on talking about demonmales wandering free in Betws. How *normal* they looked. How one was *just like* her own dream demonmale. He had a little girl, *just like* the one in her dreams. They were feeding ducks together, *just like* in one of her dreams. And the cars and the lorries were *so noisy* out there. And the river—well, I can't remember, but I think most probably Annie said it was wet.

Sometime about now, I think I told her I was turning sick.

"You will be," she said. "Because never mind them cushions, when we got to the Crown, and when I saw what I saw, and heard what I heard, well, it went and tipped everything I thought I ever knew upside down. Like turning over a cream jug in the yard. Everything I thought I knew about us and the Garden ran out onto dirty ground, so it could never be scooped back in again clean."

It was then Annie told us how she met a gray-beard demonmale in the Crown, called Sunday Mike. He was reading one of the Outside newspapers, and it had a baby face on the front, one with a blotch that Annie thought looked just like Baby Sainsbury's, and wasn't that a funny thing?

And it was then that two more demonmales came crawling out the room corner, smelling of yeast, and hungry as spiders to hear about us, because we St. Emily orphan girls were rarer than things called unicorns round these parts, they said.

And, course, they came out to spread nasty demonlies about Mother too.

I ain't going to bother with putting down all their lies, but this is a bit of what they said to Annie. They said her Ladyship made a stratospheric match in marrying his Lordship, given her background and everything, but she was a bit of a goer, so maybe that's how she bagged him—which they didn't say what it meant—but they said he wasn't a good bag, Lord Llewelyn wasn't. The craziness was deep in his blood. Which I told Annie, really weren't nothing surprising to us, was it? And anyway, them saying Mother had got married was a seethrough lie in itself, wasn't it?

And Dorothy said let Annie go on. So she did.

She said, "They said, 'He was a jealous sort. So when he discovered she had been having an affair for years, well, he hurt her in the nastiest way he could think of.' Which they said was 'the bairn,' which they said was all they wanted to say on that. Rest in peace. Except that after that, he—the Lordship—scarpered to lands unknown, and she sold up all his estate and leftover bits—them that she didn't burn— and she came home to Betws and bought up 'the old Hall,' they said, where she'd grown up, 'to grieve in peace and quiet.' "

"Well, we know all about what this nasty stinking demonmale did to Emily," I said. "Most probably they were only trying to scare you, Annie."

And she just shrugged at me at that.

Course, them demonmales shook their beards and laughed when Annie told them—which she was a total loonhead to do—about our Appendix. One of them said he had his own book with different stories in it about how everything started. The other one said the plain truth was the Sun was just a ball of fire, and we all grew out of fish, and hadn't Annie heard that? And then they stopped laughing and said what was she being taught in there? And when Annie didn't say, one of them whispered to the other that Mother had been known to be a bit of a "fruitcake," even before the loss of her daughter. That's what he said. "A fruitcake and a nutty one too."

Then all those demonmales whispered together that "Someone should take a look into all this." Which got Annie so shook up—and here I really don't blame her none—that she did the best thing for it for once in her life—well, the second best, seeing as she didn't have a blade on her to kill them all off—she went running out, with Sam chasing after.

"There weren't no time for changing into my smock, I wanted to see you all so much," Annie said. "Sam brought me to the clearing, and I came back here alone. And that's about it, sisters. So what do you make of all that?"

Well, I don't mind saying, all them lies made my head go spinning something terrible, that's what. And most probably all my sisters' heads were spinning too. Because no one said nothing now, for being too busy staring down at the Lawn and not at Annie.

During her telling the night had turned to dawn, and all our shadows had left us. A hungry thrush was tugging up a poor earthworm from the Lawn. A harvest spider was reeling a web across eighteen-year-old Emily's toes. Down in the yard, the cockerels were clearing their throats. All about us, a plain-cooked perfect Garden morning was starting up, just like always. Except this one wasn't nothing like always no more.

Dorothy said it best, course. She got up and went and snapped one of eighteen-year-old Emily's big toes right off, don't ask me why, but she did. "It's like trying to put an egg back in its shell," Dorothy said. "Nothing fits proper now."

"You told those demonmales about our Appendix, Annie," I whispered.

"Yes, I did. And I ain't sorry, Clam. I mean I've been thinking, and I actually can't stop thinking it now—I've been thinking, what is it makes us in here so right, and all them out there so wrong?"

Annie looked round us. Where Dorothy was hopping about breaking toes, and Mary was sawing her plait-end through front teeth. Where Eliza was hunched like a snail in the barrow and Nancy was knotting the worm. Seemed Annie had a good old look at my ears before she smiled at Sandra, "I've been thinking, what is it that's so special about us anyway?"

No one said nothing. Annie shrugged and stood up. "I'd better get these Outside clothes dried off. In the afternoon, I'm going back. I promised Sam."

"But what about us, Annie?" Mary cried, her plait dropping out of her mouth. "I mean golly, Annie, now you've said all this. What about us, what will we do?"

"Simple." Dorothy turned and said it in a cool easy voice that made every one of us stare. She broke a little toe off Emily, and crumbled it to dust on the Lawn. "The logical answer is quite simple. We will all go and look on these cushions, this Betws, this Crown. Once we've seen them, we can each choose the truth of it—whether they are demon-males or friends. We will go see. All of us. That is what we will do."

DISAPPOINTMENT

Well, there we all were, hurrying off for the yard, chattering about the Crown and Betws, and who might go, and when, and I was saying shouldn't we wait for Aunty to come back, and have a talk to her first, and Nancy was thumping me and saying she was off right now, she was, and she might just take the pigs, and Mary was wondering how she could push both trolleys of second-wind toddlers *and* carry the baby if the Pontefracts didn't want to come, and Dorothy was working out logic questions for the demonmales, and Annie was swiping at the Glamis Castle dead ends. So you see our brains and tongues were mighty busy. Which is most probably why we didn't hear Mother's chair wheeling screechless into the Lawn behind us.

And I'm afraid to say this is where the story turns sad. Right here.

So happen you might want to stop right here. Don't let

me stop you, if you do. Because there ain't much to tell you now, but that Mother was disappointed with us and the Garden came to an end.

That's it.

And, course, it is very sad, but we can't do nothing about it now. So you may as well shut up this book.

But if you're made something like Mary Bootle, and like to have a cry at things that can't be helped, well, you hang on and I'll tell you about Mother's disappointment. Which was big. Which was why she had to bring the shotgun when she drove into the Lawn, with Maria Liphook in front. Maria, who was attached from her belly to the arm of Mother's chair by a length of rope.

Course, now you'll probably say Maria going out north for a whiff of trees was most probably to blame for Mother's disappointment with us, but I can't really say that it was. See, Maria only wanted to go out again after Annie made the hole. And Annie had made us all make the hole.

So now you'll say we all were to blame. But I can't really say for sure that we were. See, it is also possible that Mother had been sitting in the yew path, listening to Annie's story, and maybe it was that that made her disappointed, hearing all about the demonmales laughing at her and poor Emily. And who's to say whether Sam or one of them others didn't hurry along here, after Annie left the Crown, so he could cause trouble at Mother's Glorious Abode? Or maybe that other demonmale—the one that had come sniffing in the yard after Aunty—well, maybe Mother hadn't killed him yet, maybe he was still loose in the Garden, and it was him that Mother was really after.

So you see, there weren't no telling who it was needed blaming for Mother's disappointment. You can decide yourself who to choose for it. Because, like I say, it ain't no matter now.

We didn't see our Mother coming, and we probably would have got safe to the yard without having heard her at all, if, just as we started through the Glamis Castles, the air hadn't whooshed, and the top of Dorothy's head hadn't about blown off. Bang.

"Hold it right there."

And that's when we looked round, and saw our Heavenly Mother parked up by eighteen-year-old Emily, as black-wrapped, black-glassed perfect as ever, with Maria Liphook tied to the chair, and a shotgun in her gloved hands.

Dorothy put her hand to her head, but it was all still there. The gun's eye swung onto Sandra. I whispered to Emily to wake up please, wherever she was, and please go tell Mother that the hole in the Wall was an accident. And if it wasn't the hole, but the demonmales in the Crown disappointing her, well, we could go and sort them easy. So Mother didn't need to be disappointed with us.

And maybe Emily did go and tell Mother something of this, because Mother held that gun steady at Sandra, and she didn't shoot it at her. "One has an announcement to make," she said. "Weapons will gather round."

Annie dropped her Outside clothes all quiet behind her on the Lawn.

That gun shot the air above Sandra's head, so Sandra screamed and jumped.

"Quick march forward, you worms. One doesn't have all day."

We moved closer to Mother. Twenty paces off. Nineteen. Eighteen.

Bang.

"Halt! Not one more step, if you want to keep your heads. There's gathering round, and there's reckless invasion of personal space." Mother laid her gun on her lap and undid Maria's rope. She dropped it on the Lawn. "One weapon quick march up here at once, and relieve one of this filthy thing."

Dorothy scooted up, eyes down, and took Maria's rope. They raced back down to us as fast as their toes could turn.

Mother looked up and smiled Heavenly, "Here we go, angelkins." Then she pointed them black glasses straight at us. So straight that I almost turned as dizzy as Eliza, who had just tumbled down.

And Mother spoke.

"Due to circumstances beyond one's control, one hereby announces the immediate cessation of all combat plans. Amid the mourning at this untimely end, one shall not forget the concept, which was inspired, the cause, which was just, and the preparation, which was adequate. One's daughter Emily also joins one in expressing her gratitude for playing, but says it's time now to pop the weapons back in the box."

Mother raised the gun and fired it bang bang bang over Nancy's head. "Quite right, angelkins," she said. "One other thing. One's daughter and oneself remind the weapons not to grieve for the manner of their expiration. History informs us not every soldier is so fortunate as to die in the glory of battle itself. This does not invalidate their effort for the cause. That about do it for you, angelkins? Jolly good. Therefore, without further ado, you can all bugger off back to your box. Vamoose. Scram. Go on, piss off the stinking lot of you."

And before I could think, "Well, thank goodness for that, now we'll all be safe until Aunty is back," and before I could even smile at the thought of it, my sister Annie St. Albans was only at it again.

"What do you mean?" Annie was saying, throwing words at our Heavenly Mother like common fertilizer. "I don't understand what you mean by popping back in our box?"

Mother gasped. She shrunk back in her chair and jammed up her ears.

"What box?" Annie said.

"Annie!" I whispered. "Whatever are you thinking? You know we ain't allowed to talk to Mother."

But Annie didn't hear me, course. And she may as well have been thrusting a blade at Mother's heart as she spoke, because she kept on, "What box? What box? Where's the box?"

So our poor Mother's mouth had to let out a kettling hiss of pain. "One cannot hear it." Mother shrank down in the chair. "One cannot hear it, no."

And maybe it was Emily buzzing up to me, getting cross at Mother's pain, I don't know, but next thing I was shaking Annie, "Look what you're doing to Mother! You're killing Mother, Annie! You're killing Mother!"

"I'm not doing anything to her," Annie said. "I'm only wondering about the box."

"Stop wondering, Annie. Can't you ever stop wondering? You're killing Mother with your wondering!"

"I don't want to kill Mother. I just want to know what box we're going in."

"Calm down, Clam," Dorothy whispered.

"But it's Annie needs to stop it. Stop it, Annie! Stop it all!"

Bang bang bang went the gun over our heads.

And thank the Goddess Daughter, Mother was sat up, looking most recovered. "Quite right, my angel, you're quite right as ever, Mummy can do this. It's quite straightforward if Mummy doesn't look at them." She smiled Heavenly at the air. "Yes, Mummy hears you, angelkins. Loud and clear. Yes, Mummy knows we really must get on, if we're to get a head start. No, of course, Mummy won't screw this up."

Mother pointed the shotgun. "Those two vile noisy ones will stay behind and await further orders."

Me and Annie. Course it was.

"All remaining weapons—about turn."

Mother fired the gun over Mary's head. Mary screamed and ducked. And Mother clicked the switch on her electric chair and shot forward.

My sisters turned and ran. Heads down, they ran south under the Crème arch and into the Glamis Castles, with Mother's chair chasing. Only their dew footprints were left on the Lawn. It was like an army of Cinderellas had gone off and left all their slippers behind.

EMILYS

I sighed long and hard and shook my head. "Well, thank you very much for that, sister."

Annie stared at the Glamis Castles. "Where do you think she's taking them?"

"To be safe in the dorm, most likely. Weren't it lucky Mother didn't see what Dorothy did to Emily's toes?"

"Why was she banging the gun so much at our heads?"

"I don't know, Annie. Maybe it is training for War."

"But why?"

I sniffed. "Oh, Annie, do you think Mother heard you talking about the Outside?"

Annie didn't stop from watching the Glamis Castles. "Does it matter now?"

"Does it matter that she might have heard you let demon-males stamp all over her, and poor Emily, and the Garden's purpose, and our own special purpose too?"

"Well, does it?"

Tears prickled my eyes. "Oh, Annie—"

"Listen, Clam," Annie grabbed my arm. "I'm still going out, you know that, don't you? That's the only thing that matters now. And Dorothy and Mary and Nancy and Sandra are coming out, and maybe our other sisters too. Maybe us all." Her eyes were shrunk to glass spits. "Maybe we're all going out. Maybe we won't come back."

"But look at our beautiful Garden, Annie." I looked about where a cloud blanket was draped so low and safe I couldn't even see the rim of the Wall. Damp hung on our furs and on the night's leftovers—the barrow and the petal bin, and Annie's pile of Outside clothes. "Look how safe-kept we are. What will Aunty do without us when she comes back? Who will she prepare for War if we are gone? What will the roses do, and the pigs? Don't you want to fight in Japan, Annie? Don't you want to play in Heaven's Garden forever?" Tears were jumping out of me. I went to grab her arm. "Please, Annie. Can't you wait here twenty-eight more days till it's the proper time for you to leave?"

But Annie just turned back to staring at the Glamis Castles. "What do you think she's doing down there? I can't hear anything."

I whispered that I didn't know.

Annie kept on looking. The sky lid sagged over us. All the Sacred Lawn was still.

After a bit, Mother drove back up from the yard into the Lawn. Mother had a stack of furs wedged between her lap and her chin.

Mother stopped the chair ten paces off us. She lifted the gun and rested it comfy on top of the furs. The gun's eye looked at me. "Attention!"

It shifted to Annie. "About turn."

Mother marched us north onto the yew path, and now my sorry heart flipped to instant joy. Because here was where all the past Emilys lived, all fourteen of them, going back in age to her four-year-old self. All were plinthed and polished in front of the yew hedges. Not one had rotted like pigmeat, or like Truly would have done under her mound by now, if she hadn't already been dragged down to Bowels.

Seventeen-year-old Emily had a lamb stuck to the side of her knee. Sixteen-year-old Emily was looking down over her full and happy belly. Fifteen-year-old Emily carried a baby sister in her arms. Fourteen-year-old Emily prayed under a crown of roses. Thirteen-year-old Emily was wearing wings taller than her own head. Sorrowful twelve-year-old Emily held a blooded cloth in one hand and pressed her other to her brow. Eleven-year-old Emily opened her sore bleeding heart for us to see it—a tear was stuck halfway down her left cheek.

Course, I started crying, seeing Emily bleeding there. Crying too hard to think about walking on, until the shotgun shoved me in the back. See, it weren't just poor Emily and her killing off I was remembering, it was each of her birthday parties, and how happy we had all been. How happy we all were, before Truly climbed up the Wall and Annie started wondering, and holes grew where they shouldn't, and "nothing fits proper now," just like Dorothy said it didn't.

We passed eight- and seven-year-old Emilys. I tried to dry up. "I reckon we're being taken to see Mother's Glorious Abode," I whispered in Annie's ear. "That's what I reckon. Now we're really going to see it."

Annie said nothing. She was scuffing up the pebbles on the path.

We came to four-year-old Emily, kneeling in prayer in front of the last yew bush, her eyeballs rolled up to Heaven. Mother's first and fairest, four-year-old Emily knelt by the bend in the path, which could only lead one place.

"Now we'll see, Annie, won't we?"

We walked round the corner. I took Annie's hand to squeeze.

"Didn't I say, Annie? Didn't I?"

But it wasn't the Glorious Abode with rooms of curtains and fire, like Aunty liked to talk about. There was nothing but a giant empty box in front of us. Wheeled. Its open doors blocking out the path up to the hedges. Its inside empty as a ready oven.

"Halt!" Mother said.

"I don't like this," Annie whispered. "What's an Outside van doing here?"

I touched a door. Its skin was set cold like cream. "Maybe we're going off to fight, maybe that's what's happening, Annie. Maybe Aunty got it wrong. Maybe it's not Mary and Sandra and you going first. It's actually me and you."

Annie grabbed my elbow. "Don't get in. Whatever happens, don't get in."

"Don't you want to go to Japan, Annie?"

"You hear me, Clam, don't get in."

The gun banged the air over our heads. "Weapons will get away from the doors! Grubby fingers off what doesn't belong to them." Mother drove up and threw all my sisters' furs in the van. "Weapons will wrap and pack all statues. And there will be no cracking of plaster. Break a nose and a nose gets broken in turn. A finger for a finger, that's how it goes. Quite right, my angel, eyes for eyes! Action stations, weapons! Wrapping and packing! And you'd better be quick about it!"

Mother squeezed the chair round the van door and squealed away.

"Off to her Glorious Abode, most probably," I whispered.

"I don't like this," Annie said. "I don't like this one bit."

We set to carting Emilys. We started with four-year-old Emily, who was light as a blown egg.

"Shall we play guess whose fur is it?" I said. We laid down five-year-old Emily next to her sister on the van's floor, and wrapped her in a fur so rat-nibbled it could only be Millie Gatwick's. "You have first turn, if you like."

Annie looked at me and she didn't say nothing.

"We're probably getting new furs, don't you think, Annie? That must be what it is. Like that time Mother saw the back of a lorry and it gave her a bad fit of her sickness, and Aunty said we could burn all our rabbit skins for having brand-new minks. Do you remember that, Annie?"

But Annie was already running up the path for six-year-old Emily.

"Guess something about our new coats then, Annie," I shouted after. "Come on, Annie. Do you reckon it'll be mink or fox we're having this time?"

But she didn't hear me. She looked to be wrenching Emily off her plinth more careless than a carcass off a gutting hook. I jumped down and I ran after.

We were starting on ten-year-old Emily when Mother drove back round the van door. Two big cans were stacked on her lap. Wedged behind her, a third can was upside down, spilling out on the path and the yew hedge and everywhere. Looked like it was water glugging out of its mouth. We stood aside, and Mother drove away down the path and screeched off into the Lawn.

Annie stared after her. "I don't like this one bit." She squatted down over the watered pebbles on the path. Rainbows shone on them. "It looks like slug slime," she said.

It was most probably a special fertilizing water I said. Possibly Heaven-sent, because of the rainbows in it.

Annie rubbed her fingers on them pebbles and held them to her nose. "That ain't no water, Clam. That smells stronger than Aunty's rat poison."

I tried asking Emily if she knew what it was, but she didn't say nothing, which probably meant "Keep on with what you're doing, Clam, because it's early and I've gone back to sleep after a busy night." So I said to Annie we better keep on wrapping and packing. And Annie kept on stopping and touching pebbles and sniffing her fingers, and saying, "I don't like this, not one bit, I don't."

Sixteen-year-old Emily was something hefty, never mind she was hollow inside. I took a grip on her knees and I was saying we might coat her in Nancy's fur—the one that smelled of pig and molasses, and we could maybe use Dorothy's too, did Annie think?—when Annie dropped her hold, and said, "Hush up a second, Clam. What's that?"

"What's what?"

"Something's screaming."

I stood up straight. "Why would anything be screaming, Annie?"

"It's the pigs," she said, frowning. "The pigs are screaming."

"But why would they be screaming?"

Before I could say "Don't," Annie set off down the yew path toward the Lawn.

"Come on back, Annie," I shouted. "We ain't finished here."

But, course, Annie didn't hear me. So I left Emily, and I ran after.

Well, even before I ducked through the Crèmes, I could hear them. There ain't nothing like a sore pig for wanting the whole Garden to know its pain. Scream loud enough to rattle the sky lid, a sore pig would. And they were all at it now, screaming like blades were twisting in their guts.

In the middle of the Lawn Annie stopped running. She turned and looked at me. Under her speckles her face was white. "Why are they screaming, Clam?"

My own bones had all turned to jellymeat, hearing those pigs. "I don't know, Annie. I'm sorry, I don't know."

Annie ran to eighteen-year-old Emily and pulled herself up on the plinth.

She looked about everywhere. "There!" She pointed west toward the supplies barn and Nursery Cottage. "Over there. That's why."

I followed her finger. Black threads were rising toward the sky lid like they were escaping from a poor-stitched cushion.

"It's Nursery Cottage," Annie said. "There's smoke flying out of the windows."

"Maybe Mother's having a bonfire of dead petals at the barn. Maybe that's what's got the pigs all hot and bothered."

"Or maybe it's something else."

"What else, Annie? Whatever else could it be? Annie, will you please get down off poor Emily."

"Them pigs are getting louder," Annie said. "That smoke is turning blacker. Is it just the pigs, Clam? Is it just the pigs that are screaming?"

Well, there really weren't no answer to that.

Annie jumped down. "Come on, Clam, we've got to get to the yard before that starts smoking too."

She set off running. But racing into the Glamis Castles, she skidded up.

Because here was Mother, coming up the other way, emptying a glugging can all about everywhere on the Lawn.

"Oh, one doesn't think so," Mother said, shifting aside the glugging can and settling the shotgun on her shoulder so its eye stared straight up our noses. "One doesn't think so at all."

MOTHER'S EYES

About-turned and back up the Lawn we went, the can on Mother's lap sicking out behind us, the air growing bitter to breathe, and the pigs screaming so bad, my skull felt near to cracking.

Into the yew path and back for sixteen-year-old Emily, we went, the gun's eye following us ten steps behind.

Annie looked at me. Tears were jumping out of her eyes. "This is bad, Clam. We have to do something. I don't know what to do. This is very bad."

"But this is all wrong, Annie," I whispered loud as I dared. "Mother's not doing anything to hurt us. She's just burning stuff. That's what she's doing, burning stuff."

"What stuff, Clam?"

I didn't say nothing.

"What stuff?"

"Well, maybe Mother's cooking them pigs. Maybe that's what. Maybe she's cooking them up so Aunty will have a big pig dinner when she comes back from her holiday from us. Mother knows how Aunty likes pig dinners, so that's what she's doing. Cooking up a big pig dinner. Think of it, Annie, tasty pig. Which bit of the pig do you want for dinner? I reckon a nice piece of bellyskin will do for me."

Annie shook out her tears. "We have to do something."

"Oh, Annie, Mother doesn't want to harm us." I took her hand to squeeze. "She rescued us. She chose us. We have purpose. Happen the pigs are just being silly. Pigs are silly, you know that. Scream if an eyelash is stuck, a pig does. Aunty will be back soon." Tears were leaping out of my own eyes now. "She'll sort it out, won't she? Aunty sorts everything out."

We were back at sixteen-year-old Emily.

"Aunty will be home soon and she'll sort it out. We just have to wait." I squeezed her hand bone tight, and truth be told, I didn't want to ever let it go. "Come on, Annie! Take a hold round Emily's knees with me."

But Annie didn't. She stood staring up at the sky lid. Black flakes were floating down.

"Come on, Annie, before Mother sees us dawdling."

She looked back at Mother, who was glugging the can on the plinths behind. "Listen, Clam," she whispered. Beneath her jumping tears her eyes were hard. "If this path goes off and meets them gates I saw, it might go to the road. I can go off to fetch Sam and get some help for us."

"Best wait for Aunty, Annie. She'll sort it. Aunty will sort it all out."

But Annie kept on whispering like she hadn't ever heard me. "I'm going to shove this Emily at Mother. That's what I'm going to do. Then I'm running off."

"Don't talk nonsense, Annie. You can't harm Mother."

"Listen to me, Clam. I'm shoving Emily, then I'm running. You can come, if you want, but I can run fastest, so happen it would be better if you could stay and hold her off, while I run and get myself outside the gates."

I stared at her. "Who? Hold who?"

"You know who."

"You mean I should touch Mother?"

"Hold her back."

"We ain't allowed to touch Mother, Annie."

Annie stared at me, her face all dotted black and dripping wet with tears. And I knew it then. It was a dream I was in, nothing more. In a moment my demonmale would turn up, flapping his red ears and trouble-starting like always, and after that I was going to wake up safe in the dorm with the Communicator bing-bonging and Aunty singing "Oh what a beautiful morning," with Evita's porridge pot set on the table, and our milk bowls around it, waiting for our hands to jump right in. Truly might even be back. Yes, Truly would be back, kicking and giggling in her sleep next to me. I smiled at Annie. "Everything's going to be all right."

But Annie didn't hear me. She was shoving at sixteen-year-old Emily till she dangled off her plinth and was only held up by Annie's hand on her belly.

Mother's chair came screeching up behind.

"OI!" Mother shouted. "OI! YOU! WHAT THE HELL DO YOU THINK YOU'RE DOING TO MY DAUGHTER?"

Annie let go her hand.

And sixteen-year-old Emily fell off the plinth and crashed down on Mother.

Mother went "UUU."

Her gun thumped down on the path and went BANG.

Sixteen-year-old Emily bounced off Mother onto the path and went CRACK.

Mother went, "UUUUUUUUUUUUUUUUUUUUUUUU."

Sixteen-year-old Emily's head cracked off her neck and rolled into the yew roots.

And Annie ran.

"My baby!" Mother cried, leaping out of her chair to go scrabbling under the yews for Emily's head. She snatched it up to her mouth and she kissed Emily's soiled lips. "My poor broke baby!" Mother tucked up Emily's head in her arms, and she tipped back her face, and she let out a howl at Heaven.

And just then, in this most terrible moment, it is strange to say it, but the most miracle thing happened. Mother's black glasses slid down her nose and I was shown her eyes.

Yes.

But here's the thing. Maybe it was the black smoke covering the sky lid doing it, or maybe it was Mother's grief and disappointment, or happen it was me, looking when I shouldn't—because a slug shouldn't bother a rose—but I watched them eyes, and I waited for them to shine gold at me, like Aunty's special medicine, or like a fresh-cracked egg, or a comb of perfect honey. But I am sorry to say, they didn't shine at me, not once they didn't. There was no gold in them eyes that I could see. No, Mother's eyes that I saw were made up of dead-leaf, compost-crust brown.

I was woken from staring by Annie's arm bashing the van door as she ran round it. Mother was woken too. She stopped crying at Heaven. She dropped Emily's head, and went scrabbling for her gun.

"OI! COME BACK HERE, YOU WORM!" Mother

shouted, pointing the gun's eye up the path. "I'LL GET YOU, YOU SEE IF I DON'T."

But then she didn't bother to shoot it, because Annie was already gone.

And me? Well, happen I've probably told you there's no need to bother, but if you really want to know what happened to me, well, I couldn't stand there looking at sixteen-year-old Emily's bodyless head, and Mother's eyes that had lost their gold, could I? No, my legs turned my head around for the safety of the dorm, and I set off running.

It was somewhere south of the Lawn, in the Glamis Castle rows, that I heard the bang in the air and I felt the thud in my left thigh. My leg stopped running and my body tipped over into the soil. And it was just like being a stuck pig, just like. I touched on my thigh and plummy blood pumped out.

BOWELS

Well, this was no good, was it? My face in rose roots and smoke all about me. Everything in my skull shrinking fast as a salted snail. And roaring. Yellow roaring everywhere. But never mind, it was nice and warm, so my head stopped thinking and had a little sleep.

My leg woke me, spinning sore. And my throat, crusted up for need of a drink. But here's the funny thing. Seems that Kathy Selden cat woke me too, crying in my ear.

"Go away, Kathy Selden," my mouth told her. "Go away, Kathy."

But she didn't.

I got half an eye open. Black rose canes and roaring fire. Kathy rubbing off hot stripes onto my face and crying at me. But that cat couldn't be in Bowels, could it? Which is where I was—that was clear and certain now—I had been dragged down to Bowels and I was waiting to get put on my spit, and there sure wasn't no mention in the Appendix of cats being allowed in Bowels.

Hot. Very hot. I lifted my face into the roaring. Weren't no mention of Bowels being so noisy neither. Nor so choking.

So my head got thinking then. One sister knew all about Bowels, didn't she?

"Truly Polperro?" I called. "Truly Polperro, if you're not too busy on your spit, do you know if there's any water about?"

But Truly didn't answer. The only one with an answer was that bothersome cat, crashing its head against mine and crying. But there ain't nothing for a cat to do in Bowels, so I tried to shoo it off. I tried calling Truly again, to ask her to find some bug for that cat to play with, but she didn't answer.

But just then, that cat turned and started running down the path away from me. And it was then I realized it—Truly must have sent that cat to show me to my spit. That's what. "All right then, cat," I said, and I set off after it, slithering on my belly, dragging my deadmeat leg slow as a slug down the path.

Funny thing was, we arrived at some place the Deceiving Devil had copied just like the yard. It had the standpipe and dorm and everything. But I weren't fooled, oh no. It was the Devil's fence that the flames were chewing on, the Devil's latrines that were burning orange, and the Devil's dorm that the flames were heading for.

Beneath the noise of screaming pigs and chomping flames, I heard coughing and crying. Bodies on spits, that would be, roasting in a row in the Devil's dorm. Females turning and melting and dripping their fat into trays beneath. The door all bolted down.

"Well, thank you, cat, for bringing me all this way and leaving me locked out of the dorm," I said. Though I could hear busy sobbing going on inside, so I reckoned I'd probably be let in soon enough to cook. Meantime, I reckoned on having a watch of the pretty flames right where I was lying, on the concrete by the sundial.

"Good idea," the cat said in my ear, with a hiccupy giggle.

"Truly Polperro?" I said. "Is that you? Have you been hiding in that catskin all this time?"

Truly giggled and shook off some charred fur.

"How is it, Truly? How is it in Bowels?"

Truly arched her back and bashed against me.

"You know I never sent you to Bowels with my tea with Aunty. You do know that, don't you, Truly?"

Truly pressed up to my ear. "Never mind that now, Clam," she said, "we're a bit busy down here today, so I'm afraid you're going to have to wait for your spit. There's lots of others to do first."

"Who?" I said, listening to the crying in the Devil's dorm. "Who's to do?"

"Just some naughty sisters, Clam. Never you mind about them. While you're waiting, why don't you have a rest under a barrow—like the composting barrow by the Hole door— that would do you nicely, Clam. It's cool in there. Smoke-free."

"Thank you, Truly."

"No bother, Clam."

Off she ran, and off my belly went, slithering along the Devil's yard. It was a slug-slow drag I made. Them sisters were sobbing in the dorm, and flames were dancing themselves about my eyes. "I didn't think Bowels would be so noisy, Truly," I said.

But Truly didn't answer me. Happen she was already nosying elsewhere.

The barrow was perfect for worming under. Hands tipped it over—CRASH! All in safe but for one deadmeat leg, and I weren't too bothered if the flames burned that one off. It was so warm under that barrow that my eyes closed.

Now, I hadn't slept for more than three rabbiting seconds when somebody was wanting something.

PAM PAM PAM outside the barrow.

"I am sleeping," I shouted out. "Please come back later."

PAM PAM PAM and a voice shouting, "What was crashing? Who is shouting out there?"

"I am shouting out here," I shouted back from the barrow dark. "Truly Polperro, if that's you still playing at being a cat, I ain't for it no more, thank you. Please show me your proper sisterly face or go back and get on your spit. Goodnight."

Well, that shut her up. Weren't nothing for another rabbiting second. Then it came back, the voice, all hot and bothered and roaring, "It is Maria Liphook! I am locked in the Hole. If that is a sister out there, unlock my door at once."

"Hello, Maria Liphook," I shouted back, "it's Calamity Leek! Have you been dragged down to Bowels too? You met Truly yet?"

"Calamity?" It came like a sadness. "Is that you?" That sadness again, "Just you? Well, listen, Calamity, come quick and unlock this door before we all get burned."

" 'Fraid I can't. And please don't shout so."

PAM PAM PAM. "Unlock this door."

"My leg ain't for moving no more, Maria. Sorry, I'm wait-ing for my spit. Are you waiting for yours?"

Three nice quiet rabbiting seconds.

"CALAMITY LEEK!" *PAM PAM PAM.* "COME AND UNLOCK THIS DOOR!"

"Please go away, Maria, my leg hurts."

"Clam, you must unlock this door."

PAM PAM PAM. "CLAM, UNLOCK THE DOOR!" *PAM PAM PAM.* "CLAM, UNLOCK THIS DOOR NOW!"

Well, that *PAM PAM PAM*ing went on, noisy enough to smash up my brain. Bowels turned to silent black nothing awhile. Then Bowels came back, dancing white hot. The *PAM PAM*ing had stopped. And in my barrow quiet, them words of Truly rushed back to my brain—

"Just some naughty sisters, Clam."

Whose sisters? my brain asked.

"Whose sisters, Truly?" I shouted out.

"Truly? Whose sisters are locked in the dorm?"

But Truly didn't answer me.

The only answer was something crashing down outside. Well.

Well, weren't nothing for it then. There really weren't.

Come on, Calamity's deadmeat body, pull yourself out from under this barrow quicksharp. Out to where it is bright and screaming and too hot to breathe. Never mind breathing, Calamity, there are sisters locked in there.

Come on, Calamity Leek's slug body, slither to the Hole door.

Slither, Calamity, slither. Reach for the bolt.

Too high. Come on, hands, pull this deadmeat leg up the door. Quick, quick, quick. Come on, leg, hold on, will you?

Well. Happen that one leg of mine was good enough for a second or two standing. Pain squealed up the other leg, setting my head to spinning.

Never mind that, ain't a head you need, Calamity, it's hands. Come on, hands, you'll be cooked soon enough, so don't you mind wiggling off the hot bolt quick quick quick.

Done.

The Hole door swung open and slapped me with cold air. My body fell in.

Maria Liphook caught me. She looked quizzical at my leg.

"Chop it off," I said, but she didn't hear. I was being carried down someplace cool. Which was mighty odd. There being no place cool in Bowels.

"What, Clam?"

"There ain't no place cool in Bowels."

My head turned inside out to blackness.

When I woke up, the air was filled with pigs and hens and sisters. My sisters. Maria Liphook was flapping furs at flames, like she had grown wings. Bodies were racing buckets from the standpipe, jumping over pigs and hens, throwing water at the fence, at the dorm, at the latrines.

Someone was shouting about a big injun coming down through the roses pouring out water. It could have been Maria Liphook, or maybe it was Truly Polperro come back to have a nosy, or happen it was Emily woken up and ready to start buzzing in my ear again. But injuns don't pour water. And Emily was in Heaven, wasn't she? She died and ascended straight up to Heaven when she was four years old. Emily wouldn't ever be in Bowels.

I had to laugh then. I had to laugh out loud.

Because this was Bowels. That's what we were in. The Devil's Bowels had come to the Garden. That's what had happened, I knew it now, for sure and certain. We had made a hole in the Wall and the Devil brought His Bowels in to us. And my silly running sisters didn't know it. They weren't ever going to stop them flames.

LEAVING

H ands lifted me onto white cloth.

"Not ready for the spit," I told them.

Demonmale faces, big-boned as cows, their voices rumbling thunder. "What's she saying? Easy there, Calamity, is it? Lie still now, love."

I was moving out of the yard. One cloud sat helpless above me in a Sunny sky. A stink of roasted pig and wood everywhere. So many demonboils bobbling about, that my mouth couldn't do nothing but moan. They were carting me to the spit, and there weren't one thing I could do to stop them.

Annie's voice came close in my ear, "Hush, Clam, the men are helping us. They're going to take you somewhere to make you better." Annie's face was bouncing by the side of me, Annie St. Albans, who had run away from Bowels and who was back now, her hand laid on my head.

The demonmales crunched their boots through the steaming black Glamis Castle stumps. Our white rosy army turned to nothing but puddles. We were in the Sacred Lawn now, shrunk down and melted eighteen-year-old Emily watched us go. Black tears were dripping off her melted eyes. Tears for being left behind with us to burn in Bowels. Ruined, like we all were now.

My leg was bounced so sore, I said may as well chop it off now as roast it later. Chop it off. But they didn't listen to me, these demonmales.

Crunch and crunch the demonboots went up the burned yew path. The yews frazzled to crackling stumps, like crow bones with their wings burned off.

Annie's face came over me. "Clam, listen to me. You have to go now."

We were stopped outside a white van. She kissed me on my cheek. "Be brave. We are all going. We must all be brave."

But I didn't want to be lifted inside a white box by these demonmales. I wanted to leave the Garden to fight the Good Fight, not to be roasted inside this stinking box. I tried to bite at the hands that were coming for me. I tried to growl, because everything was turned to ruin now, everything was.

A cup of poisoned air was pushed down over my mouth and strapped on me. I held my breath against it as long as I could, I really did.

AFTER EVERYTHING

My name is Elsa. That is what they say, Mrs. Waverley and the demonmale who ain't nothing better to do than stick their bottoms to the chairs in here, day after day after day.

Elsa Waverley.

They named me, they say. Do I like it, this name? they ask.

I look at them sitting there, the demonmale gripping poor Mrs. Waverley's hand. I think about telling them that it don't have no meaning at all this name of theirs. That I have one perfect one of my own, thank you very much. I think about telling them to go away and bring my sisters instead. I would write it like this—

GO AWAY

GO AWAY PLEASE NOW

YOURS SINCERELY, CALAMITY LEEK.

But it would only set Mrs. Waverley to wailing, so I don't.

Course, you come in, don't you, Doctor Andrea Doors,

and say soon we'll be talking about going home for a few days, to try out being in their house.

And right then it pops in my head, a cold little thought. Sharp and perfect as a fresh-grown thorn. So I have to have a smile at that.

"Is there a kitchen there?" I say.

And Mrs. Waverley jumps in, "Oh yes, darling! We can do some baking if you'd like."

And I give her a little nod but don't say nothing to that. Because I am thinking now about my thought. I am thinking about the Showreel. I am thinking about the Cinderella kitchen.

And you, Doctor Andrea Doors, you smile at me and stop my thinking by saying today you'd like to talk about love. These people are my parents, and they love me more than anything. Would I like to tell them what I think love is?

Well, everyone knows what love is. I loved the Garden and my second-wind sisters, and look what went happening to them. And the roses and the pigs and the hens, and even that fleabag dog sometimes. I loved Gretel—who Millie loved most of all—and look what happened to her. Millie loved Gretel, and though you have given her another rat, well, this Gretel Two can't turn no handstands, nor lick up no falling tears, can she? See, love ain't an overnight sprouting the moment a body sees a new rat. No, love needs to be sowed deep, composted regular and kept blight-free for a hope of it to bud. It needs soil and fresh air, and it needs watching over by Aunty. And happen in this white-walled place, well, that just ain't possible, is it? And if Aunty ain't here that ain't possible neither. So I reckon on not bothering with it no more.

But I don't say this. I turn away, because my eyes are filling up something busy now that I am thinking about Aunty, and I have a feel under my pillow for the envelope you gave me yesterday.

For the attention of Niece Leek,

Absolutely Private, it says. It is just for me.

I wipe my eyes and I slide the paper out from its envelope, and lay it on top of the sheet. It has a blotch on the top corner, like a creamy thumb might have sat there a second. I smooth down the paper and I read along every word, never mind it is all written inside my eyeballs now.

Dear Niece,

I'm sorry I didn't manage to tell you about your Mother's eyes, because a friend should always keep her promises. Well, they are hazel.

Now, niece, I'm afraid to say my life has suffered another Splashback. There's a perfect DNA match on the pot of spirits of salt; c'est la vie, the noose has been drawn tight around my neck. So I'm sorry to say I won't be seeing you again.

Given the circumstances, one might have hoped for a somewhat plusher locale—the Hyde Park Hilton, say—to do the deed. But que sera, sera, niece, a Brummie B and B it shall be.

And given my own extraordinary life circumstances, I have decided that my manuscripts, well, as soon as the police are through with them, I'm leaving them to you. Ophelia's reputation rests entirely in your hands.

It only remains for me to say, do not grieve for me, Calamity Leek, I shall not suffer. But do continue to cleanse and moisturize and bind back those ears at night. Watch yourself with the cake, and who knows how you might turn out. Remember even Dumbo got lift-off in the end!

And so, I bid you so long, farewell, auf Wiedersehen, adieu,

Your loving "Aunty" and dearest friend,

Ophelia Swindon

P.S. And just for the record, Calamity, I did so enjoy our teatimes together. Your little face proved quite the tonic to soothe the troubled soul.

You watch me wipe out my eyes and pop my letter away under the pillow.

"I know you loved her very much," you say. "And I know at the moment you find it hard to believe she is dead."

"Not dead, Doctor Andrea Doors. She has gone to Heaven."

"That's interesting," you say, "perhaps we can discuss that."

But we won't, Doctor Andrea Doors. Because my Aunty isn't yours to talk about. And happen I must wipe off my eyes quicksharp, because the door is opening and Annie St. Albans and Nancy Nunhead and Dorothy Macclesfield and Mary Bootle are coming in. Sam comes too. Course, they are all called other things now, my sisters, but I ain't for bothering with that, no.

"Hello, Clam," Annie says at the door. She is grinning. Everyone is grinning. Standing in their Outside clothes and shoes, and grinning.

301

They rush up to me. And I sit up taller in this bed for being with them, never mind their Outside clothes. I take a touch on Nancy's hand, and it feels just as fatty as ever. And that feels good.

Though she is sad for Baby Sainsbury's and Toddler South Mimms who couldn't be woken after the fire, Mary's eyes are popping. "Golly, Clam, did you know I have a baby sister, all my own, and two others that look like me, just like. I reckon we could even swap teeth and they would fit. What do you think to that?"

I make a shrug like I ain't bothered. Happen Mary has been took too easy with Outside ways, that's what I think, but I don't say.

Annie is smiling at Sam, who is standing behind her. He is touching her shoulder. It doesn't look like he is hurting her. Sam has brought peonies. He says they are for me. Course, his face goes all pink when he says he knows they don't smell as nice as the Garden's roses, but he hopes I will like them. Annie says she is going to stay with him when we are all let out of this hospital, on account of her real mother not being alive no more. Which she says is just how it is, but Sam's one is very nice, and Kathy cat might live there too.

Dorothy is back to her twitching ways, and I ain't surprised at that. "Eliza Aberdeen is getting new blood in her," she says. "Maria's lying under a sun but not a real sun—and she's got to go outside every day. We are all going out in the garden here tomorrow. We don't need headscarves here, you know. It is good for you, a little sunlight. For your bones. How that can be, I don't know. You know, there is so much I don't know. I don't know if I will ever know all there is to know out here." And poor old Dorothy's head near rattles off its neck at the thought of it.

Nancy swivels her knees so her shoes squeak on the floor. "My father says now they have found Mother, he is going to write and ask them to string her up. Even if bad things happened to her own daughter, it ain't a reason for her to try to use my daughter to get her revenge, he says."

"What's stringing up?" Dorothy asks.

Nancy shrugs and squeaks some more. Dorothy sets to writing in a little book she has called her "Book of Questions," which Annie says is Dorothy's very own Appendix on how things are for real. "For real," Annie says, which is words off Sam, which Annie's tongue is stacked full of these days.

"Say revenge again, Nancy," Dorothy says.

"Revenge means kill off." Nancy is wearing trousers with her squeaking shoes, and a pig-pink shirt she says is in remembrance of the boars that got killed. "Can I thump on your pot, Clam? See if it hurts?"

Well, I let her, and it does.

"Did you get a letter then?" Annie says. "Only my doctor said you did, from Aunty."

So I bring it out and I read it to them.

"You know," Annie says, when I finish and everyone is stood about quiet, "Sam reckons it was Aunty who phoned the police, and said about us being kept hidden inside the Garden and everything, just before she ate up her pills and medicine."

Sam is looking at the floor. He don't say yes or no to this. I look over at Doctor Andrea Doors. She don't say yes or no either. I will have to have a think about that, I reckon. And I look at Annie who smiles at me, and my eyes start up watering again.

"Oh, Clam, and you know the injuns?" Annie grins. "Well, there really aren't any. Not near the Garden, there're none. Only, look—see this book Sam found."

Annie shows me a hard brown book, opened on a page with a photograph inside. It is an injun—all redskinned with feathers down his back—so I shudder to see it.

"So they are real then, Annie."

"There's still some around," Sam says. "Only they live a long way from here, in a different country."

"Turn the page, Clam," Annie says. "Go on."

I don't want to, but I do. And there's a photograph of injuns that look like they are female, sitting with male injuns by a fire. And next to them are little females playing with little males and a dog.

"See, babies and sisters and everything!" Mary says.

I look at this photograph. It will take some thinking on.

"Keep the book," Sam says, turning pink-cheeked again. "It's a present."

A white-coated woman comes in the room. She says it is time for my sisters to go to their lesson about Outside, which I will be going to when my leg is a bit better.

Course, them leaving really does get my nose and eyes watering busy. And everyone comes round me, and presses in with their breath. And my eyes plop out more tears, because I can still smell something of their Garden ways. That hasn't been all lost from them yet.

"You ain't said much," Nancy says. "Would you like to try on my shoe, eh?"

"Would you like me to sing you a lullaby," Mary says.

"I've made a new one for my new baby sister. I can sing it if you like?"

"Well, Clam?" Annie says. "You haven't said what you think to everything."

So then I say it. "Sometimes I wish I had just burned up with the pigs."

GOING HOME

Annie said I saved everyone I could. Annie said, "It will all be all right in the end, you'll see. Be a bit brave if you can, Clam. Happen you were bravest of all of us." And then Annie laid a kiss on my cheek, and she left me.

And here we are. Me and Mrs. Waverley and the demonmale stuck in this white room. And, straight off, Mrs. Waverley starts up, "Oh darling, we hate to see you upset like this. Why don't you talk to us about it? Please let us help you, we only want to help you."

But I ain't for looking on her right now. Not now, Mrs. Waverley, thank you. I take a tissue for my nose and I close my eyes for thinking. I think of Aunty, lying back after eating all her pills, waiting to ascend to Heaven. I think I will think of her smiling. Most probably she was singing "I dreamed a dream" when she went up.

I think of Mother's eyes and whether they are "hazel" for sure, and whether this means some gold is hid in there for only Heavenly eyes to see. I try to see her in a white room like this, waiting to be stringed. But I can't fix her in this new place. No, I can only see her sitting on the yew path holding sixteen-year-old Emily's head, full of brown-eyed sorrow for her daughter died off horrible.

I open my eyes and I am looking straight at Mrs. Waverley, who ain't nothing like my Mother for beauty, even if she has brown eyes too. And before I know it to stop them, my lips start to curl in a smile. Which has her crying out and running at me, and the demonmale flapping his ears and coming too.

And before I think to say, "No, go away, get off me," I am being smothered up.

"Oh my darling daughter," Mrs. Waverley says, "we knew you'd come back to us in the end. We've missed you so much, Elsa. We can't wait to get you home."

I try to get away. I try to say, "Please stop. Get off me, I can't breathe no more."

But I am all coated up in hot fat and tears. And truth be told, it don't feel so bad, so I don't bother saying it. No I don't. Seeing as I can't move nowhere, I reckon on getting back to my thinking instead.

So I have a think about Mrs. Waverley's kitchen at home.

And I think about the Showreel.

I think about Cinderella in the kitchen sweeping, and those two fat sisters looking on lovingly and sharpening their knives.

And I look at the demonmale, and then I give Mrs. Waverley a big friendly smile.

And I don't bother saying nothing.

Nothing at all.

ACKNOWLEDGMENTS

I am very grateful to my friends for the support they have given me over the years. Special thanks to Anna Sadowy, Denise and Richard Harman, Gabrielle Murphy, Helen O'Toole, Nicola Peters, and of course, Simon Riley.

Thanks also to Clare Alexander for wisdom in matters editorial and practical, and Jocasta Hamilton who gave *Calamity* her first home. And a big thank you to Amy Einhorn and Caroline Bleeke at Flatiron Books for all the enthusiasm for *Calamity* and the hard work in making it happen.

Recommend

The FIRST BOOK of CALAMITY LEEK

for your next book club!

Reading Group Guide available at
www.readinggroupgold.com